THE LIVES WE'VE YET TO LIVE

MELISSA REDDISH

TP

TAILWINDS PRESS

Tailwinds Press
P.O. Box 2283, Radio City Station
New York, NY 10101-2283
www.tailwindspress.com

Published in the United States of America
ISBN: 978-1-7356016-8-7
1st ed. 2022

The Lives We've Yet to Live

VIRGIL

Amid the clatter of metal scraping meat into an edible shape, amid the orders growled by men with weekend beer-a-thon guts or women dragging their shrieking burden of children, amid the sizzle of Made with Healthy Olive Oil! (70% canola, 28% olive, 2% other), Virgil still hears the men in blue. Their shoes, a bioengineered leather-plastic hybrid, make no sound. Their jumpsuits, once described as "little boy blue" or "baby janitor blue," made from God-knows-what to withstand knives, bullets, heat, and tears, emit one tiny squeak, then nothing, like a child's toy throttled into silence. He doesn't hear the shoes or even the squeak, but he does hear the hitch from twenty well-oiled throats, the shuffles that slide into stillness. The air is thick, tamped-down, ready to burst.

The men in blue walk to the counter. Twenty bodies part to let them pass.

"Gimme two sausage-n-kale pockets. Large. TeaBerry Splash for the drink." The man who orders is taller than the other, his face cover a skin-tight cap around his head.

"Would you like to SuperHealth your order for an extra two dollars?"

"Nah." On his breast pocket, thick, looping whorls form the outline of a crib. Two buzzards. They won't fuck with anyone here; they're only after infants.

Virgil takes a breath, then clicks a few buttons on the register.

Everyone is waiting for someone behind the counter to give a sign. How fucked are they?

"Rounding up babies is thirsty work," Virgil says.

The taller one grunts his assent while the shorter one hacks up something thick and wet, then swallows it back down.

Everyone relaxes. A woman in her seventies, her gray hair shoved beneath a baseball cap, nearly collapses onto one of the molded plastic seats.

"For here or to go?"

The shorter guy fogs his face cover with his command: "To go."

Once people started reversing back to infants instead of dying of old age, the population boomed, resources shriveled, and the world got proper fucked. Talking heads pointed fingers—pollution, free radicals, not breastfeeding enough—but ultimately, the results were the same. Some politician had the idea to put a cap on the number of times a person could reverse— three—with plenty of ways to shorten that time: having a kid, selling extra years. And when your time is up? You head to the nearest Transition Center to make room for the next generation.

As soon as there were Transition Centers, there were Enforcers to gather up people reticent to die. Even though these Enforcers are only E03s, Buzzards, picking up recently reversed infants who have no one to care for them, everyone in this Health King will feel better once they're gone. Worse of course are the E01s, the Reapers, trolling the sun-slick boulevards and back-alley shanties for men and women who passed their Reversal limit. Rumor is they've started picking off the old and the weak and the sick, like a pack of wild dogs, and stealing what time they have left. Every time a video is posted on uPvoteR of some poor fucker collapsing beneath three Enforcers with electric prods, it gets taken down within the day. Usually it gets replaced with the latest rant of a Pro-birther.

The tall Buzzard is already at the door. Thank Christ. The short one picks up the bag and grabs Virgil's wrist, his grip surprisingly strong. Virgil's knees buckle, and suddenly he is eight, staring at the clump of his mother's waterproof mascara where it gathers like an accusation, her nails making pinpricks in his wrist while she stage-whispers for him to watch *Lucky Duck Detective*, even though he is far too old for *Lucky Duck Detective*, all so he doesn't have to look at the man standing next to his mother, his nostril hairs (that dark, wild thicket) beckoning so obscenely. The short Buzzard lets go, and the world reels back into focus. He pulls up his face cover to reveal two lips, thick and pink and wet. "Be seeing you."

He and the tall Buzzard share a snarfle-laugh before they're gone.

"Fuck those guys," Virgil mutters, quiet enough that their WristBuds can't pick it up.

Everyone in the restaurant nods their assent, anger packed into the whites of their eyes, futility weighting their limbs.

Around midnight, Virgil tromps through the moon-drenched streets of South Burrington, past the Nestless in their plywood and plastic shanties, past the glitter-and-nylon girls turning tricks for a weekly, past the fluorescent Time Loan signs flickering like a seedy motel, past the government-subsidized Puffy stations with their two minutes of O2 or two hits of albuterol. Ever since the government legalized selling your own time, the poor became poorer and the rich, like business tycoon Rutherford Gaslight II, basically became immortal. In the distance, the constantly changing billboard advertising everything from 90-inch home entertainment units to Ovine perfume (bottle your past to shepherd your future), shines its insomniac message to everyone below. For the last month, it's had the same phrase careening through the darkness: *Do you want something better?*

Virgil flips it the bird, his nightly ritual.

Back at the Nest Southwest, one of the city's community apartments, Virgil checks the board above the mailboxes. Those who have agreed to custodian are highlighted in green. Those close to Reversal are highlighted in red. Those who make problems or give back too little are highlighted in yellow: up for review. Virgil's name is clean: no highlighting, no resident to custodian. Yet. But the terms of the lease are clear; he won't be able to escape his duty forever. Virgil leaps up the ringing concrete stairs, past the divot beside Mr. Patrovitch's door from a microwave touchdown-slammed by his sister's boyfriend when he accidentally doubled-up on his dosage, and runs into Mrs. Silvers holding a recently reversed Karl in her arms, some kind of plastic mask covering his face.

"He could have told me he had asthma. I had already signed up, and I'm a woman of my word." Mrs. Silvers thrusts the infant towards Virgil as though they were in the middle of an argument. "But I would have checked his account. The doctor's visits, the nebulizer, the missed work—it adds up. More than what he left me. And I'm up all night, worried sick, just listening for that rattle." Mrs. Silvers rubs her face into her shoulder. "Why wouldn't he warn me?"

Virgil shrugs. "Maybe it's new." The number of commuters wearing re-breathers has leapt forward in the last decade from a handful to nearly forty percent of the train.

Mrs. Silvers sighs. Her floral blouse sags where her breasts should be. "Perhaps this was a mistake. I'm not a spring chicken anymore."

"You're not going to call them, are you?" Virgil imagines the two mouth-breathers from earlier slipping baby Karl, quiet and breathless, into their van.

She shakes her head and steps back through the threshold of the door. "I'm just tired, that's all."

"Listen, I'll come by tomorrow, give you a couple hours off. Okay?"

Mrs. Silvers nods.

Virgil touches her shoulder and tries not to imagine the skin sloughing away to reveal the small, delicate bones beneath. Everyone chose this place because they didn't have families, or their families were shit and they would rather take a chance with a bunch of strangers. Better than hoping upon Reversal that someone takes pity on them before they die of exposure or a Buzzard finds them or worse, one of the Bag Men picks them up.

When Virgil removes his hand, he notices five tiny pinpricks of blue on his finger pads. God, what now? What cancer-causing chemicals has the Health King added to their products in the name of profit?

Inside his apartment, Virgil slides into the heady perfume of nuked single-serve dinners, stale urine, and unwashed feet. He fills a glass with tap water, cloudy even through the shitty filter, and hopes everything floating inside is dead. The counter ticks down, showing the rest of the week's water supply: 40 liters remaining. If he's conservative, he might take a shower this week. Maybe he'll buy a bar of soap, make a real night of it.

Tonight, he's only on the toilet for five minutes, his ass a faucet but not a geyser. Thank Christ. When was the last time he had a solid, pain-free shit? He eyes the swirling brown lake, tasting the air like a sommelier, trying to determine if he can save the flush. *If it's yellow, let it mellow*, a dancing cartoon toilet once crooned as a childhood PSA. Now it's practically a law.

Fuck it. He flushes and watches the liquid shit turn and turn and turn. Goddamn low-flow toilets: they can't save water if they take twice as much water to flush. Virgil's prick of a landlord knows it, too. Get the tax credit and fuck over his residents. Win/win. Virgil holds the plunger down for a solid twenty seconds until begrudgingly, the water escapes. The timer ticks down.

The pinpricks on his fingers have spread to pea-sized circles, and no amount of hand sanitizer wipes them free. He flops onto his futon-turned-bed, the padding, as always, too thin for his girth.

Maybe tomorrow he'll shove his cancerous fingers right into his boss's bulldog face. Threaten to go to the press if he doesn't knock that shit off. Yeah, right. Who else is going to hire some high school dropout with a record? It was a juvie record, supposedly expunged or sealed or whatever, and yet the best job he can get is slinging the "healthy" alternative to burgers and fries.

He glances at the can of BirdBath wipes, but he doesn't have the energy. Maybe in the morning. Inside his bedside drawer, he grabs a Vitabar—all the vitamins and minerals the body needs in one convenient snack—along with a Single Pac Zoomie, a puff pastry-looking plastic baggie full of FloatAway, a government-sanctioned drug that causes the high of pot and the euphoria of Ecstasy with "minimal brain restructuring." *Float away on a sparkling sea*, the ad croons. *Please use responsibly.* Of course, the ever-increasing army of Zoombies dragging their near-corpses to government-subsidized "Rest Stations" makes the warning moot.

Before Virgil falls asleep and gives up a third of his day off to watch some wheezy kid, he clicks through his WristBud until he finds an episode of *Lock 'Em Up: Underground Edition*. Then he hits Projector Mode. Studmire and Sen have just found a twelve-year-old girl in the schoolgirl uniform of an underground sex worker, her neck and wrists ringed in indigo, her eyes staring into the colorless void before her.

"Probably picked up by a bag man and sold into slavery," Studmire explains in unnecessary exposition.

Virgil falls asleep before they can penetrate the underground ring, before Studmire poses as a customer and Sen as a Madame, before Sen holds a gun inches from the bag man's eyes and tells him to give her a reason to pull the trigger, before Virgil can slip into the fantasy of retribution and imagine his fist hitting the meat of the bag man's face, his teeth popping like fireworks, his eyes curtaining shut, Virgil's aim precise, dogged, unyielding: again and again and again.

It isn't the noiseless sweep of their shoes or the squeak of the uniform that wakes Virgil, or even the fact that the door, now ajar, is letting in the perpetual light of the hallway. It is that pair of lips, pink and wet, breathing a sour smile into his face.

"Rise and shine."

Virgil is awake and upright before his eyes adjust to the shapes in the room: the two jumpsuits, shadowed in blue. In a second that lasts for a year, he considers leaping towards the door, maybe fighting them off. He could probably take them. But he's suddenly tired, so very tired, so he just slumps back onto the pillow. He doesn't even flinch when the needle enters his neck.

PHOENIX

One red bead, two yellow beads, and a single peacock feather, purchased at the arts and crafts store five miles away, not gaudy as her father had proclaimed but beautiful, dignified, proud—a feather worthy of her name—and she's finished. Phoenix holds up the intricate orb of colored string. The spirit orb ensnares all of the bad energy circulating through a person's life. As a person lays wracked with cancer or heart disease or maybe just decades of regret, a friend or family member burns the spirit orb and releases the negative energy of sickness and decay into the heavens, so the person will have only the best, most positive energy with them as they reverse. Even though the story was from her father's heritage—repurposed, with her father's trademark skill, to suit the current times—her father made sure Phoenix knew that it was a lie. Nothing could prevent that seed of destruction from reversing with you, so long as you made it that far. Phoenix had nodded, the shadow of her mother rising, unspoken, between them.

As she admired the web glittering in the sharp desert light, she had to admit: it did look an awful lot like a calamity orb, meant to trap a person's bad luck in a crystal prison, which was one of three different complaints this month from the Hintaa tribe. They were one of the few Native reservations that still maintained sovereignty when the Reversals began, and resources began to literally dry up. Now they compete with the Natural Livers who left hearth and home to make a life free from government restriction and mandatory sentencing. Each group stays in their loosely guarded territory, a tenuous treaty in place, scratching out a life in the Sella desert.

Phoenix tosses the spirit orb into the box with the others and heaves the box into the living room. She checks the thermometer before sticking a hand outside: 110 degrees. Not yet noon. Better put on the sun suit, just in case. She massages some waterless shampoo into her hair, dragging her fingernails through the dandruff and then smelling the mix of dry scalp, lavender, and tea tree oil.

Outside, a wooden ladder leads to her father, already suited in that infallible dad way, drilling into one of their solar panels. Running in a continuous loop around him is the rainwater harvesting system. When they first moved here five years ago, the desert hit fourteen inches of rain. This year, they'll be lucky to break ten.

"Need any help?"

Her father stops drilling and walks to the edge, making an exaggerated show of looking around. In Phoenix's childhood game of Lucky Lucky Dinosaur, her father would slowly walk towards her, his arms pinned to his side like a T-Rex, rolling his head and uttering wet, guttural sounds. And she would giggle and sprint away, leading him on a chase through their living room. Whenever she hid, he would pull up short and make a show of looking for her under couch cushions or behind the refrigerator until she, near to bursting, would finally leap out and the chase would begin anew.

She freezes for a moment, her one acquiescence, before giving a long, sweeping wave.

"Ah, my little Minmi. I'm good for now, but if you want to make some Sticky Prickies, I wouldn't say no."

Phoenix gives a thumbs up and walks back into the house. Her father used to show her all his projects, leading her into the world of gears and gadgets, illuminating the harmony of a well-designed machine and the day-long puzzle when that machine suddenly ground to a halt. But as soon as her childish wonderment transformed into a more adult interest, he grew quiet, reticent, leaving her at home when repairing a neighbor's cooling unit or rainwater harvesting system, and he wouldn't even talk about sitting in the Health King parking lot, waiting with the other Sand Fleas for a black van full of prisoners and Nestless teens to take them to the latest pothole-ridden back road or crumbling overpass for a sweaty day of under-the-table construction: a man with a Master's in Mechanical Engineering reduced to yet another day laborer.

She brings out two Sticky Prickies: toast covered in peanut butter, black beans, and slices of prickly pear, her own invention. Before he can climb down, she climbs up, picking her way carefully across the solar panels and ignoring his glare.

"You should really strap in," her father says, pointing to the cord with a carabineer attached to the end.

"And you?"

He shoves half of one Sticky Pricky into his mouth. Phoenix can tell how famished he is, but he won't eat more than his share.

"Are you dropping off the spirit orbs later today?"

Phoenix nods.

"Take the Jeep. And if you don't mind, can you pick up a few things? Some more BirdBath Wipes. About ten large spring clamps. Some razor blades. There's a list inside."

Phoenix nods. She chews her Sticky Pricky slowly, savoring the flavor. The fruit is like a tangy watermelon, but it doesn't come out until late summer, so it's a treat. They'll probably do hot dogs for dinner tonight, unless she wants to play the "return damaged goods" game to get a few extra bucks for a can of corn. She'd have to loop across town to the FoodPlus that hasn't seen her this month, though.

"Don't think I've forgotten about your English session at one, either."

Phoenix sighs. She was hoping he had forgotten.

"I can speak English just fine. Better than those white boys."

"You know that's not what it's for. You want to be an engineer, yes?"

Phoenix nods.

"Then you'll need more than just a way with a wrench. You need to be well-rounded in everything: English, History, Math. That's what the universities are looking for."

"Papa, don't be silly. I'm staying here with you."

"Phoenix . . ."

"Even with these piddly little lessons, what university is going to accept a Sand Flea?" Phoenix meant for the slur to be light, ironic, but the word "flea" catches in her throat.

"Don't call yourself that."

"Well, why not?" Phoenix can hear her voice pitching higher and higher, but she can't help it. "They think we're just worthless thieves, stealing all their precious resources. Why even bother?"

Fernal is silent for a moment, his hands clasping and unclasping the wrench. Phoenix waits for the inevitable.

"Is this what you want?" His bellow ripples out into the endless expanse. "You want to live in this unlivable place begging for water, for food? You want to be a single mother at twenty-five, wondering how you're going to feed yourself, let alone your child?"

Phoenix hugs her legs. His anger is a desert storm: whirling skirts of wind and dust she just has to wait out. "You're barely sixty. You have a long time before you reverse."

"And you're almost eighteen. Almost an adult. It's time you think about your life."

Phoenix snuffles back a snot-bubble. She hates when she cries, hates not being able to stop her body's treachery. The suit gets muggy and damp and she can't even wipe her nose. She remembers how her mother used to catch her tears and raise them to the sky for a blessing. Only when she felt Phoenix had cried enough would she lower her hands and tell her the sky was already full.

Fernal holds up his hands, palm up. "Why did you go, Nell? Why am I doing this without you?"

Phoenix waits. Whenever he talks to her mother, she knows to stay quiet.

Fernal lowers his hands and looks at Phoenix. "I'm sorry."

"It's okay."

"You don't regret coming here?"

Phoenix shrugs. Her father asks her this at least once a week. By now she knows the question is rhetorical.

Fernal sighs. "Any more Sticky Prickies?"

"We ate the last two."

Her father nods. "English tutoring. 1pm."

"I'll be there." She walks back to the ladder. "You coming?"

"In a minute. I have a few more bolts to tighten."

Phoenix knows he wants to have a conversation with her mother. He prefers spaces that are both isolated and raised, as though shortening the distance will increase the reception. Once, when Phoenix was six, her mother dead for less than a week, she listened to one of her father's conversations. He started off discussing thermodynamics, how her energy was not gone but altered, transformed back into the star stuff from which they came, and then, after several minutes of silence in which Phoenix almost nodded off, he began a needling whine that grew into a scream, asking her, again and again, why did she leave him alone in the desert? Phoenix wanted to burst through the bushes and cry, *she didn't leave—she died,* but she knew her father didn't want an answer.

After grabbing her backpack and a tepid Sun Dew, Phoenix heads towards Ms. Green's house. Ms. Green tutors English, History, and Environmental Science in exchange for weekly grocery runs. Today Phoenix will be with Brandon, the fourteen-year-old with a fo-hawk and a Saving Dread shirt he stole from a clothing drop-off box, and Betsy, a sixteen-year-old with yellow teeth who hums nonstop along to her Soothing Sounds mood ring. Why is it only the weird kids who take English?

She still has ten minutes before she's expected, and there's no way she's sitting in that tiny, cloistered space with those two mouth-breathers for longer than she has to. She loops out, away from the cluster of trailers forming their make-shift neighborhood, and towards the unsheltered desert. Just a couple of minutes until she's to her first solar still, a taut piece of plastic over a hole she dug in a dry riverbed. In the direct sun, it will gather condensation and drip into the cup she's placed underneath. She learned that trick from Ms. Green during her Environmental Science sessions, which were mostly How to Survive in the Desert sessions briefly interspersed with How We Fucked Up the Planet tirades. When Phoenix gets to her first solar still, the plastic wrap is bunched to the side and the cup is knocked over, as though someone stomped it in. She checks the next hole and the next, and they're all like that: not a drop of water between them. Phoenix continues to the two trees she marked, a Mulberry and an Ash, and instead of hanging from the branches like they should be, each plastic baggie is crumpled on the desert floor, any collected water evaporated in the sun. Phoenix balls her fists and stares out at the wavering horizon.

Though she might get one or two cups of water, max, her insides still furnace to think of all this work wasted. Who is the culprit? It might be an animal, though Phoenix doubts it—the work is too meticulous, too intentional. She suspects the fuckabout twins, Joey and Jared, who never met a beautiful day they couldn't ruin.

"The Ibson girl, so deep in thought. Don't get lost in there, chicky."

Phoenix spins until she sees Patrick Davidson a couple feet away. She hadn't even heard him come up. He's suit-less, in a black shirt and jeans, his dark wavy hair slicked back. Behind him are the twins, Joey and Jared. They scuff the sand, push each other. Phoenix expects any second they'll start pulling nits from each other's hair and flinging their poo.

"How'd you know it was me?"

"What can I say?" Patrick circles her. "You have a presence about you, even in that bulky thing."

Phoenix zips the top of her suit and flips down the hood. She shoves her sweat-slick hair from her face and smiles. Why couldn't he have seen her this morning, her hair long and soft and smelling faintly of lavender?

"Knew you were in there somewhere. Brought you something." Patrick reaches into his back pocket and tosses a can at her. Phoenix holds it up: Moondrip Light.

"Something to keep you cool."

Actually, Phoenix thinks, alcohol is a desiccant, so it would make her thirstier, but she simply nods and smiles.

"And there's more if you come out with us tonight."

Phoenix taps the top of the can like she's seen people do in movies. "Where?"

"High Noon Bar. On South street."

Phoenix flips the tab and takes a short sip that is mostly foam. She smiles to show she's enjoying it. "I'm a little underage."

"Ah, they don't care. I'm doing all the buying, anyway."

Phoenix is pretty sure it doesn't work that way, but the flutters in her throat tell her to say yes. "Are they coming?" She motions towards the twins.

Patrick smirks. "Nah, I'm sure they've got better things to do. Curing cancer. Solving the reversals. That sort of thing."

Phoenix takes another sip and tries not to grimace. "Who else is going to be there?"

Patrick backs up and motions to the twins, who are trying to poke each other with cactus needles. "Come and you'll find out. 9pm. See you there."

Phoenix waits until they're all out of sight before pouring the rest of the beer onto the ground. She digs a small hole and then buries the can. Better safe than sorry. Fastest way to lose her weekly trips into town would be for her father to find the can or discover that Patrick was hitting on her.

He was hitting on her, right?

Not for the first time, Phoenix wonders how normal girls do it: flirting, dating, the whole glorious spectacle. Does it look the same as it does out here or are there hidden complexities beyond the border? The last time Phoenix was at the mall in town, she balked at the pink fuzzy legwarmers that purred with every step and the WristBuds playing a constant stream of YO TITTY KITTY. If that's what it means to be a normal teenager, no thank you. Of course, at least they had options. Maybe Patrick looks so good because he's the only viable candidate unless she wants to bat her eyelashes at a couple of knuckle-draggers or a kid who steals used shirts.

Plus, he's got that whole "already a parent" vibe going. He and his sister look after their reversed grandparents who raised them. They make it look easy too, which makes her father's handwringing about his inevitable reversal seem silly. Of course, it will probably be tougher by herself. Who knows, though? Maybe she'll be a natural.

Phoenix flips up her hood and zips it closed, hoping she wasn't exposed too long. The last thing she needs is to show up home, or worse, at the bar, with a face flash-fried by the sun. She resets a couple of her moisture catchers and then, with nothing else to do and nowhere else to go, heads off to her English lesson.

VIRGIL

When Virgil wakes, he assumes he just passed out after one too many Zoomies. But this couch, gray and unyielding, is not his comforting sinkhole of desiccated crumbs and deflated baggies. He sits up and immediately feels nauseous. After a minute of sitting with his head in his hands, his surroundings come into focus: three round Formica tables with plastic chairs, a Health4U vending machine, a refrigerator, a sink packed with mismatched mugs, and a countertop with a fingerprint-smudged microwave and coffee-maker next to a dried, puckered sponge. On the wall above the sink, a printed sign in 48-point Comic Sans reads, "We are not your custodians! Clean up after yourselves!" Beneath the lettering are clip-art smiley faces in various states of finger-wagging contempt.

Unless he's died and woken up in his own personal hell, Virgil is certain this is an office break room.

"You're awake. Excellent. We had to adjust the dosage for your, ah, size. HR was afraid you wouldn't wake up until tomorrow, but I was certain you'd be up and moving this morning." The man staring down at Virgil in a well-fitted suit and an honest-to-God cravat has the small, pinched features of a terrier. He barely comes up to Virgil's shoulders. If Virgil wanted to, he could chuck this man out an open window.

"I'm not feeling especially patient today, so you'd better tell me what the hell I'm doing here." Virgil lets his voice fall into that early morning, pre-ablution growl and is rewarded by the over-dressed beagle taking two steps backwards.

"Of course. Come with me."

Virgil considers rooting himself in place and refusing to move until his questions are answered, but ratcheting up the intimidation took what little energy he had, so he obediently scuffs behind. The man leads Virgil into a room filled with long tables and row upon row of thin, manicured women typing on virtual keyboards.

"11th and Broadway, the man sleeping on the piece of cardboard. He's a vet, so approach carefully. Has a golden retriever with him. No sudden movements, no loud sounds. Keep it civil—see if he'll come of his own volition." The woman, her eyebrows shaved and then penciled back in, touches the frame of her glasses, then types something on the keyboard projected in glimmering light on the table. "He has a daughter named Veronica who lives in New Harbor with her husband and two kids. Offer to take the dog to her, then drop it off at the pound on your way to the next target."

The tiny man claps his hands once and all the women look up. "This is Command Central. These women quite literally run the show—they find the men and women past their reversal limit and help our men secure them."

"So you can murder them."

"Voluntary euthanasia. Anyone is welcome to join one of the sovereign communities in the desert or the clean-up crews out West."

"How fucking generous." Virgil, still woozy, looks for a place to sit, but all the chairs are taken by these women with their perfect robotic movements.

"Yes, see, and this is part of the problem. We provide a necessary service, one that passed into law with public support, I might add."

"I never fucking voted."

"And did you vote for the current president? All of your representatives? And yet you are still governed by them, are you not? We are not the villains in your little story, Mr. Scott. When the power goes out, who gets blamed? The power company, of course. But the storm took out the power, an act of nature or of God, depending on your outlook. We did not create the Reversals or the inevitable shortage of resources; we are simply trying to fix the problem."

"Fine, whatever," Virgil says, lowering himself to the floor.

"Where are my manners? Let's get you something to eat. It'll help dampen the effects of the serum."

Mr. Not-the-Villain leads Virgil back to the break room. He brings over a single sealed sandwich and a glass filled not with juice or cola but with water so clear and pure, it catches the light along the beveled edge. It is like cool fingers massaging Virgil's face, his neck, his throat. The blood vessels in Virgil's head yawn open and he realizes he's had a low-grade headache ticking behind his eyes for weeks, maybe months. He downs a second glass and then a third, each one ferried by the man to Virgil's outstretched hands. Finally, after his fourth glass filled with the best water in existence, Virgil takes a deep breath, filling the dusty, deflated corners of his lungs, and, with a shudder, shakes off the last of his hangover.

"Sated?"

"Quite," Virgil says. Virgil's not sure if he's mocking this ridiculous man or, in his gratitude, falling into the role of the sycophant. Either way, he doesn't like it.

Now that his eyes are open and clear, he realizes what has been bugging him about the room since he woke up: the sink doesn't have a timer. He turns to ask, but there, standing at the doorway, ghouls at the ready, are the two Buzzards from the Health King.

"And now, the second problem. Gentlemen, did either one of you ask Mr. Scott here to come in before you drugged him?"

The tall Buzzard slips out of the doorway, leaving the short one behind. The short one pulls down his mask to reveal his gnome-like features. "Mr. Benson, uh, there was no way he was gonna come with us, so, you know, we were being proactive."

"Among Bunt's prodigious talents, elocution is not one of

them."

Bunt scratches his bulbous Adam's apple. It looks obscene.

"I'm sure you have work to do, yes?"

Bunt nods and replaces his mask. Benson turns to Virgil and clasps his hands together. "So, to recap, we have a public who sees us as monsters and an overuse of aggressive tactics. In short, we have a PR problem."

Virgil shrugs. "That sucks. Can I go now?"

"What we need is a public face for our field agents. Someone the public can empathize with . . . a regular Joe."

"Uh huh."

"You wouldn't be the only one, of course. We already have five other volunteers lined up across the country. But you would be the face of South Burrington."

Virgil pictures clean glasses of water every day, every hour, every minute if he wants them. He pictures taking deep, full breaths like a goddamn yogi master. Whatever. No way he'll sell his soul just for that.

"Nope."

"Now, don't be so hasty. You haven't heard my proposal yet. Signing on with us would mean a sizable paycheck, 85k to start. You could quit your fast-food job. No greasy fingers and a lot more money."

"No."

"Plus, we would pay your rent for, say, a year at that communal apartment you're living in."

"Nuh uh."

"And since community is clearly so important to you, we would also pay each tenant's rent for a full year."

This time, Virgil pauses. "No."

"All right, a full two years. But that's as high as I'm willing to go."

"Listen, that's all very generous, but you could offer me a harem of horny gymnastic supermodels and I still wouldn't do it."

"Charming. Well, that's all the carrot I have, but don't

worry—I also have plenty of stick." Benson reaches into his front pocket and puts on a pair of glasses. "Now, let's see. Carol Silvers. Looks like she had breast cancer a while back. Tsk tsk. It would be a real shame if her reversal limit was suddenly reached due to a clerical error."

"You can't do that."

"And then there's Anna Patrovich. Lives with her aging father. Looks like her husband has schizophrenia. I wonder if he takes his medication regularly. Doesn't sound safe for a crazy man to be living in your complex."

"All right, that's enough."

Benson removes the glasses and places them back into his pocket. "Are you ready to sign?"

"Fine. But I still want all that other stuff you promised."

Benson grins, revealing a row of tiny white teeth. "Of course."

"So what do I have to do?"

"Just show up here tomorrow at nine and wear your Health King uniform. Oh yes, and get as many people in your building as you can to sign these waiver and nondisclosure forms. We're going to be doing some promo spots for your transformation, and we'll need some background color."

This sounds like either propaganda or a reality TV show. Broke-Ass Bastard to Buzzard in Three Easy Steps!

"Where exactly is here?"

Benson chuckles. "Ah, that's right. I guess you didn't exactly walk through the front door. You can get the address from the front desk on your way out. Don't look so glum, Virgil! You're going to be a star!"

Back at his Nest, Virgil bounds up the concrete stairs, his hand nearly on the door featuring several new crowbar-shaped indentations (fucking assholes), when the smell of scorched meat drifts down. The barbecue. The one he was supposed to bring drinks to.

On the roof, thirty other residents are chatting in groups, paper plates filled with hot dogs and burgers and the occasional glob of discount potato salad, plastic cups filled with as much cheap, sugary alcohol as they can stomach. Franklin Jr., aka Tongs, is the self-appointed grill master. Smoke plumes from his grill. He stands, his face bright with sweat, his mouth open in joy. Ever since Tongs suggested the weekly barbecues, his body relaxed into purpose, and the apartment tightened its bonds.

A couple feet from the grill is Mrs. Silvers, with baby Karl in his hand-me-down stroller from Mrs. Nguyen. Virgil touches her gently on the shoulder, the papers from Benson moist in his hand. "I'm sorry I'm late."

"Oh honey," Mrs. Silvers says, touching Virgil's face, "I was just having a bad night, that's all. And we didn't decide on a time. But since you're here, I did pick up a shift at the hospital later tonight, just until 2am, so if you could watch Karl, I would appreciate it."

"I thought you were going to relax. Maybe catch a movie?"

Mrs. Silvers shrugs, her eyes tired. "Every little bit helps, you know?"

The papers are starting to wrinkle in the sauna of Virgil's palm, so he sticks them in his pocket. "What if you didn't have to worry about rent for a while? Say, two years?"

"Well, yes, that would be lovely, wouldn't it?" Her eyes narrow and she lifts one thin finger toward Virgil. "I see that look, Virgil, and don't you even think about it. I know you don't have the money and I'm not going to have you going without water just so I can watch a movie from time to time."

"No, not me," Virgil says, but suddenly Tongs is at his side with two paper plates: a burger for Virgil and a veggie burger for Mrs. Silvers. "Glad you could make it. I thought you had to work?"

"It looks like I'll be able to make all the barbecues from now on."

Tongs claps Virgil's shoulder and grins. "Hey, look at that! Your prick of a boss decided to grow a fucking heart after all."

He returns to the grill and Mrs. Silvers turns to Trinity, an East

Boatian adoptee escaping her hyper-religious, verbally abusive adoptive parents. Her accent is slight, though she still has a somewhat formal method of speaking.

"I've decided to raise him vegetarian," Mrs. Silvers says. "Maybe this time he can avoid his history of cholesterol and heart disease."

"Perhaps these attempts to avoid the problems of a former life might lead to new issues?" Trinity murmurs.

Mrs. Silvers smiles. "Perhaps. But if we can't improve ourselves, what's the point?"

Talking to everyone one at a time is definitely going to take too long. But if he's going to make some big announcement and gain the ire of the entire community, Virgil decides he'll need some liquid courage.

Tiny Tim is working the alcohol station, mixing drinks with the bartender set he "recovered" from one of his dumpster-diving sessions in the rich neighborhoods, the ones north of Lake Street. Tim is 6'3", his limbs so long and lanky they seem to move in slow motion. Most of his extended family died from cancer before reversing, and Tim lives with a quietly ticking clock in the background of his thoughts.

"What'll you have, boss?"

"Jack and coke, light on the coke." Virgil glances around at the talking, laughing, lounging group. Is he ready to drop the mood off a cliff?

Tim hands Virgil the cup, the top bubbling like molten shit. What Virgil really wants is some of that pore-opening water from earlier but getting sloshed will have to do. He chugs half the cup and waits for his lips to start tingling, followed by the feeling that maybe things aren't so dire after all. Then he'll know it's time.

"Strong enough?"

Virgil nods, then follows Tim's gaze to Trinity, who is standing at the edge of the roof, looking out at the car-choked streets below. Two more Rebuilding Zones have popped up a few blocks away, promising a couple months of extra-shitty commutes. It's all the city can do to keep up with the flash floods, windstorms, and sinkholes, but the constant one-lane roads and detours mean that everyone's walking around just one delay shy of a homicidal rage.

"Just ask her out, man. The worst she can do is say no."

Tim laughs and drops his gaze to the table. "Yeah."

Virgil knows exactly what to say, but it feels bastardly, even to him. Unfortunately, the words come tumbling out of his mouth before he can reconsider. "You really want to have that regret hanging over your head?"

Tim scrunches his nose. Then, in a couple long strides, he's next to Trinity. Virgil watches their conversation for a few minutes until Trinity touches his arm, her lips pressed together in sympathy. Tim strides back to the table, picks up his backpack, flips Virgil the bird, and walks out the door.

Now that he's fucked up one guy's afternoon, he figures it's time to ruin everyone else's. He climbs onto the mystery pile of pallets, clears his throat, then hits the edge of the plastic cup while making a "ding ding ding" sound.

A few heads turn, then a few more, and finally, everyone is standing silently and waiting for Virgil to say something. His cheeks are numb, but he's not drunk enough to start spewing whatever stream-of-consciousness enters his head.

"Toast!" someone in the crowd yells. Everyone raises their cups.

"Yeah, okay. This is a toast for a bunch of misfits who came together to make a kickass little family."

"Hear hear!" someone yells and everyone lifts their cups to drink.

"But maybe," Virgil continues, digging deep for the right words, "we could be even better than we are? Or maybe not better, but calmer, more relaxed? Taken care of?"

Everyone has paused, cups partway to mouths. They turn to each other with looks of confusion.

"I was presented with this, uh, opportunity. And the short of it is that they'll pay our rent for two years. All of us."

"Who?" Virgil scans the crowd for the person who asked but everyone has the same question on their faces.

"Uh, well, it's a documentary," Virgil explains, which is not technically a lie. "They want to film us and our community."

"That's a pretty ridiculous budget for a documentary," Tongs says.

"Okay, see, they have some investors. If we can just avoid saying anything overtly negative about the Enforcers, we're good."

"What?"

"Are you serious?"

"What the hell?"

"Is this a propaganda film for those fucking roaches?"

"No no no," Virgil says, his hands outstretched as though he can tamp down everyone's anger. "It's like a reality show."

"A reality show for what?"

"For us," Virgil feels the lie emerge, sticky and wet, "to see what we'll do with the money. To see if it strengthens us or tears us apart. To see if we really can make our own family." This almost sounds plausible.

"So we're like a bunch of lab rats?" Tongs asks.

"Yeah, but listen. This is our chance to show them just how strong we are. Just how much of a family. Then they'll have no choice but to make it one of those heart-warming tales."

People in the crowd are starting to tentatively sip their drinks. The murmurs begin to get soft around the edges.

Virgil pulls out the waiver and nondisclosure forms. Time to drive it home. "Anyone who's willing just has to sign these forms. No one's going to force you—you can totally opt out if you like."

"But we don't get paid if we do, right?"

"Exactly."

Mrs. Nguyen is the first to appear in front of Virgil, pen in hand. The day she appeared at the complex, she stood silently in front of the building, bruises on her chest and arms, her face placid. She had exactly one plaid suitcase that she wheeled behind her. Since that day, she has barely spoken a sentence. After she signs, she gives a brief nod and passes the pen to Tongs, who is standing behind her. Everyone walks up, slowly or quickly, confidently or full of nervous energy, to sign the forms. The only person who remains standing, her arms crossed, her eyes trained on Virgil, is Trinity.

"Thanks, everyone. You won't be sorry," Virgil says, which is probably the worst lie he's told today. He won't be able to hide the truth for long. Soon someone will see him in an Enforcer uniform, either in person or on TV. But by then, hopefully the free rent will lessen the blow. And who knows—maybe this will be enough to get him out of his obligation to custodian. Sometimes a significant enough service to the community is enough—Virgil just has to hope everyone feels the impact before they catch a glimpse of him in an Enforcer uniform.

The party wraps up pretty quickly, the energy depleted after everyone signs their life away. As he heads back to his room, his head spinning from the impromptu speech and too much jack and coke, he senses a body behind him. If those fuckers have come to drug him again, they'll get a fight this time, Virgil thinks as he spins around, fists raised.

"Be calm," Trinity commands, her hand raised.

"Sorry, thought you were someone else," Virgil murmurs, glancing behind her.

"Perhaps the person who is forcing you to do this terrible thing?"

"What terrible thing?"

"The documentary? But that is not the truth, is it?"

Virgil motions Trinity inside. She glances briefly at the indentations on the door. Inside, Virgil is happy to see that he didn't leave anything unpleasant simmering in the toilet. He gathers a few musty shirts and a bashed-in pizza box and tosses it into the bathroom.

"So, what is the truth?" Trinity asks.

Virgil sighs and sinks onto the futon. "Okay, last night I was kidnapped by a bunch of Enforcers."

Trinity nods like she's been expecting this.

"And the short of it is that I've agreed to become one for some reality show. Regular people turning into . . . them."

Trinity leans forward and Virgil knows he's seconds away from getting decked like he deserves.

"This is perfect," she whispers.

Trinity climbs onto the futon and suddenly Virgil is inches from her chest, the roll of her stomach pressing against her dress. He imagines her climbing on top of him, the smooth press of her legs against his stomach. He's not as hard as he would expect. He imagines instead her disappearing beneath the blankets, the tight warmth of her mouth. That's better.

"We need someone who can get close to them. We could not have planned this better!"

"What do you mean?"

"We need footage of them doing all the terrible things we know that they do. Threatening people. Kidnapping those who have not reached their Reversal limit. Stealing months and years for themselves."

"Actually, they did threaten you all. That's why I agreed."

"I knew it." Trinity's eyes are wide and gleaming. She hands Virgil one of those tiny CoolStoryBro cameras. They were initially marketed toward the skateboarder crowd but have since been co-opted by activists who prefer them to the hi-tech, ultra-surveilled WristBud. "Photos are fine but video is better."

"You want me to videotape them? Doing shitty stuff?"

Trinity nods.

"What are you going to do with it?"

"Show it to the public. We will make them lose their government contract."

"And then what?"

Trinity cocks her head. "What do you mean?"

"So you take down this company. Okay. What takes its place? Another company that's the same? Worse?"

Trinity smiles. "We have a plan. Do not worry."

Virgil waits for specifics, perhaps some kind of flowchart, but instead Trinity stands, winks, and saunters out the door.

He waits a couple of moments after the door clicks shut, his boner wilting. At least he didn't betray Tiny Tim, even in his mind. He pours a glass of water. It tastes metallic and sour, like a robot fart. He fills the glass again and again, trying to ignore the steadily diminishing timer. Now he can afford all the water he wants, right? Maybe he can even weasel a few renovations from them: a nicer stairwell, some new pipes. Of course, that'll probably all disappear if he follows Trinity's plan. But wouldn't it be great if he could somehow get the benefits AND stick it to those assholes? He touches the camera inside his pocket and hopes that when the time comes, he can make the right decision.

PHOENIX

After an entire English lesson spent daydreaming about Patrick's softly muscled arms, Phoenix trips back to her house, where her father has finished tinkering with the solar panels. Her father stands at the plastic basin they use for a sink, scrubbing the afternoon's plates with a scrub brush and waterless soap.

"Heading into town? I hate to ask, but can you sequester that?" Fernal nods towards the bulging trash bag. Sequester is their euphemistic phrase for illegally pitch in the first dumpster they can find.

"Sure, but I have a lot of homework. A five-page essay on my relationship to the earth. I'll have to go out a bit later."

"Okay," Fernal says, peering at her, "but not too late. The Enforcers get more aggressive at night."

"I'll go after the town meeting. Easy peasy."

"Don't forget your passport. I hear they're starting to pull people over more frequently."

Phoenix rolls her eyes. She makes these trips every week and she's never forgotten her passport. Why would she start now?

Fernal grabs Phoenix's shoulder and spins her slowly toward him. For a moment, as he stares into the wavering pool of her eyes, she thinks that he's found her out, that he can flip through the last two hours like a projector and see where she's really headed. "I know you think I'm being ridiculous, but I worry."

"I know."

"I don't know what I would do if something happened to you."

"Okay, Papa."

Fernal smiles and pulls her in for a hug. "Okay. Now get to that essay."

In the close quarters of their shared room, their sharp family odors still perceptible through the air freshener, Phoenix flips on the window A/C and flops onto her bed. The lie was easy to tell because it wasn't technically a lie: she does have a five-page essay to complete, but she has no intention of starting it now. She pulls open her dresser and roots in the underwear drawer for her old journal. She started shortly after her mother died and her father suggested putting her thoughts on paper. The last entry was dated June 23. She flips to the newest clean page and stares at the thin blues lines.

Dear Diary, she writes, then scribbles it out. Too juvenile.

I met a boy, she writes, then scribbles it out. She's known Patrick for years. And though he's been semi-flirtatious, it was always familial, almost brotherly. She wonders what has changed.

She holds the thick red journal up to the window light. If her father ever became suspicious, this would probably be the first place he would look. Better to leave things unsaid. She starts again, this time with one of her characters created in the lethal heat of August after weeks in the same tiny square cell: Juniper Barb, a jungle warrior who shoots poisonous darts from her fingertips and doesn't take shit from anyone. Juniper Barb used to have a partner-in-crime: Betty Go Boom, a femme fatale created by her best friend, Nuna. But Nuna left, so no more Betty. Phoenix creates a story in which Juniper Barb falls in love, though the man turns out to be a secret agent trying to extract the formula for her deadly darts, so she lures him to an isolated outcropping, ties him to a rock, and leaves him for the rest of the tribe to do with as they wish. She leaves the ending open, so it is up to the reader whether or not the man lives or dies.

The town meeting takes place in the high-ceilinged tin shack set up for communal events. It is where the Feast of Independence is held that marks the day they freed themselves from government tyranny, and it is where the newly reversed naming ceremonies take place. Each person brings their own chair and a beverage. In the back is the spread from Jim Hutchins: ten party-size subs and a tub of off-brand cola from Mike's Sub and Sandwich Emporium, one of three fast-food places where Jim works for the employee discount.

Francis Harcourt stands in front of the podium and waits until everyone is seated. He does not bang a gavel or make any other noise to signal the meeting has started; instead, he lifts a hand, and everyone falls silent. "Thank you. Now, we have a number of items to get to tonight, including Tim's proposal for an additional well and committee assignments for this year's Feast of Independence. But I think we're all a little anxious to hear the report from Barbara, so I'll yield the floor to her."

A woman sporting a perfect blonde bob and a form-fitting sleeveless dress strides up to the stage and places two hands on the podium. Her arms are tan and muscular. Everything about her is sharp, precise. She is the only woman in the building currently wearing make-up.

"I'll get right to it. The Native lobby is too great: we weren't able to re-negotiate the treaty to include the right to build a casino."

Phoenix clutches her father's arm. She and many others weren't keen on trampling on Native territory or making money from other people's addictions. However, they still need some legitimate business, or each family would have to continue to work illegally under the table for a third of what they should be making.

"Unfortunately, the news gets worse. Our bid to become sovereign territory was denied again. We are still classified as 'unincorporated territory,' even though we need a passport to cross into the border, a passport that, as we all know, carries severe restrictions on employment, travel, and resource consumption. As such, we are still controlled by state rather than federal legislature, which makes it nearly impossible to create a business that would incentivize citizens to cross the border. And the representative I met with warned that any further infractions would get us classified as a domestic terrorist organization."

Phoenix nervously sips her off-brand cola, clicking her tongue against its syrupy sweetness. She was foolish to get her hopes up: the country doesn't care about them, a bunch of traitors who chose to leave. Good riddance, everyone said after the marches and riots were over, the fires put out. And whenever they have problems, a camera crew is all too eager to catch their worst moments on tape, so families cozy in their air-conditioned living rooms can say I told you so.

Most of the men and women are grumbling while others leap from their chair to scream at Barbara, who remains at the podium to absorb their abuse.

"They can't fucking do this!"

"What the hell, Barbara?"

"Did you even try?"

"Maybe it's time for a new representative."

The last voice is Davie Lynn, named after both of his grand-parents. He is head-to-toe in camo, has a wall of compound bows and a Black Lab named Boomer back at the trailer he towed all the way to the desert.

"You want to replace me? Be my guest." Barbara grabs a tuft of hair and pulls, the entirety of the bob shearing off her suddenly bald head. She tosses the wig and it lands, like a small dog, right in Davie's lap.

Davie flicks the wig onto the floor. "You're fucking nuts."

Barbara gives the peace sign and strides off the stage.

Before Francis can take the stage, Phoenix is out the back door, shoving two sandwiches in her coat: one for her and one for Patrick. There's no chance that Tim's well proposal will pass, now that all hope for a legitimate source of revenue is gone, and Phoenix doesn't care about any other trifling issue, including Granny Hattie's monthly complaint, usually involving the twins and her sad desert garden.

"Phoenix! Where are you going?" Fernal jogs to catch up to her.

"To town, remember?"

Fernal picks at some dirt underneath his fingernails. "Maybe it's best you don't go."

"Because of some blowhard bureaucrat? He's just frightening us so we keep begging for table scraps. And who are these bureaucrats, anyway? A bunch of pathetic white boys who can barely stand under the weight of their own hypocrisy."

Fernal smiles and touches Phoenix's arm. "My little Minmi, now a ferocious raptor. Your mother would be so proud."

"I'll be careful Papa, don't worry."

Fernal nods, clasping her hands in his. Finally, he lets go. Phoenix can tell he wants to touch her hair, her face, keep some small part of her with him, so she turns and walks away before she can change her mind.

Ten minutes across the desert by car, and she pulls onto Mile Wide Road, which leads into town. About eight miles south is the toll booth, intended not only to track visitors from the desert but also to earn a little extra revenue. She hands her passport to a bored woman in a beige uniform.

"Business or personal?"

"Personal," Phoenix declares, wondering if she should have hidden the box of spirit orbs. But, as usual, the woman doesn't even glance into the backseat. She stamps the passport, takes Phoenix's money, and waves her through.

Phoenix pulls into downtown Chartreuse and manages to find an unsecured dumpster behind the Forever Lux. Most of the local businesses started securing their trash after the Natural Lifers moved in, which was both insulting and annoying, but usually Phoenix can find at least one lazy shop owner a week. After she parks, she carries the basket of spirit orbs into A Gift in Time. They made a deal with Sandra Nin, the owner, to sell their items for a share of the profit. Inside, oversized suns and hummingbirds battle it out for space among the shelves of pottery and jewelry and other kitschy knickknacks. Phoenix walks to the back wall, the local artist section, where the Native spread, woven baskets and calamity catchers and even a full-size rug, threatens to overwhelm their small space. Phoenix is dismayed to see an entire basket of spirit orbs. Have they even sold one since she was last here?

"Hey, honey." Sandra, a middle-aged woman with bleached blonde hair, squeezes Phoenix's shoulder. "This is gonna need to be the last shipment for a while."

"The spirit orbs aren't selling too well?"

"None of your stuff is. I guess the novelty's worn off."

"I could bring you some of our new handmade soap. I've been experimenting with a recipe featuring cacti." That is a lie—she has only recently considered the possibility—but they can't lose two sources of revenue in one day.

"Sorry, doll. No can do." Sandra pulls a shirt off the rack: an outline of the state with a small heart inside. "This looks like your size. Want me to wrap it up to take with you?"

"No thanks." Phoenix isn't feeling especially in love with Arridia today. "You'll call when you're ready for more items?"

"Sure, honey."

Phoenix scoots out of the store, her face hot, trying not to let the tears slip out. She sits in the car, the A/C on high, some bass-heavy song thumping in the background.

"Goddamn it," she finally says and wipes her face with the back of both hands. Then she turns the ignition and pulls out, not even looking behind her.

Even though she's nearly forty minutes early, she heads to the High Noon Bar. She passed it a couple times when heading to the YumYum Express with Nuna on one of their sweet tooth runs. Nuna and Phoenix always competed to see who could eat their ice cream the most seductively, with each round getting more outlandish, until Nuna would jam the nub of leftover cone up her nose and then snake her tongue into the opening, making her the de facto winner. But after years of sewing clothing for herself, her younger brother, and her mom, Nuna left her family and the Natural Lifers for good to pursue her dream of becoming a fashion designer. That was nearly a year ago, and Phoenix hasn't heard from her since.

The bar is in a more rural part of town, just at the outskirts of the desert. Phoenix pulls into the gravel driveway that the bar shares with a hair salon specializing in wig care for the woman who wants beautiful locks without wasting her weekly water stipend. Phoenix has toyed with the idea of cutting her hair, but her father says they aren't animals—they can afford basic hygiene. Of course, Phoenix is also fairly certain he's been using the hose on site to wash off like the other workers, leaving the bulk of the water for her. She pulls down the visor mirror and checks her teeth, finger-combs her hair, and then, with a deep breath, heads inside.

In the small, dark space, the wooden baseboards creaking beneath her feet, it feels like she's descending into the bowels of a ship. The small grimy windows let in very little light. She stands near the bar where two man, gray and hunched, sit several seats away from each other. They finger their glasses and don't look up. She glances at the cluster of tables, uncertain whether she should wait to be seated. The few times her father took her for a surprise dinner at Paulie's Tex Mex or Noodles², they always had to wait, usually behind three or four other families. But here there is no hostess stand, no large sign instructing her on what to do.

Near the back, five people sit at a table next to a raised platform with a karaoke machine. One of them turns and waves. Patrick. Phoenix, her heart rat-a-tat-tatting, walks over to him.

"You're early."

Phoenix shrugs, hoping she can dam the tears threatening again. "Sandra doesn't want our stuff anymore."

"Man, that sucks. I'm sorry."

Phoenix nods, ready to turn to more pleasant subjects, but the words spill from her lips before she can stop them. "And Barbara couldn't get us even one business. Not one. And those government goons threatened to label us terrorists if we keep getting caught over here."

And, goddamn it, here are the tears again, and worse, now that she's finally said it all out loud, her body releases everything, every quelled frustration, every stopped wail, and now she's sobbing, a loud and ugly spectacle, and when her body has finally emptied itself of sound, she ends with a series of gasping hitched breaths, trying to get air.

Five faces watch her break down: Patrick and four other strangers. She thinks about muttering some excuse and leaping towards the door, or maybe burrowing into the creaking floorboards and starting her new life as a stowaway, but before she can say anything, a woman with spiked blonde hair and a tank top that says "Eat Pussy: It's Good for You" leans across the table.

"They're assholes, every last one of them. Don't let them make you feel like shit."

Phoenix nods and manages a hiccupping smile.

The woman turns to Patrick and scowls. "You gonna let your girl be upset or you gonna get her a drink?"

"Sorry, Ruby—you're right." Patrick jogs over to the bar.

"And check on our actual customers while you're there!" Ruby leans over the table again. "Since your boy's an asshat, I'll do the introductions. Over there is Adam." A muscled guy in a white tank top and jeans nods. "And that's Jongmyung, but he goes by Gabe." The long, lanky guy sitting next to Adam, head to toe in matching Thresher gear, smiles. "And that's Jose." Jose, his hair in tight cornrows, sits at an adjacent table by himself.

"He's a b-boy, but we don't hold that against him," Adam says.

"Least I'm not a meathead," Jose says with a smirk.

"I'm sorry, who beat who on Jeopardy last week?"

"Man, you know I can't do that Before and After shit. And you just won 'cause there were two different Sports categories."

Adam shrugs and leans back in his chair. "Can't help it if I'm quicker than you."

"And finally," Ruby says above their bickering, "that's Danny."

"People call me Danger," Danny says. With his short brown

hair and light blue t-shirt, he seems the most forgettable of the five.

"Nobody fucking calls you that," Ruby says.

Phoenix nods. Though her face is probably still puffy and red, at least she can breathe. "Nice to meet you. There's no chance I'm going to remember all of your names."

Ruby laughs, an open-throated celebration. Phoenix likes how loud she is, how she takes up as much space as she wants. "I like your girl, Trick. She's got balls."

Patrick sets down two beer bottles slick with moisture. Phoenix knows she will actually have to drink this one, so she takes several long gulps. The beer is cool and frothy down her throat and only tastes a little like bitter soap. Her fingers work at the label.

"Feel better?" Ruby asks.

Phoenix wonders how a beer is supposed to make her feel better, but everyone seems to find this plausible, so Phoenix nods.

"All right, ladies and gentlefuckers, who's going to be first?" Ruby nods towards the karaoke machine. "It was your idea, Trick."

"I'll go," Danny says, already leaping onto the stage. He fiddles with the machine and then steps back.

"I thought it might bring in more customers on Sunday, our dead night," Patrick explains. He looks toward the two men sitting at the bar. "So far, no luck."

Danny clears his throat and glances out at them to make sure they're listening. Then he launches into a soulful rendition of "My Heart Beats for You."

"My heart's an open secret, it's hidden beneath the floor, my eyes are blue and open, won't you come in through my door?"

"Boo! Boo!" Jose calls. He lifts an empty bottle and then lowers it when Ruby glares at him.

"You break shit, you're gonna pick it up with your fucking teeth."

Danny begins hamming it up, reaching out to the audience, clutching his chest, his voice growing higher and more pitched, amid an ever-growing chorus of boos. Finally the song ends and

Patrick takes Phoenix's hand and leads her up to the stage.

"I don't know," she says, pulling away.

"Don't worry—I have the perfect song." Patrick grips her hand tighter and pulls, gently at first, and then with more pressure, until she's up the stairs.

The words flash on the screen: When I first saw you, I thought oh well. When you first spoke to me, I thought, gee, that's swell. But now that you're here in the cover of night, the world has burst open like a dream come to life. And I say oooh oooh baby, I can finally see. Yes oh yes baby, you're the one for me.

Phoenix sings, quietly at first, her lips nearly touching the microphone, but watching Patrick belt out the lyrics and gyrate his hips emboldens her, and soon she's matching him in pitch and volume. They finish the song to a small thunderclap of applause from the closest table.

Back at the table, Phoenix lifts and then immediately sets the beer back down. Maybe she can sneak it into the bathroom and pour it down the sink when no one's looking.

Patrick leans in. His breath warms her neck. "You don't like beer very much, do you?"

Phoenix shakes her head, embarrassed.

"Why didn't you say something? No reason to suffer through it." He smiles and grabs the half-full bottle. "I'll make you something better."

After he leaves, Adam fixes his gaze on her. It is cold and penetrating, almost predatory. "You're one of those Natural Lifers too, huh? You work in town like Patrick?"

"Not really. I come into town about once a week, though."

"Damn, only once a week? I would get so fucking bored," Jose says. He takes out a sharpie and begins sketching something on the table. Phoenix waits for Ruby to yell at him, but she doesn't seem to notice, or if she does, she doesn't care.

Phoenix glances at Gabe, who is sitting with his hands primly clasped. "You don't say very much."

Gabe blushes and looks down, and Phoenix immediately feels

bad—she knows what that kind of unwanted attention feels like, the assumption that if she isn't braying like a mule, she must be shy.

"Gabe here thinks his English is jacked. But it's fine—probably better than mine," Jose says.

Patrick returns with a glass full of thick, syrupy red. A slit strawberry straddles the rim. "Strawberry daiquiri. Enjoy."

Phoenix takes a sip that is sweet and tart and sharp. She swallows quickly so she doesn't choke. She waits a second for her nostrils to clear and then takes another.

Ruby leans in to Patrick, and Phoenix feels jealousy burbling in the now-warm pit of her chest. "You know the deal—beer only. That one's coming out of your pay."

Patrick shrugs and motions for Phoenix to keep drinking.

Ruby takes the stage and sings several screaming punk songs Phoenix has never heard before. As Phoenix downs the daiquiri that is becoming easier and easier to drink, she imagines herself in the restroom, shearing her hair into spikes and tearing her top into a tight-fitting tank. She imagines herself emerging, her face scrunched into a scowl, to a whistle of admiration from Ruby.

She turns to Patrick. "So is Alana watching your grandparents?"

"Yeah, though they're not really our grandparents."

"Oh," Phoenix says. How could she have gotten that wrong?

"I mean, physically, they're them. But Siobhan's just an infant and Liam's a toddler. They're nothing like the people who raised us."

"Maybe when they're older, you'll start to recognize them."

Patrick shrugs. "Maybe. But by then, they'll probably be totally different people from our shitty caregiving."

"I think you guys are doing great." Phoenix feels that familiar flutter in her chest at the thought of Patrick rocking an infant to sleep.

"I guess. But it's fucking brutal, raising two kids. There's always some emergency, and you have no time, no money. It's just go, go, go from morning 'til night. Working here is the only break I get. Most guys my age have their own apartment, a full-time job, maybe even a girlfriend. I've got two needy kids and a sister in a house the size of a trailer. I can't remember the last time I went home and it didn't smell like piss and spit-up."

Phoenix fingers the rim of her glass. She had no idea how miserable Patrick was. If raising a child is this hard on him, and he has help, how can she possibly do it alone? Maybe her father is right. But what will happen to him if she leaves? Who will take care of him? She grabs the strawberry and bites it whole.

"It drives me crazy when you do that," Patrick whispers in her ear. Phoenix sits upright. When she does what? Eats a piece of fruit? And how can Patrick go from mourning his lost bachelor-hood to horny in a matter of milliseconds?

"Looks like you could use a refill." He grabs her glass.

"Are you sure? I heard Ruby say—"

Patrick turns back and winks. "Don't worry, I got you."

Phoenix relaxes into the chair. The edges of her vision go soft. How nice that she's here with Patrick and all of his cool friends. Ruby and Adam start debating the most underrated punk bands, Ruby shouting names of all-female bands over Adam's suggestions. Phoenix takes another long drink and it is cool and sweet. Patrick's friends climb the stage and sing and gyrate to rock songs Phoenix half-remembers from her father's old CDs. One of them might be The Greybeards. Or maybe all of them all. Who cares! Phoenix drifts in time to the music. What does CD stand for again? Patrick tells her, because apparently, she asked this question out loud. She has already forgotten his answer, so she decides to make up her own name later and patent it. Cool Data. Conditional Dancing. Controlled Danger.

Phoenix stands. "I have to pee."

"Bathroom's back and to your left," Ruby says. She narrows her eyes. "You want some company?"

"No, I am an excellent pee-er." Phoenix walks until she sees the familiar outline of a woman. Why is this woman wearing a dress? Phoenix isn't wearing a dress. Does that mean she isn't a woman? But Ruby isn't wearing a dress, and she's definitely a woman. This door is an antique. Antiquated. That's it.

Inside the bathroom, Phoenix squints at her reflection in the mirror. Her face looks wrong—her eyes too big, her skin too shiny, her cheeks too flushed and apple-round. She pokes her cheek but doesn't feel it. She gathers all of her hair on top of her head and tries to imagine herself with a pixie cut.

"Bye bye, hair," she whispers to the mirror.

She stumbles into the stall and pulls down her shorts. Her stream comes in spurts. She tries to release it to the tune of the last karaoke song, but she doesn't have that kind of control.

She washes her hands with BirdBath wipes and tosses them onto the floor next to the trashcan.

"I'm drunk," she chirps to the mirror.

When she returns to her table, she finishes the second drink in one long gulp. Ruby makes a slicing motion across her throat. Maybe they are ninja assassins and they are here to kill her, Juniper Barb. If so, she'll have to seduce them all first. Phoenix imagines walking up to Ruby's chair first, since she is obviously the leader. She imagines Ruby's hand on her stomach, her back, Ruby's tongue following her trickle of sweat wherever it may lead.

No, that's not right. She climbs into Patrick's lap and puts her lips on his neck. "Are you here to kill me?"

Patrick chuckles. "Maybe."

And then the door slams open and they all jump. Six girls in sequined tops and too-tight jeans hover at the doorway, clutching each other's arms. The one in front with the cheap plastic tiara screams. "I told you they had karaoke!"

They stampede toward the table, two of them breaking off midway to the bar. Ruby reaches into the seat behind her and picks up two button-down black shirts, one of which she tosses to Patrick. She begins buttoning hers over the tank top. "Party's over."

Adam, Gabe, and Jose rise and start heading to the door. Danny remains seated, his smile one of childish glee. The four girls not at the bar grab Jose's table and drag it toward an adjacent one.

"Oh my god, this one has a dick on it!"

"Goddamn it, Jose," Ruby mutters. Jose shrugs, grinning.

The girl with the tiara shrieks, "That's just what I need!" She looks over to Adam, who hesitates, his gaze shifting from the girls to the door.

"But you're getting married," a girl with streaked mascara and tangled blonde hair whines.

"Not 'til tomorrow. Tonight, I'm free as a bird!"

"And as horny as one!"

All the girls collapse giggling into their chairs.

"Helloooooo," one of the girls calls, leaning over the bar.

"Yes, coming," Ruby says, and Phoenix feels a pit in her chest to see Ruby cow-tailing to these tragic glitter bombs.

Patrick grips the shirt in one hand and grabs Phoenix's hand with the other. "Give me a second," he says to Ruby and then to Phoenix, "I have something to show you."

"Hurry up," Ruby says, her hand waving in small circles.

Patrick pulls Phoenix into a small back office. A faux wood and metal desk belching manila folders, uncapped pens, and an ancient brick laptop stands next to stacks of liquor boxes, some empty, others not. In the corner is a single-sized mattress with a light blue fitted sheet, the corners scuffed and several bleach stains near the center.

Even as the rough ocean waves of the strawberry mojito make the room pitch and swell, Phoenix wonders what she's supposed to be looking at.

And then Patrick is mashing his face into hers, his hands yanking her shirt, her shorts. "God, you're sexy," he murmurs into her neck, each word a puff of humid air against her skin.

"Thanks," Phoenix says, though it comes out more like a question.

He pulls her shirt over her head and drops it onto the floor. "Do you even see how perfect you are?"

"Um." She wants to cover her chest, her small yellow bra with the sewn-on bow. She looks at the door.

"Don't worry—nobody's coming in." He quickly sheds his

own shirt and his chest is almost white in the fluorescent light. It looks caved-in, sallow. She wonders if hers looks the same.

And then he's unzipping her shorts, pulling them to the ground. He stands and cups the back of her head. "Do you like me?"

Phoenix nods.

"I like you too." He pulls down his own shorts, the elastic twanging over his hips, and suddenly that hidden darkness is lit, and it is a twist of springy black hair and something else, something Phoenix isn't yet ready to name, thick and bulbous and stuttering towards her.

Phoenix looks up and into his eyes. He is looking at her but not really—it is as though he is looking through her at something much more interesting. She is standing, then she is on the mattress, then he is on top of her. She grabs his back to steady herself—every part of her feels off balance—and then feels a sharp sting. She holds her breath until he starts moving and it doesn't hurt anymore. Now she is numb there too.

"Tell me you like it." He bites her neck, gently at first, and then a little harder. "Tell me you want it."

"I'm not—" she begins to say and then takes a shaky breath. She looks across the dusty floor at a stress ball painted to look like a globe. The blue of the ocean is flaking off in places, revealing a dull grey sponge beneath. As his body presses into hers, she starts hearing a song her elementary teacher used to sing: "One Little Planet."

One little planet, is it enough? One little planet all used up.

"Don't worry—I got you, baby girl, I got you." Patrick is above her and shuddering and she thinks that maybe he too is feeling uncertain. But then she recognizes his pleasure moving over her on a solitary course, a cruise liner leaving her capsized in the middle of the sea.

Her eyes trace the contours of the stress ball, the edge of each continent lost in the thick gray foam. The end for him is like a seizure or maybe a sneeze. Is it even pleasant or just necessary? Then he is buttoning up the black shirt, trading the shorts for a pair of jeans. Next to Phoenix's legs is a small dark stain. She remembers when their community brought in a volunteer medic to give everyone check-ups. The man with broad shoulders and a gut poking out of his lab coat would splay her legs and gently touch her skin with an "ah, hmm; ah, hmm." Phoenix felt the press of his fingers turning her body into a series of parts, divorced and foreign from the rest of her. Afterwards, she wanted to touch her stomach, her arms, her thighs, and bring them back into a unified whole, solid and irrevocable, but she couldn't. That is how she feels now, lying on this dirty mattress, Patrick already standing, already dressed, already whole again.

Patrick leans in and kisses her cheek. "Gotta go. Don't miss me too much."

Once he's gone, she dresses and slips out the door, past the drunk women screaming into the microphone, past Ruby and now Patrick shaking cocktails behind the bar, and into the dark solitude of her truck. She had hoped that Patrick took the ocean with him, but here it is again, pounding in her ears, her throat. Her car is a flood site, her dashboard floating up and away from her. No amount of gripping the wheel can hold it still. Oh no.

Phoenix bursts from the driver's seat and runs to the nearest tree, where she hits the dirt, vomit searing through her nose and throat. She pukes again and again. Finally, blissfully empty, her stomach quivering, she stares up at the moon-dark branches. It is a walnut tree. She feels like that means something, but she can't remember what. As she sways gently on her hands and knees, she makes up a song:

Walnut tree, walnut tree, tonight at least, you're my puking tree. Walnut tree, walnut tree, I know that you'll never leave me.

She stands. Thankfully, the tide is finally out. The water is trembling and calm. She can probably drive home now.

On the now-motionless dashboard, the clock reads 10:48. Shit, when did it get so late? She has absolutely no excuse, no alibi, and with each passing second ticking against her skull, she has no other option. She is ready to be in her room, curled into her pink and purple comforter, in the close, familiar space of home.

VIRGIL

The South Burrington Enforcer building is ordinary: just another windowed tomb in the office district. Virgil expected something ominous and oppressive, a sleek black coffin glossed to an evil sheen, not another faceless bureaucrat. Inside, guards flank two scanners, their bodies hard and gray, a breastplate full of hammered divots. Beyond them, a woman in a sleek bun sits behind a mahogany desk. The wood grain flashes a tickertape of information that the woman reads then swipes away. She gives Virgil a visitor's keycard that will call down the elevator and allow him to choose a floor.

On the fifth floor, Virgil heads to the break room, his fingers touching the camera hidden in his pocket. Three Enforcers sit at one of the tables, drinks sweating through their cardboard. Virgil considers turning the camera on to catch a little audio, but as soon as he steps into the room, they all clam up. After several awkward seconds where Virgil is uncertain whether he should sit down or not, the Enforcers toss their trash and file past him silently. No one makes eye contact.

Benson appears at the doorway. "Good, you're here. Come with me."

He leads Virgil to a large closet. Oblong gray stains along the floor along with the lingering smell of ammonia suggest this was once a janitor's closet. Now, towering industrial lights illuminate a single folding chair. Behind the chair stands a woman with a ponytail of teased blonde hair and a face contoured to appear sharp and dramatic. She holds a giant puffball and motions for Virgil to sit.

"Doreen is going to do your make-up."

My what, Virgil thinks, as Doreen begins to pencil around his eyes, puff powder on his cheeks, comb his stubble, and color his lips with what he hopes is not lipstick.

Benson peers at Virgil's face, slowly, appraisingly. Virgil imagine Benson standing in his bedroom, examining a line of women in negligee—touching their necks, spreading their legs, shaking the skin underneath their arms, all the while stroking his small, puffy cravat.

Benson nods. "Good. Let's go."

The elevator ticks down, past the entrance at ground level and into the bowels of the building. The doors open onto the basement, a darkened space of concrete and exposed brick occasionally punctuated by fluorescent lights. Benson leads Virgil into a familiar scene: an expanse of stainless steel splattered with grease and bits of tomato and kale. It looks like a cleaner version of the prep station, grill, and fry station from the Health King. Voluminous tripod lights cocooned in umbrellas surround the scene and cast it in a yellow-orange glow.

A man wearing all black, his hair gelled to a single soft-serve point, lifts his camera. Immediately, Virgil hates him.

"We're going to get some before and after shots for the first PR splash," Benson says. He motions for Virgil to stand behind the grill. "It's a normal day at work and you've just received your first order. Go."

Virgil grabs a metal spatula along with a handful of kale and some pre-cooked sausage. He's used to the sound of sizzling and the beeping of timers merging together in a pleasant, mind-numbing cacophony, but here it is quiet, and five pairs of eyes watch as he flips the kale and sausage, the thwak of food on cold plastic interrupted only by the clicking of the camera.

"Sad. Saaaaaad," the photographer instructs.

Virgil pulls his face into a pantomime of unhappiness, slumping his shoulders and grimly pushing the mush around.

"Now you are wishing for better times."

How the fuck does a person look like they are wishing for better times? Virgil remembers all the times he stood at the grill, imagining a better life, one involving a cushy office gig and a busty secretary in a tight-fitting cardigan. This is definitely not what he had in mind. He gazes up and to the right, trying to look wistful.

"Now you are angry. Angry to be working this horrible job."

Virgil imagines throwing the spatula right into this asshole's face. Who the fuck is he to judge?

At this point, Virgil is no longer pretending to cook anything—he's just banging the spatula against the stainless steel, creating a sharp ringing that makes everyone cringe.

"Okay, good. Now customers."

Doreen appears, her teased hair now free of its ponytail. Even in her stained khaki pants and tucked olive t-shirt, she looks too careful and put-together. Plus, she's about fifty pounds shy of the Health King's usual clientele.

"All right, exchange money."

Doreen complies, a crisp twenty held between her thumb and forefinger. She freezes in place. Virgil closes his hand around hers.

"No, no, no. We need to see the money."

Virgil pulls his hand back and awkwardly freezes. The photographer circles, snapping shot after shot. Virgil imagines him as a boy, surrounded by two beaming adults who cooed over his inscrutable crayon drawings as though the spasmodic scribbles signaled the arrival of a new child prodigy, while Virgil's mother simply let his drawings fall to the floor, two manicured fingers pressed to her forehead to signal yet another migraine. His parents probably indulged his every whim, signed him up for expensive enrichment classes and bought all the latest flashing gizmos hocked by sugar-corrupted brats on Channel 4. They probably didn't drop him off with the 62-year-old neighbor upstairs who fell asleep by noon, forcing him to learn pretty fucking quickly not to play with knives or hot stoves. His parents probably only fucked each other once a month in a lukewarm, fully-clothed tumble and did not lead rows of grinning, pot-bellied men through his goddamn living room. And now here he is, their pride and joy, a douchebag pretending to be an artist, taking mediocre pictures for the roaches' latest vanity project. Whatever. Next go around, someone at the Nest will take Virgil in and all those memories will disappear. Poof.

The douchebag circles again and waves a hand in Virgil's direction. "Now she is giving an order and your face is dead."

Doreen gestures above us to a fake board. Damn, she's good. She's going to look totally natural and Virgil is going to look like a lumbering fool.

"Dead face," the photographer repeats.

How the hell does he make dead face? Virgil closes his eyes.

"No, not sleepy. Dead."

Virgil snaps his eyes open.

"Not angry. Dead."

Virgil slams his fist onto the cash register. Doreen flinches but recovers. Her expression is frozen in place. Virgil stares out across the subterranean damp, past her, past Benson, past the douchebag photographer, to the possibility nestled in the aching thrum that nobody will want to take him in, that he's too much of a fuck-up, that this is his one and only shot.

"Finally, yes. Now with backdrop."

Doreen strides off. Virgil wants to apologize but she's already gone. The photographer points him toward yet another set-up, this time a plain white screen.

"Again, wistful."

Virgil stares off into the distance, the spatula drooping uselessly by his side.

"Arms crossed. To me."

He complies, feeling the muscles tense around his neck and back, imagining his hands popping the photographer's head clean off his body. Benson whispers something to a woman with a clipboard who wasn't there a moment ago. She nods.

Benson claps. "Okay, good, now let's get some after shots."

Doreen brings Virgil a square of folded fabric. Baby blue. Oh shit. Virgil knew he would eventually have to put on the uniform, but he assumed he could postpone it for days, maybe even weeks. It looks like the moment has arrived.

Virgil ducks into a small bathroom, the overhead light flickering with a soft tsking sound. His sallow face is reflected in the mirror. He slips off his shirt and pants, setting them on the sink. He has the distinct impression that everyone is watching, even though the door is closed. Part of him wants to run from the bathroom screaming. Another part wants to jerk off. He stands for a moment, cupping the bulge of his stomach, noting how the coiled black hairs of his legs grow however they choose, ignoring all design and symmetry. Still, there is probably some deeper law, some mathematical construct, some invisible hand of the universe leading them, inexorably, to a predetermined destination. Virgil slides the fabric, cool and stiff and surprisingly light, over his body. He zips it all the way up. It fits perfectly—like his own tailored suit, or a body bag.

Virgil flings the door open before he can create an indelible image of himself as a man in blue.

"Good, good," Benson says, clasping Virgil on the shoulder. Instead of feeling terrified or in awe of his presence, the uniform seems to put everyone at ease. Suddenly, everyone is standing much closer. That's not good.

Firm, guiding hands lead Virgil back to the white backdrop. His bares his teeth in unadulterated menace, but the photographer simply instructs him to look straight at the camera, this time with a look of confidence.

The photographer pauses. "This is not good."

"Okay," Benson says, walking beside the photographer. "Imagine all the good you're going to do in that uniform."

The photographer looks through the lens and then back at Benson. "Worse."

"Then imagine the people in your building. What can they do

with two years of rent?"

Virgil doesn't want to follow his direction, but he's suddenly picturing Mrs. Silvers putting baby Karl to bed and then flipping through the channels until she finds an old episode of *Buttercup Brigade*—not putting on a pair of scrubs to work yet another night shift, her body tick-tick-ticking away the hours until its inevitable collapse— but calm, happy, well-rested.

The photographer clicks away and then nods. "Got it."

Benson walks up and slaps Virgil on the back. Virgil's got to get out of this uniform and into something less approachable. "Great job! Just super. Let's take five, and then we'll head over to your complex to get a few interior shots, some local color, et cetera."

"What should I wear?"

Benson gestures to the uniform.

"I don't think that's a great idea. I mean, I'm supposed to have a transformation, right? Shouldn't everyone see me just as a regular person first? Before . . . "

Benson smirks. "All right, fair point. Why don't you head home, and we'll meet you there?"

Virgil walks toward the bathroom when Benson calls, "You can return the fast food uniform, but keep the Enforcer uniform. It's yours now."

Back home, after sliding the treacherous blue fabric into his dresser and taking a few hits of a Zoomie to calm his nerves, Virgil opens the door to three cameramen, a guy holding a boom mike, two women carrying small black bags, and Benson.

"Well, this place certainly is . . . charming," Benson says. Virgil follows his gaze to the water stain shaped like a pot-bellied pig, the drywall ripping off in strips, the piles of dirty laundry he didn't have time to hide. It's definitely a shithole, but it's his shithole, and Virgil's ready to throw down over the next passive-aggressive comment.

Benson claps his hands, and the men and women begin setting up. "Let's get some everyday shots."

The women begin mussing Virgil's hair, rubbing something slick and oily across his face. If he wasn't so uncomfortable, it would almost be sexy.

Benson directs Virgil into bed, where he strips down to his boxers. One of the cameramen pulls three Zoomies from his bag and sets them on the nightstand. Virgil chuckles—if they want to give him free drugs, more power to them.

"You're just waking up, and go."

After a few seconds of laying with his head on the pillow, smelling his own musty scent, Virgil slowly sits up and swipes the alarm clock off the stand. He yawns, stretching his arms comically wide, and then takes a long toke of the Zoomie. Nearly half the baggie is gone by the time he's done.

"And cut," Benson says. "Good work. Very, uh, authentic."

Virgil runs through the rest of his morning routine while the second camera zooms in on each unpleasant detail, like the pile of toenail spears on the nightstand or the spray of toothpaste and popped zits on the mirror. Each time a cameraman pauses, each crusty sock or rancid wrapper suddenly set aglow, Virgil sees this place through their eyes: a bubbling pit of excrement, endlessly swirling. Might as well lean in. As he brushes his teeth, he adds in some disgusting bachelor behaviors: belching, scratching his balls, excavating ear wax with his pinkie. The final shot is Virgil, dressed in his Health King uniform, walking out the door. They get a shot of him from inside the apartment, and then they reset and get a shot of him from outside. At the end, he's exhausted and ready to climb back into bed and finish off that Zoomie.

But the women poking through Virgil's closet tells him they're not done yet. After a few minutes of whispering to each other, they finally pull out a pair of ripped jeans and a shirt featuring a busty space alien with a comically large blaster saying, "Here Comes the Boom." God, when was the last time he wore that shirt? Virgil was 19 when he bought it at Mayonnaise Salad, a crappy store selling t-shirts, magnets, and posters with obvious sexual innuendo written in comic sans.

With everyone staring at him expectantly, he takes the outfit into the bathroom. It takes a few minutes to struggle into the shirt, which suctions to his chest and stomach, clearly outlining his gut. Terrific. When he emerges, the women look at each other and nod. So, this what they want—some chubby asshole in a chauvinistic shirt? Naturally.

Benson leads the group to Mrs. Silvers' door. She answers on the first knock like she's been expecting them. She glances at Virgil's shirt, then up at his face with a look of flickering concern. He gives her his best what-can-you-do shrug and she motions for everyone to come inside.

Inside, the place is immaculate: the scuffed and yellowing linoleum has been scrubbed, the carpet has been vacuumed, the television stand and bookcase have been dusted, the porcelain knickknacks centered perfectly in the shadowbox, and the afghan that usually blocks the breeze from the doorway is now carefully laid across the back of the couch. In the center of the room is baby Karl in a bouncy chair, happy and burbling, no nebulizer in sight.

Virgil grins at the brief flash of disappointment on Benson's face. Only one pathetic loser on the agenda today. The cameramen get shots of the kitchen, the living room, the bedroom, and baby Karl, but they spend far less time focusing on the minutiae than they did in Virgil's apartment. Not enough pathos to this poverty, Virgil supposes.

Then they set up for an interview: Mrs. Silvers on the floral couch, hands clasped in her lap, her face small and gray.

"Okay Barbara, we're going to ask you a few questions." Benson speaks in a voice usually reserved for children.

Mrs. Silvers nods.

"How did you wind up at The Nest?"

"Family is something I've always struggled to keep." She tucks a lock of hair behind her ear. "My parents died young. No brothers or sisters. And my husband, well, he had a heart condition."

"How did your parents die?"

"In a car accident. Father was on the board of the hospital, and they would attend all sorts of galas. I remember she always wore shiny black dresses and perfume." Mrs. Silvers closes her eyes and tilts her head, as though the smell has drifted, undiminished, through time. "It smelled of jasmine and oak, and always reminded me of moonlight drifting through the window." Mrs. Silvers opens her eyes. "Well, one night they didn't come back. I was eleven. I went to live with my aunt. Life was different with her—quiet, austere. Church every Sunday, meals in silence, that sort of thing. It wasn't bad, it just wasn't very warm."

Virgil sits, his hands clasped just like hers. This is the most he's ever heard her talk about her past.

"And your husband?"

"He had a heart condition, as I said. I don't like to talk about that."

"Any children?"

Mrs. Silvers swallows, her hands working at something invisible. Virgil isn't sure why she's taking so long to answer. If she had children, she would have mentioned it by now.

"One. A daughter," she finally says.

Virgil shifts in his seat.

"What happened to her?" Benson asks.

Mrs. Silvers swallows again. She picks up one of the throw pillows and fingers the fringe before setting it back down. "She was the most beautiful baby—yellow hair that was almost white. Soft, pink lips. And those big green eyes that would make you give her whatever she wanted. I knew she was going to be a willful child, but I underestimated just how willful. I mean, I assumed her hatred of dresses was just a phase. Her tomboy phase. And her crying fits whenever I took her to a department store to shop for bras were just low self-esteem, like any girl. I told her it was time to grow up, stop letting this childish hysteria rule her. It was time to become a woman."

Everyone inside the apartment is silent, waiting.

"By the time she reached high school, there was this rift between us. She had cut almost all of her hair off, her beautiful blonde locks, and she was wearing this leather jacket she found in a thrift store. Looked like something more appropriate to a biker gang, and I told her so. Then she left for college and never returned. She sent postcards from different places, Grantsburg and Binville, and signed them Ocean. Asked me to use 'he' when speaking to her. I refused—when your child is lost in the woods, you don't pack them a sandwich, you go and bring them back. Then one month she wrote that she and her therapist had decided it best she cut ties with me. When I was diagnosed with breast cancer, I wrote to all of the addresses I had for her, but she never responded."

"Did she ever have surgery? Fully transition?" Benson asks.

Mrs. Silvers snaps her head up. "That is none of your business." Then, as the camera zooms into her face, the anger streaking behind her eyes fades, leaving her small and hunched. "I'm sorry, but I am quite tired. Is this sufficient?"

Benson nods and motions for the cameramen to wrap it up. "Thank you for your cooperation, Barbara."

Mrs. Silvers nods and then stands by the door, waiting for everyone, including Virgil, to leave. Virgil tries to catch her eye, give her a sympathetic nod, but she doesn't look up.

In the hallway, Benson has a slow-creeping smile, and Virgil realizes what he's going to do: he's going to find this Ocean, this estranged child, and get his perspective. He's going to juxtapose his memories against Mrs. Silvers' narrative, turn the floral couch and linoleum floor into something nefarious and oppressive, maybe even arrange a surprise meeting, a confrontation. Virgil glances back at the closed door—no matter what this kid has to say, Mrs. Silvers doesn't deserve that.

Benson and the camera crew knock on door after door, but everyone is out or they're pretending to be. He turns to the girl in the headset. "Call them all—arrange interviews. Make it a condition of their rent. Let's see what else is skittering underneath the floorboards of this place."

After Benson and the others leave, Virgil strips the too-tight shirt and smashes it into the trash can. He feels coated in grime, worse than any shift at the Health King. He considers finishing the two and a half Zoomies left on the nightstand but decides against it. He doesn't want to mellow out—he wants to grab something by the neck and squeeze. With nothing to do, nowhere to go, and no money to do it, he grabs the Health King uniform and heads out. Anything to get out of this suffocating apartment.

The Health King is past the lunchtime rush and in the no-man's-land of 2:00 pm, so Virgil slides past the handful of customers drinking Kale Berry Smoothies or crunching on fried zucchini sticks and heads to the back. Flies flit lazily from customer to customer, clustering around the puddle of soda on the table near the restroom. The tables are molded plastic meant to resemble kale leaves and carrots and other healthy vegetables, beckoning patrons to eat their oily slop and then leave as quickly as possible. Becky's at drive-thru, which is amusing since she's slow as hell and gets the order wrong half of the time. Jerome is on the line today, and as usual, Terese is pushing the bucket towards the bathrooms. Maybe he's imagining things, but Virgil swears they're glaring at him as he passes, even Terese, who never speaks above a whisper and whose gray hair forms a permanent frizzy halo around her head.

In the office, Virgil slips past the boxes of ketchup packets and napkins made from recycled paper and sets his folded-up uniform on Jim's desk. Jim is everything Virgil tries to avoid: he's the manager of a shitty fast food joint, wears khaki pants belted over his gut, shaves his head to hide his receding hairline, and claps his hands to get everyone's attention. Not to mention the posters. Behind him is one that says, "Eye wouldn't do that" with a wide, unblinking eye and a series of angular shadow-men doing things the eye doesn't like: chatting during work, stealing, failing to wash their hands after using the restroom.

"Was wondering when you'd show up." Jim is writing something on a pad in front of him, but Virgil wouldn't be surprised if it was just a bunch of squiggles. Perhaps it is power move number 10, always keep your subordinates waiting, from the copy of *Boss Bitch: 50 Power Moves for the Motivated Woman* that he keeps hidden in his top desk drawer.

Virgil is about to respond but then stops. How did Jim know he was coming in?

"You can come pick up your last paycheck on Friday. Is there anything else?"

Virgil shakes his head, though Jim hasn't even bothered to look up. Another boss bitch move. Whatever, Virgil has better things to do now than tangle with this buffoon.

When Virgil turns to leave, Jerome is blocking the door. He's leaning against it, arms crossed, in a posture of forced relaxation. "Guess you wanted something better, huh?"

What the hell? Is today National Asshole Day? Virgil places a hand on Jerome's chest and waits. Will he move on his own or is Virgil going to have to get physical?

Jerome straightens so he's flush with the doorframe, enough for Virgil to squeeze past. Virgil recalls two weeks ago, when he and Jerome sat on his lumpy couch drinking Insanifizz (uppers and downers mixed in a sugary, carbonated soda) and watching shitty action movies from fifteen years ago. Jerome's the kind of guy who should be celebrating Virgil quitting, not posturing like a goddamn bouncer.

After Virgil clears the door, Jerome follows him, and it takes all of Virgil's willpower not to turn around and clock him.

"Hey," Jerome says. Virgil turns, ready for either an apology or a fight. Jerome points a shaking finger at Virgil. "You're not fucking better than us. Remember that."

Virgil waves his hand dismissively and strides past the gaze of Jerome and Becky and Terese, past the customers slurping up their greasy slop, through the double-doors and into the oppressive city heat.

He's walking slowly, trying to remain calm, so no one will know they had any effect on him, when he sees it: lightning-bright, even in the afternoon sun, and the size of a building. *Do you want something better?* The same question from last week is still there, but now there's a picture of Virgil, sweaty and focused, flipping imaginary fast food on the grill. Then the picture transitions to Virgil, spatula in hand, staring out at nothing, his eyes flat and empty. God, he looks like such an asshole. And then, even though he knows it's coming, it still turns his bowels to soup. Coming Next Week: *Becoming Blue*. And under that teaser is a picture of Virgil dressed as an Enforcer. No, not dressed as one. Virgil, an Enforcer.

Well, shit.

PHOENIX

As soon as Phoenix wakes, she regrets it. The light is an assault—it arrows into her head and lands, quivering, in her temple. Her throat is parched and the space between her legs, well, she doesn't want to think about it.

She scuffs into the main room, hoping to find a can of cola, something thick and syrupy that can coat her throat. Everything hurts. Everything is too much. If this is what drinking feels like, she's never touching a goddamn beer again.

At the kitchen table, her father is sitting, hands clasped, head lowered. Five curling beer labels are spread like a cornucopia of shame before her. She blinks and then remembers peeling them off one by one as the others finished their drinks. She must have put them in her pocket. She looks down—she's wearing pajamas. When did that happen?

"Sit," her father says.

She sits.

"So, not only did you sneak off to a bar while you're still underage, but you lied to me and put yourself in danger. Does that about cover it?"

Phoenix doesn't say anything.

Fernal shoves his chair back with a screech. He begins pacing the tiny kitchen. "We're not like other people, Phoenix—we can't mess up like this. If you had gotten caught, we would be a bunch of sandworms stealing from hard-working citizens or worse, terrorists. They'd lock you up and throw away the key. Is that what you want?"

Phoenix shakes her head. It reverberates, an unholy ringing. Big mistake.

"You're grounded. For a month, possibly longer. You'll go to your tutoring sessions, all of them, and then come straight home. And you've lost your truck privileges until I see that you've gotten your head on straight again. Any drop-offs of our merchandise will be made by me."

"Sandra doesn't want our stuff anymore," Phoenix mutters.

For a moment, Fernal's eyes are open wounds. Then he shakes his head. "Problem solved, I guess." He looks at Phoenix, who doesn't meet his eyes. He opens his mouth and then closes it. "I'm going to work now. You will stay here. Take some time to think."

Fernal grabs his backpack and slams the door behind him. Phoenix hears the engine turn over and the four-wheel drive kick in as it rumbles over the sand.

She gathers all the beer labels in her fist, wanting nothing more than to throttle them out of existence. After she throws them out, she sees a bag of Health King next to a sweating fountain drink on the counter. "For hangovers," is scrawled in sharpie on the bag.

Phoenix's eyes water and she lets several tears creep down her cheek. How much of their special occasion money did he use on this? Her stomach turns as she opens the bag, but she forces down the Sausage-n-kale and fried zucchini sticks along with the entirety of the large coke. Though her head still pounds an awful score, she feels a little steadier.

It is 7:23 am. Another hour before her History tutoring session. She climbs onto the couch, one arm wrapped around her waist, the other pressed to her forehead.

It is only a moment before she opens her eyes and sees that an hour has passed. Crap. Phoenix springs from the couch, her headache now a murmuring stream, and vaults out the door. She's halfway to Mr. Barron's trailer when she remembers that he moved their sessions to 9 am. She still has half an hour.

Without a pause in her step, she heads out to the high desert to check her water catchers. If they're busted again, she's not sure what she'll do. She can't afford even a tiny camera to catch the thief in action. A part of her is ready to give up, shut it all down. What does it matter, anyway?

Before her, the air wavers. The sun is relentless on her head, her neck. She should have worn her sun suit, but she didn't think she'd be outside this long. If she gets sunburned, she'll be in even more trouble. Then again, how much worse can it get?

She finds her first solar still, which appears intact. She carefully removes the plastic wrap and raises the cup with a shaking hand. Success. The water is warm and humid down her throat. She drinks slowly, but still, in a matter of seconds, it is gone. She does the same for her other three solar stills. She maybe gains a cup of water in the process. Then she carefully places the cup back inside the nestle of plants and replaces the plastic wrap. She'll need new plants and new plastic wrap soon.

So much work, so much effort, and for so little. Her eyes are hot and her throat aches. She sees Patrick moving toward her, reaching for her waist. Her stomach turns.

"No," she whispers. "Enough." She will get new plants. She will get more plastic wrap. Not everything is ruined.

She begins walking in the direction of the tree she marked for her next solar still. She recalls the branches of last night's walnut tree, moon-dark and tidal. She swallows the image, mucus-thick. It sits heavy in her stomach. She walks until the heat on her arms is a warning: too much longer and she will be burned.

"Yo," a voice says behind her. It takes a moment for her to recognize it. It is not the very worst voice she could hear right now, but it is close.

She turns to face the twins. Joey and Jared. Both with dorky bowl-cuts from their disabled grandmother, both with muscles hidden beneath their fat. Their lips part to reveal rows of yellowing teeth. Joey steps closer to her while Jared grabs a fallen tree branch and draws something in the sand.

"What're you doing?" Joey asks.

"Calculus," Phoenix snaps. "I'm doing a vector analysis on the amount of intelligence displaced by two black holes."

"Know what I heard?" Jared asks. He points the branch at Phoenix. "Heard you went out with Patrick last night."

Phoenix's stomach dips. "That's none of your business."

Joey steps a little closer. "I heard something too. I heard she spread her legs for him."

Phoenix steps back. She looks around—no one's out here. It's at least a five-minute walk to the nearest house. How long would it take to run?

"Think she'll spread her legs for us?" Joey asks. "If we ask real nice?"

Phoenix's throat has gone dry. Her head swims in sunlight.

"Say pretty please?"

"With sugar on top?"

"Nah." Jared finishes his drawing: a dick and balls, the kind scrawled by bored kids in math class. It points toward Phoenix. "We're gonna have to open 'em ourselves."

Jared drops the branch.

Phoenix turns, and before the branch hits the ground, she's running as fast as she can away away away it doesn't matter where oh yes back towards trailers and people and sounds she can hear their footsteps one two one two behind her and she isn't sure how close they are but she can't turn around or they'll be on her and her mind goes white and blank and makes a sound like krrrrrrrrrsh-hhhhhh but it doesn't matter because she's running and running and her lungs are hot and dry and screaming and she tells her lungs her heart to shut up and dig deep until yes up ahead she can see it a house the house the outlier the one furthest from camp Davie Lynn named after his grandfather swell and his grandmother a real fine lady and when he's away visiting one of his women from town she feeds Boomer he leaves the key he leaves the key he leaves the key oh god where does he leave the key underneath the hollowed-out rock the one that's spotted and black she needs to be careful

now she needs to be quick she can't stumble or hesitate or stop
    Find the rock
    Grab the key
    Turn the lock
    Push the door
And then, miraculously, she's inside. She tries to close the door but there are hands on the other side, and they are strong, too strong. She flings the door open and Jared flops forward, enough of a pause for her to run into the living room, to the wall of compound bows. She grabs the one glimmering blue and white: a sleek promise, a star on a journey to its end. She fits the arrow, pulls the mechanism back—it is easier than she expects—but Joey has run past Jared and his hands are reaching, he's almost there, and she squeezes the trigger and—

   Joey, his neck pouring
      red, the sound of liquid
         leaving a small space.
           Jared at Joey's side, blood
              on his hands, blood on the floor,
                 his head thrown back and howling,
                    a pure animal sound: a brother
                       slain, a body not brother.
                        Twin heart: halved
                        and bleeding.
                         She did this
                           she did this
                             she . . .

Phoenix backs up, drops the crossbow. She sprints past Jared, whose fist now grips the arrow. He's going to pull it out. She's out the door before she can hear the sound.

Out in the bright white light, she looks at her hands. They are small and shaking and bloodless. How are they bloodless?

She takes a breath. In a minute, Jared will be outside, his hands at her throat. Since his plan was thwarted (say it: rape), what will he do now? She can't go home—he can find her there. She has to leave. She glances around and notices Davie's truck. He must be inside, sleeping off a bender. But even the heaviest sleep won't mask Jared's animal keening for long.

Phoenix yanks open the truck door and flips the visor. The keys fall in her lap. For someone so suspicious of the government, Davie is very laid-back about locks. She starts the engine and puts the truck in drive.

VIRGIL

Virgil's dreams that night are sweaty, grueling things. He's coming after the Nest with a wrecking ball and everyone—Mrs. Silvers and baby Karl and Tongs and Tim and Trinity—is running from the building. They stand a couple feet away, their faces set.

"I knew it," Tim whispers to Trinity, "I fucking knew it."

"I thought you were better than this," Mrs. Silver says.

Baby Karl floats away on a thin blue cloud and nobody stops him.

When Virgil opens his eyes, Trinity is inches from his face. He flails and yelps, kicking away the covers. For a moment he's certain she's there to exact retribution for the decimation of the building, and then the morning light burns away the last vapor trails of his dream.

"You are a light sleeper. I did not even touch you."

"Yeah, well, sneaking into my bedroom tends to put me on edge. How the hell did you get in here?"

She shrugs. "I have a key."

Apparently, Virgil is just supposed to accept that, because then she crawls onto the bed. "Do you have something we can use?"

"It's only been a day."

"So, nothing then."

"Listen, I don't know what your game is, but I'm the one with his neck on the line. If they start beating some grandma to death in front of me, I'll try to get some video. Until then, back off."

Trinity nods and smoothes the edge of the covers. Virgil hopes there isn't anything crusty beneath her hand. "Things are progressing quicker than we expected. So, here is my offer. I have contacts on the board. If you are able to capture something useful, you will not have to custodian."

Virgil sits up. "What? Are you serious?"

Trinity grins. Her teeth are dazzling in the soft yellow light. "I will be back in two days. Please capture something by then."

At the office, Benson is waiting with the camera crew. Virgil was hoping to have a moment to sneak into the break room and record some casual conversation, but it looks like that won't be the case. Today Benson's suit is light gray, his cravat pink. Virgil wonders how much of his outfit is an affectation.

"Today you'll be starting as an Enforcer."

Virgil takes a breath to quiet the pounding of his heart.

"Don't worry, you'll be on light duty for now. I hope you brought your uniform."

Virgil motions towards the backpack. The longer he can keep that fabric from touching his skin, the better.

"Good, get changed. And from now on, just wear the uniform here."

Gone are the merciful minutes from his apartment to the train to the office when he's just another faceless schlub off to grind his bones for bread. Gone are the moments he can forget the uniform even exists, tucked away in a drawer. Now he will truly be one of them, ignoring the hitched breaths, the glares, the furtive shifting away. He will be as repellent as the guy on the train covered in open sores.

After swaddling himself in death, Virgil follows Benson to the parking garage, where a four-door Barreler is waiting, a black tank of death that often lurks in bad neighborhoods, the independently contracted Soothers in full riot gear just waiting for some action. Benson opens the passenger-side door, revealing a cream leather interior, and motions for Virgil to climb inside. Benson revs the engine and peels out.

In the morning commuter traffic snaking through downtown Burrington, it takes about twenty minutes to reach their destination: BRMC, Burrington Regional Medical Center. They walk through the waiting area where soon-to-be patients and their families are ignoring the wall-sized projection of BRMC's latest medical innovation: The Dual-Life Lockbox, which allows a person, for a nominal fee, to store a sample of their stem cells upon rebirth to grow new body parts, should they need them.

Up the glass elevator that makes Virgil's head go woozy, past the nurse's station, and down the long hallway, they arrive at room 402. Inside, a man with spotted skin glances up at their arrival and takes a long, shaky breath. He is hooked up to machines that trill their minute calculations to the monitor above his bed. The mounted TV is turned to a daytime talk show: Grace, the first agender talk show host. They are in a floor-length beige shift, simple yet voluminous, threaded with a rainbow of color. Yellow, green, red, and violet gleam iridescent with each sweep of the hand or twist of the torso: a private wink amid a stately public speech. Grace shows everyone how to make environmentally conscious cake bites and interviews whichever celebrities want to rebrand themselves as activists that week.

Moments later, two of the cameramen join them. Everyone shifts in place, the heat from too many bodies and the naked roil of decay making everyone feel claustrophobic. A man in a white lab coat, his face leached of all expression, strides into the room.

"Hello Mr. Samson, it looks like you've been transferred to me for your end-of-life care," the doctor says in a practiced drone.

The man in bed nods. Pain flickers across his face.

"And it looks like you've waived your right to religious or secular counsel along with any request for legal representation."

Mr. Samson nods again. He swallows.

"All right. Then if there is nothing else." The doctor reaches into his lab coat and Benson steps forward, his hands raised.

"Whoa, whoa, whoa. We haven't had time to set up yet, get

an interview. We'll need at least twenty minutes, maybe half an hour."

The doctor snuffs, one quick, low burst through his nose, the first sign of emotion since he arrived. "Mr. Samson's departure was scheduled for 10:15, and it is now 10:02. You have ten minutes."

Benson laughs, a high note that sounds like distress. "Since when are doctors on time?"

"If we miss our window, he'll have to be transferred to a Pediatric Portologist, which is a mountain of paperwork. Mr. Samson's organs are in failure. The time is now."

Benson grabs Virgil by the shoulders and shoves him toward the man. "Grab his hand."

Virgil touches the back of the man's hand. The skin feels slippery and dry and loose, as though it is no longer connected to his body. Virgil never imagined a reversal before—the prismatic shimmer, like an oil slick or the air just above bubbling asphalt, drawing the body back through time—but what he imagines instead is the man flopping onto the floor, an oversized pupa, pink and naked and wet, leaving behind a layer of sandpaper-thin skin perfectly preserved in the hospital bed like a cicada's exoskeleton, that pale, ghostly remnant, still clinging to a tree.

Both cameramen have set up. One man is perched on the padded chair in the corner. The other squats below Virgil.

"Speak," Benson says.

Virgil glances at the man's sallow face. His eyes are closed, and if not for the steady beeping of the machines, Virgil would think he's already dead. "Any thoughts on your life?"

Mr. Samson takes a long, shuddering breath. Virgil tries to keep his face neutral, maybe even compassionate, when really, he wants to take a running leap out the window.

"I've lived two good lives," Mr. Samson says. He takes another long, shuddering breath. God, this is going to take forever. "I had one child. She was . . . " another breath, "an only child. I felt a little . . . bad about that . . . I didn't want her . . . to have a deficit

. . . I served my country . . . for my first life . . . and for my second . . . I served myself . . . In the end, I guess . . . things evened out."

"Where's your daughter?"

"We had . . . a falling out . . . "

Virgil waits for more, but Mr. Samson has turned his face to the wall.

"All right, that's it. Safe travels, Mr. Samson." The doctor squeezes a clear liquid into his IV bag.

Virgil reaches forward instinctively, his heart racing. Those can't be his last words. They have to ask him something else, something meaningful. But it's too late. Mr. Samson closes his eyes, takes one long breath, and then another . . . and then with a wheeze, he stops. The machine trills one long note synonymous with death before the nurse flips it off.

"Time of death, 10:13," the doctor says. A nurse pulls the sheet over Mr. Samson's face.

Virgil places his hand, heavy and limp, on the blanket. This man literally died in his arms. Where was his wife? His child? At the end, all he had was some washed-up fast food worker turned corporate shill. He should have had something better.

Virgil glances toward the camera and realizes it has been zooming in on his face. Fucking fantastic.

"Well," Benson claps his hands, a loud punctuation to the sudden silence. "If everyone could be as responsible as Mr. Samson here, our job would be a lot easier."

Virgil snorts. "Yeah, you wouldn't have one anymore."

Benson nods. "Exactly."

After an additional twenty minutes of getting exit shots, they arrive back at the office. Benson leads Virgil and one of the cameramen into the hair and make-up closet. A tripod faces a single folding chair. Benson motions for Virgil to sit and stands behind the cameraman. "We're just going to get a few reaction shots to juxtapose against the scene from earlier. So, your first day on the job. Tell me—how are you feeling?"

"Fine, I guess."

"It's all a lot to take in, I'm sure. How about helping Mr. Samson transition to the other side?"

"I didn't really do anything. The Portologist did all the work."

"Yes, but you were there to ensure the transition went smoothly and nobody lost their nerve." Benson peeks out from behind the cameraman. "Wouldn't you say Mr. Samson led two good, full lives?"

Virgil can feel Benson's attempts to steer him toward a good sound bite, but he doesn't feel like playing dice. "No idea. I barely knew the guy."

Benson drums his fingers on his arm. "Listen, Virgil. I know you want to be a good little protestor, but I don't feel like threatening your Nest every five minutes, so from now on, just imagine that conversation anytime you're feeling antagonistic."

Virgil lets his face go slack. "He led two very good lives."

"That's better. Now, tell me about that experience. In detail."

Virgil sighs, then straightens. "Listen, I get it. I get why it's necessary. The planet would be sucked dry if we could just go on living forever. And it's not in our DNA to kill ourselves, so we need someone else to do it. And I get why you started me off with Mr. Samson, some rich white guy who follows the rules. You want me to start seeing this as natural, maybe even good. But buddy, I gotta tell you—it ain't natural what we're doing. In another minute, Mr. Samson would have been a baby again. He could have had another life, a whole new set of experiences. Maybe he would have even had someone with him in the end. But now he's just another body for the incinerator." Virgil shifts in his seat. "We killed him. We fucking killed him. And no matter what you show me, no matter what you have me do, I'm never going to be okay with it."

The tiny red light of the camera blinks off. Great, now he's done it. He's screwed everyone he cares about.

Benson emerges from behind the camera, a slow smile sliding up his face. "That'll do."

PHOENIX

Phoenix drives down Route 409, her sweat-slick hands kneading the wheel. She glances behind her every couple of minutes for the red and blue lights she knows are coming. The silence doesn't make her feel better—it makes her even more panicked and jittery. All she can hear is the glup glup of blood exiting a wound faster than the space allows. After about twenty minutes, she takes exit 15, and it isn't until she pulls up to A Gift in Time that she realizes where she is headed. Stupid, she mutters to herself. This would be the first place they would look.

But then again, she needs to ditch the truck, and fast. And where better to hide it than in plain sight, among all the other weekend shoppers or, as her father would call them, spoiled Summit Market families? She finds a side street, one that dead ends at a patch of sage brush. Probably won't be noticed for a week, maybe more.

She's debating whether or not to wipe down the car of her fingerprints when she notices the arc of blood on her chest. She reaches down to touch it, but the street grows wobbly at her feet. Bile rises up in her stomach, her chest, her throat, and all she wants to do is empty herself, just like before. But not here, not now. Okay, she whispers. You're okay. She sits up, and the street is solid again.

Even so, there's no way she can go walking around with a shirt covered in blood. Quickly, before she has time to change her mind, she takes the shirt off, flips it inside-out, and puts it back on. Her chest quivers where the blood touches her skin. Anyone who gives her more than a cursory glance can see the stain. She's going to have to ditch this shirt too. She glances in her wallet: twenty-two bucks and some change. That's barely enough for a shirt in these overpriced tourist traps.

Then again, if she knows Davie, he's probably got a small roll of cash squirreled away somewhere for a situation exactly like this one. She pulls down both visors, roots around in the glove compartment, pushing aside suspiciously moist papers and greasy fast-food wrappers when her hand wraps around something cold. Metal. She pulls out a handgun and nearly screams. Her fingers close and then pop open, the gun shaking in her palm. Great, now her fingerprints are on this too. That was what the cops were always talking about on *Lock 'Em Up* — they were always looking for fingerprints or DNA at the scene. The few episodes she saw were with Nuna when they snuck into a CompleteMart and switched all the TVs from some football game to a *Lock 'Em Up* marathon. Then they sat in the rows of leather recliners, hopping from one to the next until they found the most comfortable one. They were often able to watch an entire episode and part of the next one before they were kicked out. She could try to wipe her fingerprints off the gun, but she's desperately afraid of it going off. Instead, she places it carefully back inside the glove compartment and closes the latch.

One of the basic rules of living in their community is no guns. But everyone knows that out in the desert, with no police trolling the streets, sometimes the best way to ensure your safety is with a little personal protection.

Another rule, of course, is no murder. Killing in the name of self-defense is one thing, but she would have to prove it, and now it is her word against Jared's. And if she was found guilty, her father would stand up and take her place. They would confiscate his car, and then she would have to watch her father walk with only the items he could carry out into the high desert. Could he make it to the border in time, or would he die a slow, agonizing death of dehydration or heat stroke?

So that's it, then. She can't go back. And then, without warning, she remembers one autumn evening, a town hall meeting where Granny Hattie took the stage and with a wavering voice described how two nights ago, Joey and Jared had slipped through her rusted screen door and into her bedroom. Nobody would meet her eyes as she talked. When she finished, a murmur rumbled through the rows and swelled to a din, each person discussing, among other things, the series of failed attempts by Granny Hattie to hold the twins accountable for pulling up her plants, for emptying her water cistern, for drawing lewd pictures on the outside of her house. Phoenix remembers leaning over to her father and whispering, but she's so *old*. And eventually, the entire community agreed, after Joey's wrinkled-nose "no way, man" and Jared's exaggerated eye-roll defense.

But now, Phoenix knows that desire was never a part of the equation. Or if it was, it was only the brief flare of the reptile brain before other, more basic needs took over. Phoenix's stomach churns with the image of Granny Hattie alone in her house, the covers tucked around her like a child, listening for soft sounds outside her window.

Maybe a little self-defense wouldn't be a bad thing. She pulls out the handgun, surprised at how a second handling feels lighter. She examines the whole thing, wishing she had listened better to Davie's never-ending lectures when she took care of Boomer. She knows the gun has a safety mechanism, but all of the buttons and levers look the same—small and innocuous, a uniform gray. It is unclear if she would be making the gun safer or cocking it, so she says a little prayer and slips it into her backpack. Hopefully she won't have to use it at all, and if the time comes, maybe instinct will take over and she will know what to do.

She continues to examine the truck, reaching under the seats, touching the roof, sliding her hands down the armrest, when her fingernail snags on a rough bit of fabric. It is a hole in the passenger side seat. She pokes two fingers inside and pulls out a small roll of cash, exactly what she was looking for. Hurriedly ripping off the rubber band, she counts sixty dollars. Combined with her twenty-two and some change, that comes to eighty-two dollars. If she is careful and thrifty, that could last maybe two full months. She sticks the cash in her pocket and zips up the keys in her backpack. No telling when she might need to make a quick exit, assuming the truck hasn't been found yet.

Outside, the sun grips the back of her neck, so she power-walks to A Gift in Time. Inside, Sandra is gesturing dramatically to a woman with a long white braid that reaches to the middle of her back. For some reason, Phoenix feels like this woman is knowledgeable, wise, that she is here to tell Phoenix what to do.

Sandra turns and when she sees Phoenix, drops her hands. "Hey, honey. You know we can't take any more product, right?"

Phoenix nods. She's finding it difficult to open her mouth without bursting into tears. She wants to nestle her face into Sandra's chest and spill every last detail. "You mentioned a shirt?" she squeaks out.

Sandra stares at her blankly. The woman with the braid walks out the door.

"A shirt I could have?"

"Oh sure, sure." Sandra grabs the shirt, size small, and hands it to Phoenix. "Honey, are you okay?"

Phoenix nods. She swallows the quick-forming tears, hot and prickly down her throat. "Thanks," she says. "See you."

With the shirt gripped tightly in her hands, she walks out of the store before Sandra can ask any more questions. She turns the corner and keeps walking, down the side street where the truck is parked. Quickly, though no one seems to be looking, she ducks behind the truck, rips off the old shirt, and puts the new one on. It is cool against her skin, though she feels even more naked beneath it. She can't shake the feeling that as soon as she emerges, dozens of hands will be reaching for her.

She keeps walking, passing three trash cans before stuffing the blood-soaked shirt in the fourth. That fourth can is only half-full. With any luck, by the time the trash is taken away, the shirt will be buried under a mound of cardboard drinks and plastic bags. She passes families with children reaching for a bite of their parents' fries, middle-aged women holding armfuls of stiff, rectangular bags, and a group of floppy-haired boys who look like they're about to do something stupid. She imagines sneaking herself into one of these groups. How hard would it be to follow one of those families into their home, change her last name to Smith or Jones? Instead, she keeps walking, until the ordered grid of streets grows sparser, and then it's just her and a line of cars whooshing by on a two-lane highway.

She passes a pharmacy and a Time Loan store, then a United Together Meditation Center, and finally a tiny shuttered storefront that simply says Feisty. She imagines a row of cats in dapper suits serving platters of fish sticks and milkshakes to tables shaped like scratching posts. A basket of fish sticks costs three belly rubs while a milkshake is two flops of a feather wand. She and Nuna would sometimes make up stories for different stores when they passed one they didn't recognize. It was easy to start feeling like an outsider, a freak, someone so out of touch they didn't even know what a freaking Feisty was, and this allowed them to paint the world in bold, fantastic colors. But now, without Nuna, she realizes how childish this game is. All she has to do is walk inside and she'll know what Feisty is. It is probably just another clothing store full of fuzzy leg warmers with generic pop songs blasting through the speakers. And if she is going to stay, maybe even scrabble out a life here, she'll need to figure these things out.

She learned a lot from her father: basic carpentry, plumbing, how to break down complex systems to their basic components and then fix them. What she doesn't know is the equally complex systems that make up the world across the border, the world she now inhabits. Can she learn before someone discovers her? Her father told her about the Nestless shuffling the streets in one of his many lectures about the dangers of the world across the border.

If they can do it, why not her?

Eventually the highway widens into a four-lane road. She follows the sidewalk, the rumble of cars making her body vibrate. On the opposite side, she spies a CompleteMart. That's exactly what she needs right now. There is no crosswalk, so she simply walks down the middle of the road when the light turns red, her stomach held tight as she watches cars come screeching to a stop before her. As she reaches the other side, she is nearly run over by cars leaving the parking lot. The drivers gesture wildly at her and a few blare their horn. She is the only person attempting to navigate this busy intersection on foot, yet another red flag that she doesn't belong.

Finally, she's in the parking lot, and the cars are a little more forgiving of her presence. A plastic bag catches a gust of wind and twirls once, twice in the air, before slipping beneath the wheels of a sedan. A man with arms covered in sores stands at the entrance and holds out his empty hands, a magic trick gone wrong. Nobody looks at him, including Phoenix, who scoots past him to the exit-only set of doors.

She's learned a few tricks over the years:

1. Always buy something. Place 1-2 items in the hand basket and pay for them. Still the trembling of your heart and wait in line like an ordinary customer.

2. Don't steal too much. Only steal food and preferably things with labels that can be peeled off. Never steal high-theft items like makeup or candy bars or cough syrup or fancy soap.

3. Don't hit the same place twice in the same week.

4. Don't be dirty or shifty or otherwise conspicuous.

5. Engage at least one other customer in conversation, even if that conversation is brief. Pick a middle-aged woman, someone likely to be watching you.

Most of these rules Phoenix learned from Nuna, her fingers warm in Phoenix's palm as she led her down the aisles. Her curly brown hair flashed golden underneath the fluorescent lights. "Tell me who looks suspicious," she would whisper. And Phoenix would search until she found him, a man in a large puffy coat standing in the middle of the aisle, looking left, then right, then left again, every movement telegraphing his intent, before pocketing a single beer. Once, she and Nuna watched as the man ran from the security officers, out the door and into the wide expanse of yellowing grass. He was surprisingly speedy, and finally the security guards gave up.

"He got away," Phoenix said.

"Yeah, but what does he look like? Do you remember?"

Phoenix nodded.

"Me too. So do those men." Nuna gestured toward a man speaking into a walkie talkie and another at the edge of the grass, watching the man's diminishing form. "Now that store is ruined for him. And for what? A single beer. We have to be smarter than that."

With the memory of Nuna's hand in her own, Phoenix makes several laps around the store. She manages to pocket two apples, a granola bar, and a package of beef bologna. Inside her hand basket is a small tube of lip gloss and Platinum Blonde hair dye. She will decide at the register that she doesn't actually want the lip gloss. After one more trip around, she is about to pocket the scissors she needs for her new pixie cut when she feels heat on her neck. Someone is watching her. She puts the scissors in her hand basket and waits a total of three seconds—one baby kitten, two baby kittens, three baby kittens—before turning around. A woman in gray sweatpants with bleach stains is watching her. She's in her late fifties, maybe early sixties, and her thinning hair sticks straight out. They stare at each other for two beats before Phoenix steps forward. "Excuse me, but do you have the time?"

The woman takes a step back as though she has been caught. She looks around her while trying not to take her eyes off Phoenix. "I wasn't going to give them all away."

She needs to put this woman at ease, keep her talking. Otherwise, this conversation will make her look more suspicious. "Of course. I was just wondering, have you ever dyed your hair before?"

The woman touches her hair, a wisp of golden-white. "Hank doesn't like short hair. He told me that." She turns and walks down the aisle, glancing behind her.

Well, that didn't go well. Like Nuna always said, conversations with strangers were a gamble. No telling how they might turn out.

Before giving anyone else time to grow suspicious, Phoenix gets in line behind a woman with a cart full of food stacked haphazardly. Self-checkouts were watched more closely; slower was always safer. If Phoenix is careful, and if the woman now talking loudly on her WristBud is distracted enough, she might be able to snatch an item out of her cart after they exit the store. That was the trickiest grab of all, though, and it was much easier to do with two people.

The cashier taps one very long, sky blue nail against the register. She pushes back a strand of her hair. Before she can even say the total, Phoenix hands her a twenty-dollar bill. The cashier holds the twenty up, and for a moment Phoenix's throat constricts. What if Davie's money is counterfeit? Maybe that's how he affords all those compound bows.

But the cashier is holding out her change, so the twenty must have checked out. She tells Phoenix to have a nice day. Phoenix squeaks out a "you too," which the cashier doesn't even register because she's already scanning the next set of items.

Just a few more steps until Phoenix reaches the door. Off to her left, a man in a red CompleteMart shirt is walking toward her. Striding, actually. Maybe it's his shaved head, or maybe it's the muscles tensed beneath his shirt, or maybe it's just the fact that he's white, but he looks dangerous. Phoenix imagines his hands, the dirt encrusted under his fingernails, the way they could easily hold her down, and the world capsizes. Phoenix's vision is winnowed, shrunken down to the size of a small gray ball. Where is her body? It is a diving bell beneath the water, it is a balloon in the sky, and Phoenix cannot reach it. Phoenix slumps, almost falls forward, but then she catches herself. The last thing she needs is to collapse. There would be a police station and questions she couldn't answer. Someone would sift through her backpack. She needs to be more careful. She needs to be smarter.

She takes a long, steadying breath. What would Nuna say? Right, Phoenix has two choices. She can continue to act as though nothing is wrong and hope that the man walks right past her. Or she can run. For a moment, her body poised between the two extremes, she considers what will happen if he catches her. She feels a trembling start in her legs and knows that she will not be able to outrun him.

She does have one other option.

She strides forward until she has closed the distance between them. The man stops and stares down at her.

"Excuse me, sir? I was wondering if you could tell me where the bathroom is."

The man points behind him.

"Oh my gosh, thank you so much," Phoenix says in a high, breathy voice. But just like the cashier, the man has already turned away. He walks down the fruit and vegetable aisle and grabs the woman with the stained sweatpants, who has just stuffed a whole plum into her mouth. He is not being gentle. She feels the woman's body become her own, feels her bones, light and hollow as a bird's.

Phoenix turns before she can see what happens to the woman and walks to the in-store restaurant, I've Died and Gone to Chevre. She orders a Chevreburger and coke. With that, the change she received from the cashier is gone, and in less than a day, she has already spent twenty dollars. She's going to have to get better at this. She fishes an apple out of her backpack and eats it with the cheeseburger. After she's done, she grabs a half-empty container of fries that someone left on the table and walks out before anyone can stop her. Looks like it's cold fries and a granola bar for dinner.

Okay, she thinks to herself. Okay. She can do this.

Once outside, she walks the length of the parking lot and backtracks to the gas station she saw a few blocks back. Everything in her body screams at her to move forward, but she needs a private bathroom to cut and dye her hair. It is only a matter of time before they start looking for her. By now, the community is sitting in the town hall, listening to the charges being brought against her. Her father is storming the stage. Everyone else has already decided their verdict: guilty. Someone is calling the cops. Once they start their search, she'll need to be tougher to find. The t-shirt was the first step. The next step is removing her long brown hair, the thing they'll notice at a distance.

Inside the gas station, Phoenix squeezes past the tight rows of candy bars and potato chips and travel-size toothpaste to the one-room bathroom in the back. She's been here once or twice when stopping to refuel the truck, and the place is almost always deserted, thanks to the sprawling ten-pump gas station/Health King combo just down the street.

Inside the bathroom, Phoenix rips open the box and reads the instructions. She'll need to mix the chemicals together in a small bowl. Then she'll need to apply it evenly over her hair. After twenty minutes, she'll wash it out.

She glances around the bathroom, but there isn't anything like a bowl. A grime-coated toilet, a sink, a toilet paper holder (empty, of course), and a hand dryer.

Phoenix pulls the plunger on the sink and pours the chemicals inside. She plugs a few coins into the timer and turns the tap to let a little water in. Then, she mixes it with her finger.

She reaches into her backpack and pulls out the scissors. In the mirror, her face is pale and sweaty. She takes a deep breath and then cuts off a chunk. She keeps going, surprised at how long it takes. After she gets through the first layer, shortening her hair to a bob, she continues cutting until she has a rough, uneven pixie cut.

If she squints at herself in the mirror, the rough edges look almost intentional, almost punk. It looks nothing like Ruby, but that's to be expected. She pictures Ruby in her pussy shirt, her head thrown back and laughing. The memory is a bright spot of gold tinged with grey. Well, at least the blonde dye will make it look better. Probably.

The finger she used to mix the dye is starting to tingle. Weird. She grabs globs of the dye and rubs it into her hair. Once she's covered her entire head, she rinses of her hands, which are now throbbing. The whole room smells sharp and acidic and wrong. She's desperate to open the door and get some air, but she knows this is probably not the sort of thing one is supposed to do in a gas station bathroom.

Now all she has to do is wait twenty minutes, then rinse it out. There isn't a clock in the bathroom, and she doesn't have a watch, so she'll have to guess. She hums her father's favorite song, the one he played on loop when they moved to the community: My Girl, Time. It's about four minutes long, so if she can loop it five times, that should be about right. She reaches the bridge of the second verse—*And when they say, ain't life sublime, I know I'm running out of my girl, time*—when her head starts to feel weird. It begins as a tingling, like when her leg falls asleep during an especially boring History session, then starts aching. Pretty soon her entire head is aflame, and she is leaping from the toilet seat to dunk her head in the sink. But she doesn't have any change left, and she's not leaving the bathroom like this. Phoenix is certain she is burning alive. Soon she will be nothing but bleached bones.

Finally, her body blossoming into panic, she runs to the only source of water she can find: the toilet. The seat is coin-operated, just like the sink, to make sure visitors don't pump and dump. Phoenix opens the back of the tank and is greeted by the faint smell of sewage and metal. Every flush, the water runs down the pipes, through the treatment plant, and then back into the city's water supply. But the same water is being treated again and again and again, and just like a copy of a copy, reproduced endlessly, the result is a streaky, noxious mess. Of course, now is not the time to be picky. She dunks her head inside. The fire cools a little, and as she washes the chemicals out, a little bit more. It takes a couple of minutes before her scalp finally calms down.

Once she rises, she peeks at herself in the mirror, and her heart drops. Not only is her hair still mostly brown, but the semi-circle of dyed hair on her scalp is more of an orange yellow rather than the platinum blonde she was promised. Not exactly rocker chic. In fact, with her rapidly staining tourist shirt and her butchered dye job, she looks exactly what she is: a runaway.

Phoenix's eyes well up. Maybe she can't do this after all. The leftover dye has disappeared down the sink and she can't waste money on more. Plus, as her fingers gingerly massage her scalp, she knows she can't go through that again.

Is this what normal girls do? She always thought the girls tramping the mall were prissy little things with their fuzzy legwarmers, jeweled eyelashes and stereo-loud WristBuds. She thought that she and Nuna were far tougher, their lives buffeted by sand and hunger and isolation. But maybe the make-up and clothing fortified those girls, turned their bodies into a carapace ready to withstand the world. And maybe the hunger and sand did nothing but hollow Phoenix out, erode her away, one layer at a time, leaving nothing but a soft, pliable center. So easy to grab and twist whichever way you wanted. Nuna, wherever she was, had probably figured all this out.

And then, Phoenix is crying, really crying, just like at the bar, and the memory of the bar and everything that came after is making her gasp and stumble and retch. She stops herself before she barfs up the cheeseburger. She can't waste that money too, or today will have been a complete failure.

"Nuna," she whispers, her voice hoarse. "I need you."

There is a knock at the door. All noise zips tight in her larynx: breath, ache, cry.

"Everything okay in there?"

"I'm fine!" Phoenix clears her throat and wipes her eyes. She opens the door to the concerned face of the cashier, a teenage boy with wide-set eyes and a shaved head with a lotus blossom inked on his forehead. She hadn't pegged him as part of the Unity movement, but it was becoming more and more popular, especially with young adults. The Unity movement's motto was to emphasize our sameness rather than our differences. After all, you can't have discrimination based on gender or race or sexuality if the distinctions are all smudged out. The news called them hippie wannabees and her father said they were just a bunch of bored white kids with too much time on their hands. Phoenix liked the images of men and women gathered around a bonfire, rows upon rows of canvas dresses and shaved heads, but she had to agree that they were the whitest white people she had ever seen.

"All yours," Phoenix says, even though she knows he isn't waiting for the bathroom. She strolls away as though she hasn't just left a horrible mess for him to clean up, as though her entire body isn't aching for her father to place a hand on her back and tell her it's going to be okay.

She walks out to the main road, where cars zoom through the intersection as though no time has passed. And then, like a vision, she realizes how naïve she's been. She can't build a life here. She can't even dye her hair right. She'll be lucky just to survive. Her whole life, she's been a baby bird flitting about the nest, pretending it's ready to fly, and now that she's been kicked out, she landed, splat, right on her face.

Even so, she can't go back.

So, she trudges forward, one step at a time, for ten, then twenty, then thirty minutes. Her mind goes blank: she is simply a body in motion. The road becomes a smaller, one-lane road and she follows it into a residential district. The houses are squat one-story ranches in the colors of the desert—beige and brown and red—surrounded by small scrub bushes. They are jammed close together, chain-link fences splitting one property from the next. Sometimes, to break up the monotony, there is a rusted tricycle or a three-legged table with a sign proclaiming it "free." Otherwise, all is sand-blasted tedium. She follows the road until it turns into a neighborhood. Another sign proclaims, "No Exit."

She isn't sure where she's going, but she knows she will need to stop and rest soon.

Finally, she sees a house with a thick white fence, tall enough to hide her. There are no cars in the driveway — it's only 3 pm, after all. She scales the fence and drops herself onto the other side. The backyard is dirt with a few sprigs of grass pushing through. There's a deflated kiddie pool and a rusted toy wagon tipped onto its side. A mystery toy is jammed deep within the ground, the blue loop of the handle the only part to break the surface. The handle points to a sliding glass door, through which Phoenix spies several kicked-off sneakers and a stuffed rabbit. And then, Phoenix almost cries when she sees it: a water spigot. There is a counter on the spigot, but the read-out is low, so the family can probably afford a small loss. Next to the spigot is a plastic gallon jug. Phoenix can't believe her luck. She fills the gallon jug halfway, drinks, and then refills it. With a place to sit and her eyes no longer ticking her pulse, she feels a little bit better. Maybe this is how the Nestless do it—just tackle one problem, one moment at a time.

She places the jug in her backpack. Hopefully this family won't mind if she borrows it for a bit. She bunches up the kiddie pool into a makeshift pillow and closes her eyes, the sun a warm reassurance. She can almost feel Nuna's fingers on her cheek. *Close your eyes. When you open them, you will be someplace far, far away.*

When Phoenix opens her eyes, the sun is below the tree line. It takes her a moment to struggle out of sleep. At first, she can't figure out why her bed is so hard. But then the world zippers itself open, and she remembers. Her backpack is still beside her—she reaches inside to feel the food, the sun suit, the water jug, the gun. But something is not right. Her eyes travel to the sliding glass door, where a toddler in a polka-dotted dress, the loose hem just brushing her knee, is pressed against the glass. A woman in a rainbow bandana walks up and yanks her away, speaking into her WristBud, her eyes locked on Phoenix.

Shit! Phoenix leaps up, her legs wobbly with adrenaline. She grabs the backpack and reaches for the top of the fence, but the gallon jug and her still-sleepy muscles make it impossible to scale.

She tosses the backpack over and manages to wiggle up and over herself. Then, backpack secured, she hobbles off.

Once she is a block away, she slows down. Nothing looks more suspicious than running. If she sees a police car, she'll duck.

The sky is streaked with orange and purple and red, a none-too-subtle warning that time is running out. As she walks, Phoenix imagines a front door opening to a room bathed in yellow light, a perfect Phoenix-shaped space just waiting for her. She shakes the image from her mind. She is one of the Nestless now, and she must remember the lesson from earlier: tackle one problem at a time. The first problem is getting away. The second problem is where to sleep tonight.

She walks and walks until she feels like collapsing, her body whispering treacheries: just sit down for a minute, you're so tired, doesn't that house look friendly, I'm sure they won't mind if you sneak inside. She ignores each promise leading directly to ruin.

Finally, she's back downtown, where she began. Only a few people walk the sidewalks, their arms full of bags. The shops are closing for the night. As the color disappears from the sky, the streetlamps blink on.

Phoenix sits on one of the cast-iron benches, just another shopper taking a break before heading home. Except for her ridiculous hair and her dirty shirt, she looks normal. The heat of the day is finally beginning to break. But Phoenix knows that as the night turns from blue to black, it will get cold—colder than she would have thought possible before she moved out here. She always thought the desert was perpetually hot, an oven that never turned off. Her first night in the trailer her father built, she shivered beneath a pile of blankets, feeling utterly alone. At her old school, there were too many bodies pressed into too small a space. She remembers endless worksheets of numbers and letters that were never corrected, eraser-less pencils worn down to the nub, the smell of throw-up covered with bleach, kids screaming unsupervised down the hallways, the feel of the janitor's mop between her toes during yet another lockdown drill. There, among so many bodies, so much chaos, she was nearly invisible. Out here, the silence surrounds her, watching her every movement, every breath.

Of course, she wasn't alone then—she had both of her parents, and then, after her mother died, her father. Now she has no one.

She reaches into her backpack for something soft to lean against. The metal is hard on her back. The only thing she has is her sun suit, the most conspicuous piece of clothing she owns. Maybe if she gets far enough away from the people and cars, she can put it on. The smart thing would be to take the truck and drive across state lines, put some distance between the community and herself. Maybe tomorrow.

She takes another long swig of the gallon jug. She should really start conserving, but her head aches from so much time outside unprotected. She leans on the backpack, trying to look casual, before finally just laying down. The last few shoppers are gone. Nobody seems to notice her. She won't stay here long—just long enough to rest for a moment, consider her next move. Just long enough to close her eyes.

VIRGIL

After watching Mr. Samson take his final breaths, Virgil is ready to get blitzed. Nothing he has is strong enough to create the void he needs. Maybe Tiny Tim has something a little more obliterating. While he's there, he can find out if Tim or anyone else has seen the promos yet.

Tim opens the door as though he's been expecting Virgil. Everything he does is cyclic, precise. Last time they had a batch of shroomadooms—mushrooms laced with a synthetic LSD—he turned into an accountant of hallucinations, carefully cataloguing each one by tracing his wetted finger along the wall. Now he stands holding the door, a careful non-expression on his face.

Maybe it's the dead guy Virgil just left or maybe it's the image of Mrs. Silvers on that freshly made couch, the camera zooming in on each dirty secret, or maybe it's the thought of traipsing through Downtown Burrington in search of another Nest, but Virgil's throat is raw and it's all he can do not to start crying.

"B-bombs?" Tim asks.

Virgil clears his throat in what he hopes is a manly way.

Inside is the familiar leather sofa, a crimson rug with several oil stains, a thick glass cabinet filled with tools and packets of Insta-soup, and further back, a long oak dining table covered in gaskets and gears. The place smells of ranch dip and kerosene, which means that Tim's been working on his motorcycle again. Even though it's pungent, it's preferable to the usual old person smell, grassy body grease with just a hint of persimmon, since all of Tim's furniture is from his dead aunt. At the time of her death, EMTs had to literally cut her out of her apartment, since she was almost four hundred pounds. Now each austere item plants itself in the room, an enervating totem, until Tim's jaunt becomes a shuffle and then a slow, steady creep. The only time Tim seems to snap out of it is when he's tinkering with something mechanical, like the bike he bought from one of the residents.

Tim walks into the bedroom and then returns with two green vials. Zoomies are for kicking back and relaxing. B-bombs are for demolishing the evening.

Tim grabs two cokes from the kitchen. Virgil grabs the headsets and chooses SICKO Slayer 2 from the menu. In the series, a virus is making people into bloated meatsacks that eat everything—plants, animals, lampposts, houses, you name it—and you have to kill them all before they destroy the Earth. You can customize the SICKOs with trucker hats or valley girl accents or whatever, but Virgil's favorite is the prep school accent with its catchphrase, "Wait until my father hears about this." Shoving TNT right down that cocky meatsack's throat is incredibly satisfying.

Virgil and Tim slouch on the sofa, tie themselves down with the safety straps, and then let the Home Experience Portal transport them to an irradiated wastescape where they can slice and dice a bunch of corpulent assholes. They dismember about twenty SICKOs before Tim speaks.

"Saw you on TV today. Commercial for *Becoming Blue*."

Virgil clears his throat and nods, even though Tim can't see him.

"So that's it, then? The documentary?"

"Yeah." Virgil slices two SICKOs head to toe with a machete. "Am I gonna get kicked out now?"

Tim grunts. "A couple of them will get on their high horse about it. But most of us won't look a gift horse in the mouth, especially one that brings us two years of free rent."

Virgil exhales a whoosh of relief. He didn't even realize he had been holding his breath.

"Shit, man, I'm helping a bunch of tycoons at Conoco Phillips rape the earth. Not like I can say shit." Tim shoves a homemade pipe bomb down one SICKO's throat and the bright ticking attracts a whole swarm. Tim and Virgil back up to the nearest tree and watch the explosion of viscera and body parts.

"But you know, this pretty much seals it. You're going to have to sign up to be a custodian now."

"Me? There's gotta be a few women left."

"That's sexist, man."

"I haven't seen your name on the board."

Tim chuckles. "What can I say? I'm sexist too."

Virgil decapitates two prep school meatsacks, their coiffed hair waving in the breeze. "Seriously, though, why me?"

"Your grace period is gone, man, especially with this Enforcer stuff."

"What about your whole raping of the earth?"

Tim laughs. "I'm set until the next big oil spill kills a bunch of fluffy seals. Until then, you're the new pariah."

Virgil's about to do a really complicated move where he jams a still-wriggling SICKO into another's gaping mouth, but at that moment, a third SICKO, one he didn't see, grabs him from behind. He jams the distress button, which should call Tim over, but it's too late—two more SICKOs have joined the first, and now there's a whole swarm around him, ripping his body into pieces. They're playing the Foaming at the Mouth mode, so once you've got one SICKO on you, it's pretty much all over.

"Fuck it," Virgil says, tossing the headset onto the carpet. "Let's get bombed."

It's close to midnight when Virgil shivers himself awake. It's a pleasant shiver, like fingers on the back of his neck. He's half on, half off the couch. It takes him somewhere between a minute and an hour to sit up and the same length of time before he stands and stumbles into Tim's bedroom. Tim is asleep on the ground with his legs wrapped around the bike like a night of drunken mistakes. Virgil chuckles and flings the comforter onto his back. Then, his legs still quivering, he takes a swig of warm, flat coke and leaves.

As he stumbles down the hallway, his legs wobbly and uncertain, he's hoping no one will come out—the last thing they need to see is a newly minted Enforcer blitzed and wandering the hallway.

He walks for what feels like hours but doesn't seem to be getting anywhere. There is an ocean of concrete between him and his futon. Through the billowing curtain of his blitz, he keeps his eye trained on the naked white light at the end of the hallway. He can't look down, because small worms are burrowing in the holes in the concrete, and they are fleshy pink pigs, rooting and squealing and grunting, ready to devour him down to his bones. And then, without warning, Mrs. Silvers opens her door. She points a long knobby finger that grows to the length of the hallway. Then Virgil is sitting on her couch, the afghan covering his bare feet. Where are his shoes? All he wants to do is lie down, but Mrs. Silvers opens her mouth and inside, the sky is filled with stars.

"Where is your new uniform?"

Virgil gestures vaguely behind him.

Mrs. Silvers nods. Then she stands and walks to the kitchen.

Virgil waits. Has it been a minute? An hour? A week or more? The afghan on his lap rustles its disapproval. Mrs. Silvers returns carrying a small teapot and cups with a delicate floral pattern. The flowers sway a bit in the breeze. She pours them each a cup.

"Best cure for hangovers."

The tea tastes like mushrooms and moss with just a hint of dandelion. Virgil quickly down the rest.

Mrs. Silvers takes a slow sip of her tea and nods. "Now to business."

The room comes into sharper focus. The flowers on the cup are still. What the hell is in that tea?

"I understand that you have joined the Enforcers."

"Temporarily." Even to Virgil, that doesn't sound truthful.

When the reality show is over, will they let him leave? And if they do, where will he go?

Mrs. Silvers holds up a hand. "And the rest of us have signed a contract to appear on a television program with you."

"Yeah." His stomach flops with guilt. "I should have told you."

"Yes, you should have."

The comforting shimmer of the B-bomb is starting to dissipate, dumping Virgil into the hard angles of the room. "I didn't have a choice! They were threatening you, all of you, with eviction!" The back of his throat is aching, partly because this is the last conversation he will have with Mrs. Silvers, and partly because everything she is about to say is justified. He did have a choice. He just made a shitty one.

Mrs. Silvers sighs. "I have a request."

Virgil snaps his head up. This wasn't what he expected.

"You know about my daughter, Marybelle. I would like for you to find her."

"Marybelle?" Virgil thinks back to the interview. "Do you mean Ocean?"

"Yes, that is what she is calling herself now."

Virgil reaches for his empty cup. On cue, Mrs. Silvers pours him some more tea.

"Okay, you want me to find your daughter, who is now your son." He searches the bottom of the cup for more information. A cluster of tea leaves hangs suspended in the last dregs of golden-brown liquid. If there is meaning in this sign, Virgil is not the one to interpret it. "How, exactly?"

"I imagine your new friends have the technology to find someone who doesn't want to be found."

"Probably, but why would they—"

"I will agree to a reunion on your program. I imagine it will help with ratings."

Virgil sinks back into the sofa. This is exactly what Benson and his cronies want. "They'll use you."

Mrs. Silvers' eyes narrow. "You think I don't know that?" Then she coughs into her arm. The sound is thick and wet, productive. Virgil stands to help, but she waves him away.

"So, do we have a deal? Will you find my Marybelle?"

"You know, even if we find him, there's no guarantee he'll agree."

"Yes, you will have to convince her."

Virgil pours himself one more cup of tea. He's completely alert now—it's like he didn't get blitzed at all last night. Even the taste has grown on him. "I have one condition."

Mrs. Silvers raises an eyebrow.

"You have to start calling your son by his name."

Mrs. Silvers nods. "It isn't as though I don't want to. But when you carry a child for nine months and then guide them through the world, teaching them how to walk, how to use a spoon, rocking them to sleep at night, comforting them when they are scared, cleaning the dried milk from the tiny folds of their neck, it is quite a blow to be told you do not know your child, that this person you spent the last two decades of your life with is gone and a stranger has taken their place."

"I know," Virgil says, though of course he doesn't, not really. Not unless he agrees to become a custodian. "I think the important thing is that you try."

Mrs. Silvers nods. "So, you like the tea, then?"

Virgil laughs. "I do, actually."

"My grandmother taught me how to make it. No matter where you have drifted, how lost you are, this tea will help you return."

A smile creeps across Virgil's face. "You do a lot of drifting back in the day?"

Mrs. Silvers returns the smile. "Please do let me know when you find my child. Ocean."

Virgil nods and leaves Mrs. Silvers sipping her tea, her frail body buoyed by the couch, adrift but hopeful.

PHOENIX

Time passes on the park bench when Phoenix feels a prick on her arm. Once. Twice. She startles awake, her back a crumpled mass of muscles, her eyes crusted with gunk. It is dark, completely. The moon, a sly smile, barely lights up the sky.

A girl stands in front of Phoenix: a pale, dirt-smudged child somewhere between eleven and fourteen. Her hair is short and she's wearing at least three different jackets over a pair of purple tights. She's holding a backpack—Phoenix's backpack.

"Hey! Get off!"

The girl drops the backpack and steps back, her head cocked to the side. "I was adjusting for maximum velocity. Don't needle off."

Phoenix rubs her eyes and grabs the backpack. The girl doesn't look dangerous. Crazy, maybe. Big-eyed and hollow-cheeked, definitely. But not dangerous. Still, better to be careful.

"You shouldn't stay here. Soon the lightning will catch you."

Phoenix looks around—the street is completely empty. No one is here.

"You are covered with light. Shake off that voltage and come with me. I'll help you disappear."

Phoenix looks at the other benches, all empty, and then back at the girl. The bench was supposed to be temporary, not a place to sleep. And it is likely the police will make their rounds soon, make sure there aren't any vagrants hanging around.

By the time Phoenix looks up, the girl is walking away. "Hey," she calls, "wait!"

The girl looks back and shakes her head. "There are too many steps to keep still. But if we keep moving, we can use to our advantage."

Phoenix follows a couple paces behind. The girl definitely has a screw loose, but maybe she knows someplace safe to stay the night. She looks like she's been out here a long time. "Do you have a name?" Phoenix asks.

"You are still too bright." The girl grabs a clump of dirt and smashes it on Phoenix's chest. "There. Better."

Phoenix brushes the dirt off and frowns. "If you wanted me to be quiet, you could have just said so."

"I'm Briga," the girl says. She smiles and then, her eyes darting around her, begins walking forward again.

"Phoenix. Nice to meet you. Where are we going?"

Briga doesn't answer but begins muttering to herself. Phoenix can hear occasional words and phrases but nothing that makes any sense. After a while, it becomes comforting, a murmuring stream that she doesn't have to listen to. Briga leads them away from the main road, cutting across lawns and wide-open fields and the occasional side street. Phoenix holds her breath as she crosses each lawn, but no one seems to notice them, or if they do, no one seems to care. Finally, Briga leads them down a long dirt path that ends at a two-story brick building, a long-abandoned mill. Several windows are broken. Shattered glass speckles the dirt outside. Rope-like vines have curled up the entrance and through the broken windows, reclaiming the structure for itself. Near the entrance, a sign bolted to the brick exterior says, "Report all unsafe conditions to your foreman."

Inside, the cement floor holds piles of bricks and a few overturned barrels. Phoenix looks up at the latticework of rusted ceiling beams. It is the same temperature in the building as it is outside. Further in the building, their bodies outlined in moonlight, Phoenix sees a dozen other kids, some still children and some teenagers. They are sitting on sleeping bags or blankets, many held together by duct tape. A tall, scrawny teen in a cinched hoodie strides up to Phoenix and leans down until he is eye level. "Who the fuck are you?"

"She was in the light. Now she is hidden."

"Goddamn it, Briga, stop bringing your runaways here."

"I'm Phoenix," Phoenix whispers.

"Who the fuck asked you?" the hoodie kid bellows, his face centimeters from hers. He pushes his hoodie back, revealing olive skin and a birthmark the size of a nickel below his right eye. Now that she can see his face, it is obvious he is no older than thirteen.

"Listen, this isn't the place for rich kids trying to piss off their parents. If you have a home to go back to, you better go." The speaker, a young kid wearing gloves a size too large, sits crossed-legged on the ground. A girl his age sits next to him, prying open the back of a WristBud with a pair of pliers.

"I don't," Phoenix says. She waits for the olive-skinned kid, the de facto leader, to make some motion that she can stay, but he doesn't move, doesn't say a word.

When she looks over at Briga, hoping that she'll say something, she sees Briga opening the package of beef bologna.

"Hey," Phoenix cries, "that's mine!"

The leader blocks her movement. He reaches forward—

—and all she can see is a globe, green and blue, on a dusty floor. There is a sound like someone moving something heavy. And down in her chest, in the pit of no air, a skein of pure noise splits open.

The leader backs up a step, appraising her. Something about his expression has changed. "The food's payment for one night's stay." He points a finger at her, but he's no longer trying to touch her. His nails have been chewed down to nubs, the skin around peeled off in tiny strips. "You leave in the morning."

"Fine," Phoenix says. She crosses her arms, presses them to her chest. She doesn't want to stay in this shitty abandoned mill anyway. She walks over to the corner, away from the other kids.

A skittery sound makes her jump back. She wishes she was back on the park bench—at least there she was off the ground.

She unpacks her sun suit, making sure the gun and jug of water stay hidden. No one approaches her to demand further payment. No one even looks at her. She is truly on her own here.

Phoenix has just gotten herself halfway comfortable using the backpack as a pillow and the sun suit as a blanket when she hears footsteps near the entrance. The entire room stills: a dozen bodies hold tight, ready to fly. A girl in her late teens, maybe early twenties, appears. She's in a tank top and jeans with shoulder-length rainbow hair. She is thick and curvy, but not in a bad way.

"Special delivery," the girl calls. No one moves or acknowledges that she spoke. The girl reaches into a tote bag and pulls out cans of fruit and vegetables along with a few sodas, which she places in front of each sleeping bag. "Some asshole just threw these away. Not expired or anything. Can you believe it?" The last can she sets in front of Phoenix.

"Thanks," Phoenix says. She pulls the tab and dips her finger into the slimy sweet potatoes.

The girl stands near Phoenix, eyeing her. "This your first night?"

"No." Phoenix answers quickly—too quickly. She tries to think of an appropriate amount of time to be out here. A week? A month? But she's taken too long to answer. Whatever, it's not this girl's business anyway.

The girl smirks. "Okay."

Phoenix sneaks a peek at her. Her dark skin, the cluster of freckles at her nose, and her thin green eyes are some weird hodge-podge of bloodlines. She's unlike anyone at the compound, unlike any of the teens Phoenix has seen in stolen moments at the mall. With every dip and twist of her face, her ethnicity changes like a chimera. Now that she's closer, Phoenix notices the plastic sheen of her perfectly straight hair—she's wearing a wig.

"Until next time." The girl waves and is out the door.

"She isn't staying?" Phoenix asks to no one in particular.

"She's a recruiter. Don't listen to her—she's bad news," the kid in the oversized gloves says.

After everyone finishes their food, the room gets quiet. Phoenix doesn't want to be the first one asleep—she doesn't trust these kids not to rifle through her backpack. But the drone of beetles and the sound of small animals searching for food form a kind of ambient noise that swallows Phoenix in darkness.

Phoenix wakes to a pair of overalls, thick and grimy, leading to a hard, lumpy face. Before she can rub her eyes or sit up or say *huh*, the man with the lumpy face is grabbing her and shoving her against a metal pillar. He yanks her hands behind her and zip-ties them.

Phoenix's first thought is that the police have arrived, that she's getting arrested for trespassing, but policemen don't wear overalls and tie people to pillars. She looks around the room. The windows are dark, so it must still be night. All the sleeping bags and blankets are gone. So are the others. It's just her and this man.

No one could wake her up first? What a bunch of assholes.

The man rifles through the empty cans, tossing each one clattering down the concrete. His back is to her, a thick wall of muscle and fat, solid and impenetrable. Finally, he finds Phoenix's backpack, and Phoenix holds her breath. He's going to find the gun. He roots a paw around and then shakes it. Empty.

She's never been so glad to be surrounded by a bunch of thieves before.

"Well, girly, looks like all your friends have left you."

His voice is higher than she expected, and it has the tenor of thoughtfulness. Based on his wardrobe and his potato-sack body, she was expecting a series of grunts and groans. Her heart chugs in her chest. Should she be less afraid, or more?

"You a virgin?"

A laugh rips violently through her throat. "No."

The man shrugs. "Too bad."

And then, all at once, she knows who he is. Her father used to warn her about the men who grabbed abandoned children and sold them into slavery—grueling manual labor, sex work, the worst things you could imagine. Bag men. She always thought they were boogeymen, stories created by her father to keep her from wandering off. But the man standing before her definitely looks real.

Now her breathing comes fast and shallow, her heart sending its danger signals too late. She glances around to see if there's something she can use to cut the zip-tie, but there is nothing. She tries to rub the plastic against the metal pillar like she's seen in movies, but all she does is scratch up her wrist.

"It's just you and me, chickadee." The man giggles like he's made a joke.

All she can do now is wait. If she's lucky, maybe he'll just kill her.

The bag man reaches into his back pocket and pulls out a Zoomie. He puffs it directly into her face.

"Nighty night, baby bird. See you soon."

When Phoenix wakes again, her wrists rubbed raw and her left shoulder aching, she sits up with a start and immediately throws up. Her head ticking a countdown, she whips her body right, then left, then right again, so quickly she doesn't actually see anything. Another wave of nausea hits her, and she sits with her head between her legs. That makes the ticking turn to pounding, so she sits up, slowly this time, and looks straight out in front of her. She's in a room. More like a cell, actually: scuffed beige walls, twin-sized bed. Not room for much else. Her hands aren't tied together anymore, at least. Surrounding the bed is a sea of trash—plastic bags and empty bottles and single-serve bags of chips and greasy wrappers. And her backpack. She jumps forward, ignoring the pounding, and roots around inside. Empty. The sun suit, the jug of water, the cash, and the gun, all gone.

She looks around again, slowly this time, but there is nothing more to see. It's odd the bag man didn't leave her tied up, but maybe he doesn't need to. Maybe he's just waiting for her to wake up and walk into her new, terrible life. Should she try the door or pretend to be asleep a while longer in this breathless limbo?

Finally, her mind and body resolved, she reaches for the doorknob, but the door swings open on its own. And sailing through the air onto the twin-sized bed lands the girl from before: the ethnic chimera with the rainbow wig.

"Hiya!" she says, her legs crossed underneath of her, smiling like they're at a slumber party.

Phoenix glances around, waiting for the man to appear, but it's beginning to dawn on her that he's gone.

"I rescued you," the girl says, as though reading her mind. "That grabboon was going to, well, we don't have to talk about it."

"What happened to him?"

"Don't worry about it," the girl says, all smiles. "I'm Aisha."

"Phoenix."

"Rebirth. Energy. How appropriate." Aisha reaches beneath the bed and pulls out a half-eaten hoagie. "Hungry?"

Phoenix's mouth immediately salivates, and she tears into the sub. She doesn't care how many lips have touched it, how gray and rainbow-slick the meat is. Aisha reaches beneath the bed again and pulls out a can of Sunburst. Phoenix drinks the entire can. The sugar coats her throat, whispers away the headache forming behind her eyes.

"Do you have any water?"

Aisha laughs. "What am I, the Queen of Belvadia?" She reaches under the bed again and pulls out Phoenix's sun suit. "Cool threads. You spend a lot of time outside?"

Phoenix grabs the sun suit and stuffs it in her backpack. "I used to."

"Well, stick with me and you won't have to spend the night in any more abandoned mills."

Phoenix glances at Aisha. She's not sure she trusts this woman, but anything is better than the bag man. "Can I . . . stick with you?"

"Of course."

Phoenix smiles. This close, Aisha smells like moss and daffodils and sweat, like she's just rolled through a forest after a summer storm. It isn't unpleasant.

Aisha wades to the corner of the room, roots through some trash, and pulls out a white mannequin head. Phoenix assumed the sea of trash was laziness, but maybe it's a clever way to hide things. Aisha grabs the top of her rainbow hair and pulls it off. It is a wig! Underneath, she is completely bald. Phoenix resists the urge to touch the smooth skin, feel the tiny hairs tickling her palm.

Aisha leaps back onto the bed. "This is one of my tuckaway spots. We should stay a couple more nights before moving on. Just in case."

Just in case the bag man is looking for them? Phoenix grips her backpack. "Did you happen to find anything else of mine?"

Aisha shakes her head. "Nope. But if you're with me, you don't need anything else."

Phoenix nods, though she's not keen on this enforced dependence, grateful as she is not to be dead or worse. Her life is beginning to feel like a series of shutter clicks: she can only see one developing image at a time. Everything before is hazy, a wash, and everything after is simply darkness.

With his head clearer than it's been in a while, Virgil heads to work. Partly because it's silly to resist, and partly because he's curious, he wears his Enforcer uniform through the morning commute. There isn't much difference. He's still a small bit of debris whirling along the eddy of workers, easily ignored. But after a while, he begins to notice the space around him is quieter. The silence is weighted: there seem to be fewer breaths, and not just because today is a mid-level smog day. Amid the close, suffocating air of the subway are faint strains of lilac and rosemary. Several commuters are wearing Pocket Full'a, small sachets of fragrance that mask the smell of sweaty, unwashed bodies. And through the haze of smog and scent and breath are furtive glances: one from a pregnant woman, another from a man in an absurdly thick scarf. Every time Virgil meets their gaze, they're already looking away.

A 3-D ad flashes out the window: Embryos, Not Egos with an image of a zygote surrounded by shadowy men in trench coats. Just more pro-birther propaganda, the religious right's answer to the reversal problem. They believe people should give their additional lives to their kids, like God intended. Sounds good until you're faced with the choice: a newborn or the needle.

Once he's upstairs, Virgil walks past the women in long rows whispering treacheries into their headsets and into the kitchen, where he pours a mug of cool, clean water. Then, rooting in the fridge, he finds a saran-wrapped sandwich and a Nutribar. Who cares if they were meant for someone else—if he's going to sell his soul, he's going to get all the damn perks.

Once he's finished, he sits at one of the tables. For once, he doesn't have a low-grade headache pulsing behind his eyes, a rumbling in his stomach threatening to turn into a monsoon. In fact, he feels a complete absence of shittiness throughout his body. Is this what it feels like to be healthy?

Three men in blue enter and sit at the table with Virgil. The two knuckle-draggers who kidnapped him aren't among them. In fact, these men look like the upper echelon of murderers.

"Had six runners yesterday. Christ, where do these assholes think they're going?" The speaker pulls back his hood to reveal a long face: clean-shaven, square jaw, a real Joe-next-door kind of killer.

"That's nothing. I found a woman last week with ten kids. Ten. Kids were starving, living in filth—sores all over and plastic bags for diapers. I hate cunts like her, living on welfare and stealing time from the bastards as fast as she can pop them out." The voice, a deep rumble beneath the second hood, brokers no argument.

This is exactly the kind of conversation that Trinity is looking for. Virgil makes a show of coughing into his hand as he clicks the button on the recorder.

Joe Serial Killer runs a hand through his hair. "I'm getting too old for this shit. As much as I hate those Pro-birthers, they're right about one thing: mandatory sterilization."

"Fuck sterilization," the hooded man says, "Let's just chuck 'em into the desert with the other sandworms and call it a day. You wanna pop out ten babies you can't take care of? Fine. No more government Zoomies for you."

"Then we'd be out of a job," the third man says. He's smaller than the others, with large gray eyes and a shaved head. A small lotus blossom is inked on what would be his hairline. His face is round and soft, not quite masculine, not quite feminine. Something about it feels off, like a practical joke that hasn't reached its punchline. Virgil wants to shove his fist against the man's face until it shifts into a more recognizable shape.

The hooded man flips back his hood. His shaved head has the beginning of wiry dark hair. Virgil imagines the hair curling, dark and sinewy, around the man's face. "Got a joke for you. What's the difference between a bad day at work and a promotion?"

The handsome serial killer shrugs. The man with the soft eyes doesn't respond.

"About 50 ccs."

The smaller main straightens. "I have a joke. A bus full of children is dangling off the edge of a cliff. You have the power to save them, but you would have to abandon the criminal on the other side of town who is about to get shot." He turns to Virgil. "Who deserves to live?"

Virgil glances at GI Killer Joe and the dark-haired man, who are rolling their eyes. "Uh, okay. The bus full of children, I guess."

The smaller man nods. "Okay, same situation, but now the bus is full of criminals, and the person across town is a child."

"Still the bus," Virgil says.

"So, each life is worth the same?"

"Yes?" Virgil mutters, feeling led into a trap. Word problems were never his strength in school, though he spent most of ninth grade, before he dropped out, in the peaks and valleys of low-res, mercury-tainted drug paranoia.

"All right, so let's say the bus has a single criminal, a child molester, and across town is the child."

"Well, then I guess the child." Killer Joe is tipped back in his chair, staring at the ceiling.

"Ah, so each life is not the same. I wonder, then, how many criminals equals the life of a child? Two? Twenty?"

"Fine, who would you fucking save?"

Killer Joe sits upright and motions toward the door. "Come on, let's hit the Training Module." The hooded man grunts his assent and they leave.

The small man smiles. "That's the punchline. No one."

Benson pokes his head into the room and smiles. "All right,

ladies, it's time to earn your salary."

Benson, the man with the soft gray eyes whose name turns out to be Phren, and the cameramen all pack into the double-wide Barreler, the same one from the hospital.

"We need a little action this week, and things have been quiet in South Burrington. So, we're heading to Arridia. This week you'll be a E02, working with local law enforcement to catch a bad guy."

"Couldn't we bust up one of those Time Loan scams? There are at least four storefronts downtown," Virgil says.

"Time Loans aren't illegal. Plus, they're pretty popular with the multi-life poverty set. Can't afford to alienate a chief demographic."

"They might not be illegal, but they're . . . they're . . . "

"Usurious?"

"Yeah."

"Of course they are," Benson sniffs. "That's their chief modus operandi. Buy a couple years for a song, sell them for a mint. What else do poor people have but time? And if they're dumb enough to give up their future for a drawer full of Zoomies and a WristBud MagnumPro, then they get what they deserve."

Phren glances at Virgil and raises an eyebrow. Despite his annoying riddle earlier, it feels like he's on Virgil's side.

"Besides," Benson continues, "we need something with more action and more pathos. Human trafficking will get the heart racing, make the audience feel like warriors from the comfort of their couch."

The Barreler drops them off at the entrance to the Bullet, an express train meant for speedy cross-zone travel but so prohibitively expensive, thanks to the near-constant track maintenance, that it's mostly used by the multigenerational rich. Inside, the train further discriminates: Business, Luxury, and Zenith. They board the Business section, settling into red velvet chairs with in-seat infomercials on constant loop. Throughout the car, men in tailored suits travel from one time zone to the next, brokering business deals across mahogany tables and home in time for dinner. Here, there are no re-breathers, no cacophony of coughs, no quiet desperation of too many bodies packed together. Here, everything has that new car smell.

Through the window, gray-blue streaks turn to green, then to a reddish-brown. They are bullets fired without a target, slicing untouchable through the air. Once they near the South, a thick, lead-coated screen drops down, covering all the windows. They are a few miles from the Dead Zone, an irradiated wastescape populated with "volunteers": the men and women with no time left, who are given a choice to die instantly in a Transition Center or die slowly out here. Every so often, the news flashes pictures of faceless Hazmat suits push-brooming irradiated muck across vast, open fields. Everything from broken WristBuds to medical waste ends up here, the plastic and glass and mercury and lead and cadmium and blood all forming a slurry to be shoved into lead-lined pits deep within the earth. The sky flashes brilliant streaks of orange and red, the slit wrist of the universe. It is almost too beautiful to watch.

As they pull into Arridia, Virgil glances at Phren, at his silent equine face. His features are smooth and soft, a memory foam pillow that molds to your touch. Virgil follows the loops and whorls of the lotus blossom. Does he draw it on in marker every morning or is it a tattoo?

Outside the station, another Barreler drives them past reddish-brown expanses dotted with green hills. After the train, the car feels too slow. If Virgil concentrates, he can see scraggly bushes keeping pace with the car. He wants to hover above it all, move through the landscape without touching it. He wants to see nothing but red.

It is sunset when they finally pull into a small, two-story motel. It is a grimy beige with a sun-bleached red roof. A single twisted acacia sprouts from the dirt out front. Up the ringing concrete stairs, past a woman leaning over the railing in a halter top that shows the bulge of her stomach, Virgil wonders why the Enforcers would spend so much money getting them here and then put them in such a shitty, STD-infested motel. Down the street, a strip mall holding a Time Loan store, a liquor store, a Hoagie King, and a Unification Center blinks in the quick-moving night. The hotel is surrounded by empty dirt fields, as though they are at the edge of everything.

Virgil drops off his duffel bag in the room. There is a queen-size bed on wood-paneled floors, a rickety bureau holding a WristBud port. Inside the bathroom is a sink with a timer and a basket of BirdBath wipes. No shower. It's too early to turn in for the night, so he wanders back downstairs until he finds Phren and the camera crew at the motel restaurant. The crewmen are sitting at a table with a pitcher of beer while Phren is at the bar. Phren motions for Virgil to sit next to him. Virgil glances at the crewmen, who don't even acknowledge his arrival.

The food is just as mediocre as the rest of the hotel. Virgil inhales an overcooked burger while Phren picks at a salad that is nothing more than iceberg lettuce and two watery slices of tomato.

"Where's Benson?" Virgil finally asks.

Phren chuckles. "Probably at a hotel with half the number of prostitutes."

"Why would he put us here?"

"Cheaper? Give us the full dirtbag experience? Who knows?"

After Virgil finishes the burger, he orders a beer. Phren follows suit, half of his salad uneaten, and orders a gin and tonic. He flashes a credit card and mentions something about a per diem. Virgil changes his beer to a whiskey.

They are two drinks in when Virgil finally feels his tongue loosen. "So, are you one of them?"

Phen lifts an eyebrow and Virgil realizes one reason his face looks so smooth: his eyebrows have been removed and penciled back in. "One of whom?"

"The uh . . . the uh . . . " Virgil can only think of the slur: clamheads.

"Unity movement," Phren supplies.

Virgil nods.

Phren sips his gin and tonic. "Do you know it takes seven seconds after meeting someone to form an impression? Seven seconds. Doesn't really allow for a lot of gray area, does it?"

Virgil shrugs.

"What if we could take away all of those preconceived notions and be judged as a person, instead? Not as rich or poor. Not as a man or woman. Not as white or black."

"Well, you're pretty damn white."

Phren nods and swirls his glass. "For now."

"You're going to do the skin pigmentation?" One of the news blasts from last week, before Virgil instinctively swiped it away, was an image of a man with dark splotches across his face and neck. Most of the headlines joked that he was transitioning into a giraffe.

Phren shrugs. "Maybe, maybe not. But someone has to support progress. Imagine a world where we aren't divided into these tidy little boxes, where we can all just exist."

Virgil tries to focus on Phren's face, but the whole room is tilting. "But aren't our differences what make us great?"

"Says who? Our differences are what allow us to engage in this primitive tribalism: us vs. them. The good guys and the bad guys. The normal and the weird."

"You're not weird," Virgil mutters.

Suddenly, Phren grabs Virgil's face with both hands. Even as he holds Virgil in place, his fingertips are gentle, soft. Virgil glances towards the table of crew members, but it's nothing but empty beer glasses and smashed peanut shells. When did they leave? He glances across the bar, but it's empty as well. The bartender is on the other side, tapping on his WristBud and chuckling at the distant sound of car crashes.

"Underneath this uniform, do you know what you are?" Phren's voice is a whisper.

Virgil opens and closes his mouth. His skin prickles underneath Phren's touch.

"You're nothing but a walking corpse."

Phren releases his hold, leaving tiny pinpoints of flame on the side of Virgil's face.

In the morning, Virgil's throat is dry, and his head is the familiar shape of pounded meat. He turns on the tap, but instead of fresh, clean water, there is only the scream of dry pipes. He pulls on a uniform, not even bothering to comb his hair. Time to get this over with.

Benson is waiting downstairs, next to the complimentary breakfast nook: a carafe of coffee, individually wrapped muffins, and a porcelain bowl full of plastic-shiny apples and a single bruised pear. Phren is nowhere to be seen.

They drive until they reach the industrial section of town. A sewage plant, flimsy office buildings, and U-rent storage units are interspersed against vast, empty fields. They stop at an abandoned mill with several shattered windows and a pile of toppled-over bricks out front, as though a small army of cockroaches had been building their own warehouse and scattered at first light.

Inside, two policemen are waiting. Directly behind them is a body. Even here near the entrance, Virgil can smell death. A couple steps closer, and he would see the maggots and blowflies and small scooting beetles. He would see the empty eye sockets and the flesh grown loose. He would see the soft places chewed down to bone.

A few feet away, Phren is writing in a small notebook. Virgil's breath catches.

"Dead for at least 30 hours," one of the cops says. "We found the gun. Perp didn't even stash it—he just left it next to the body. Prints have been wiped clean. Ran it through the system, but it's not registered to anyone. We're thinking either a scared kid or an amateur hit."

"Who was he?" Virgil asks, motioning toward the body.

"Low-level creep. Mostly human trafficking."

Virgil swallows. "Did they find any of his victims?"

"EO2s found six girls in a storage unit nearby." The cop shakes his head. "Those girls would have been dead by the time anyone got close enough to hear them."

Benson claps his hands. "All right, I assume we can have the northeast corner for filming?"

The cop nods. "Just try not to disturb the body."

"Frank, run him through the routine, okay?"

Two men walk up behind Virgil: a thin, balding man in a track suit and a mountain of a man in dirty overalls.

"All right," the balding man says, his voice a perpetual sigh, "Jerry already knows the fight sequence, so I'm going to need you to pay attention."

He leads Virgil through a series of moves, punches and dodges, slow at first, and then faster and faster. Benson feeds Virgil dialogue from the side, and gradually, a showdown between Virgil and the faux-trafficker takes shape. There is a lot of slow circling while he throws out dramatic one-liners. In the finale, Virgil whips out his electric prod and slams it against the trafficker's back, knocking him to the ground, and then he electrocutes him, again and again, while the camera remains trained on his face. Of course, Virgil's prod is just a prop. They'll edit in the electricity and the trafficker's screams later, Benson explains.

Because the fake electric prod is just an empty tube of plastic, Virgil is instructed to hit mountain man full force. The man absorbs the blow every time, and Virgil imagines the rainbow of broken blood vessels emerging on his back.

They run the sequence a couple more times, until Virgil stops flinching when the mountain man advances. Then they clear everyone out, and one of the crew sprinkles dirt and sawdust on the floor, erasing their tracks. A tight-lipped man washes the grime off of Virgil's face while another slices a careful tear in mountain man's once-white shirt.

When mountain man enters the space and crouches on the floor, looking off in the distance with a sneering scowl, he looks every inch a bad man. For a moment, Virgil forgets the pitiful state of his flesh and he sees him as the audience will: someone who deserves to be punished.

They do the scene three times. Each time, the crew resets the floor, and the cameraman moves to a slightly different position. Virgil shivers with a mix of adrenaline and fatigue, pleasure and guilt. Each time he slams the plastic wand on mountain man's back, he feels a tremor throughout his body, like an itch that burrows to the bone. He wants to scream into the void. He wants to raze this whole condemned building to the ground. He wants a good hard fuck. But mostly he wants a goddamn sandwich—he's starving.

When they finish, Virgil braces for the thunder of applause—a sudden swell, a monsoon—but everyone just begins cleaning up.

He walks toward Phren and the certainty of praise. The corpse's skin is white and wet and unreal. Small bugs are nestling into shallow places. Phren stands close: the perfume of decay surrounds them. Virgil claps his hand on Phren's shoulder. He means for it to be a friendly slap, but with his muscles primed from his pugilistic fugue, his clap is more like a punch. Phren staggers, and Virgil grabs both arms to steady him. Even when Phren recovers, Virgil doesn't let go. He imagines slipping through Phren's skin into the pulse of his blood: the warm, oceanic pull of his breath, in and out, rocking him to sleep.

Phren's eyes narrow. He grabs Virgil's hands and places them at his side.

Is that a giggle behind him?

Virgil's vision tunnels. In the dark void surrounding his sight, he sees his mother: body slumped, head propped against the sofa cushion. She's wearing a white slip, and he wants to cover her, but the men are already here, taking pictures, leading him away, even though he's thirteen, already a man—Becky Lynn made sure of that earlier. He tries not to see Becky's pursed lips and the way her head flopped onto the bed when he came quickly, too quickly. Later, the men will ask Virgil questions—did any of his mother's clients seem dangerous, did any of them take a particular interest— and later still, he will drown this day and all the days after it in B-bombs until his synapses spark themselves dark, but for now, one of the men is giving him a Suzy Q snack cake. The officer tucks Virgil into a corner of the room until he can just see the tip of his mother's perfectly still, perfectly white toe. The officer puts a finger to his lips: our little secret. Virgil pops the snack cake in his mouth, the icing gritty against his teeth. Somewhere behind him is the word "whore." He doesn't hear anyone say it—it is just in the air. It slips between his teeth like something he can chew.

Virgil turns and walks back to the crew. Someone brought in several greasy bags from Hoagie Hero. Virgil's stomach is hollow and pulsing: it needs to be filled. He tears into a hoagie and then a second. He devours a bag of chips and large cola until his stomach swells. He no longer feels the desire to rip off his skin in one long skein. He glances towards Phren, but he's gone.

Benson walks over and slaps Virgil on the back. "Ready to rescue some damsels in distress?"

Virgil stares at him, open-mouthed. A small clump of meat falls from his lips. "They're still in the storage unit?"

Benson chuckles. "Not until we put them back."

The U-rent storage units are a five-minute drive. The sun ricochets off the rows of corrugated metal. Outside unit 103, six young girls—mostly pre-teens—sit cross-legged on the dirt. They are surrounded by half-empty water bottles and Vitabar wrappers. They blink in the light and tense at the sight of Virgil. Three officers stand in a circle around them, though Virgil isn't sure if they are protecting the girls or preventing them from running away.

"All right, ladies," Benson says to the group of girls. "Time to get back inside."

A girl with shoulder-length brown hair stands. Her hair is matted into a thick snarl at the back of her head. Her arms are thin and bony like a child's. "Fuck you. There's no way I'm getting back in there."

"Fine. Five girls is enough." Benson motions to the other girls, who stay seated.

"Not unless you pay us," the first girl says.

Benson sighs. "Fifty bucks. But then you have to play nice."

"A thousand."

"A hundred. That's my final offer."

The girl huffs. "Fine."

Benson reaches into his wallet and hands out hundred-dollar bills to each of the girls.

The girl with the long brown hair grins, revealing teeth stained purple. "Look at this milleniarre, raining dollar bills. You ain't afraid of getting robbed?"

Benson narrows his eyes. "All right, ladies, back in your cage. Remember, you are delicate fucking flowers."

The girls shuffle back into the storage unit. The way they hold their arms and glance around, it is obvious they don't want to go back. The cameramen set up, and Virgil slams open the metal gate to six pairs of bright eyes.

"Girls," Virgil says with a dramatic pause, "I'm here to rescue you."

"What?" the girl with the matted brown hair gasps. "Can it be? We're saved?" She runs into the light, stops for a moment, and then leaps into Virgil's arms. It all seems a little melodramatic. "Thank you," she screams inches from his ear.

Two more girls walk to the edge of the unit. They look around uncertainly. The rest sit cross-legged on the concrete, staring out at nothing. Nobody else speaks.

"You don't have to worry about that man ever again. He's dead," Virgil says.

A blonde girl with a line of dried blood on her forehead looks up. "Really?"

"Yeah, really."

The brown-haired girl purses her lips together. Her arms are shaking. "Good."

Virgil glances down at his uniform and remembers the whole reason he's here. "Don't just thank me. Thank the Enforcement Officers that are here to serve and protect young people just like you."

He waits for one of the girls to say something, anything, but they all stare silently into the hot desert sun.

"Okay, cut," Benson says. "That was a bit heavy-handed, but we can use it. You all are done."

The girls look up but don't move. The girl with the brown hair smiles, but her smile disappears when the officers grab them and lead them to the waiting vehicles.

Back in the Bareller, Benson gives Virgil a thumbs-up. "We did some good back there. You should feel proud."

"What'll happen to those girls?"

"The officers will get a statement to see if there are any other traffickers or if the man was working alone. They'll get medical attention and get returned to their parents if they have them or get put into the system if they don't."

Virgil nods. He can't shake the feeling that they screwed those girls over in some way.

Benson seems to read his mind. "Would it be better to return them to the streets or let that man sell them to the highest bidder? Maybe that feisty one could spend the rest of her life servicing Huntian businessmen in an underground sex shop?"

"Yeah, okay," Virgil says. "We did good."

Benson points a finger at him. "Don't forget it."

Back at the hotel, Virgil wakes around 7 pm. He's still in his Enforcer uniform. The lunch he gorged himself on earlier has disappeared and his stomach rocks back and forth, an empty ship at sea. He doesn't feel like going downstairs and possibly seeing the crew or Phren, so he wanders the hallway until he finds the nook of vending machines. He swipes his WristBud and pounds selections for syrupy soda and candy bars and greasy chips and peanut butter crackers. His arms loaded with a feast of simple carbohydrates, he turns and there, a few feet away, is Phren.

Virgil freezes with his arms full of junk. It would be a simple thing to step around Phren, but he is caught, a moth struggling against the light. The hum of the vending machines rumbles through him.

"That your dinner?" Phen asks.

Virgil coughs and nods. His throat feels slick, treacherous.

"About earlier. I need to remain professional when I'm in the field. You understand."

Virgil nods again. Despite the late hour, the corner is lit with unnaturally bright fluorescent light.

Phren takes a step forward. "But now that it's just us . . . "

Virgil's finger is inside Becky's cunt, surrounded by wet, warm muscle pulsing like a heartbeat. His mother's glazed-over eyes are staring out at nothing. The officer is handing him a snack cake, the wrapper moist from his hand. Becky is straddling him, and he can't help it, he's already coming. Phren is standing over the body. The bugs are nestling into dark crevices. Becky is standing up, leaving him spent and cold and shivering. *You could have at least waited.* Men are circling and circling his mother. Phen is unbuttoning his shirt, and inside is an entire galaxy. *Come on in.*

And then Phren is reaching forward and all Virgil wants is to press his face against Phren's hands and tell him what a piece of shit he is, what a load of human garbage, but instead Virgil is hitting him once, twice, in quick succession, *pop pop*, the last two fireworks to end the show. Phren slumps against the wall, his mouth open, eyes glazed over in shock.

Virgil stoops down and gathers all the candy—he can't leave a mess—and runs to his room. He will spend the rest of the night with his WristBud blaring noise and his bed covered in slick, shiny wrappers. He will not close his eyes until he doesn't have a choice.

PHOENIX

Phoenix stays in the room, tucking into the subs and burgers and salads and extra-large smoothies that Aisha brings her. She's pleasantly full, but still, a fist-sized gnarl of worry grows. Who is this girl? What is her endgame? And where will Phoenix go from here?

Aisha disappears for most of the day. Phoenix spends most of it napping on the bed or flipping through a water-logged issue of *GrrrrlFriends* she finds among the wreckage of the room. She stirs only when Aisha returns, bags of greasy fast food in hand. She thinks about going outside, wandering around, maybe just picking a direction and walking, but she decides to ride this train as far as it will take her. The second she leaves, she'll be faced with the same daily dilemmas: finding food, finding a place to sleep, avoiding the prying eyes of nosy white women.

Inside this tiny, sealed-off space, time hovers just out of reach. Without a watch or a window, Phoenix can hardly tell how much time is passing until Aisha punctuates the endless stream with breakfast or lunch or dinner.

On the fourth day, Aisha creaks open the door. Phoenix sits up; she didn't even realize she had fallen asleep, but the burning in her eyes tells her that it's late.

"Sorry, didn't mean to wake you." Aisha glances up. "You can turn off the light, you know."

Phoenix nods. She knows she's safe here, or at least some

semblance of safe, but the last time she fell asleep, alone in the dark, a bag man got her. She prefers the quick catnaps of daytime until Aisha is asleep on the floor beside her. On the nights Aisha doesn't return at all, her sleep is light as a hummingbird.

Today, Aisha's usual joviality is gone: she is quiet and somber. She removes her wig and climbs onto the foot of the bed. Everything about her seems weighted. "Mind if I stay?"

Phoenix glances down at a single-serve Froyo cup. She's having trouble making eye contact. "It's your room."

Phoenix follows the line of Aisha's tights, neon green, to a small area of pilled fabric at her inner thigh. Aisha's dress, a soft gray wool, rides up just high enough for Phoenix to imagine where her legs meet. Phoenix's breathing is quick and shallow. She doesn't know where to put her hands. She thinks that maybe, in the short time she's spent in this room, she's forgotten how to be a person.

Aisha reaches over and touches Phoenix's foot. Phoenix whips it underneath her.

"I didn't mean . . . " Aisha shakes her head, a quick, violent spasm. She grabs the wig off of the mannequin and slams the door open. "Screw it—let's go out."

"Is it late?" Phoenix asks, meaning, *Is it safe?*

"Yup. Nobody out but us vagabonds." Aisha laughs and flips her rainbow hair, and she sounds happier, lighter. "You want to stay cooped up in this room all night or you want to get some air?"

Phoenix follows her out into the hallway, a narrow space with pea-green walls and a stained yellow carpet leading to dozens of closed doors. Phoenix pauses, glancing around. Why hasn't she heard anyone else moving around?

Aisha leads her down a staircase and pushes open what looks like a security door. When they emerge outside, the cool night air slips down Phoenix's throat like a waterfall. She stops and takes a deep breath. She can feel her shoulders relax, the veins in her head loosen. She looks up at the building and recognizes it as a high-rise built by a local philanthropist to take care of the homeless population. Each room was barely more than a closet, her father had said—Phoenix can see now that wasn't hyperbole—with twenty rooms to a floor and ten floors to the building. All a person had to do to receive a year-long contract was fill out paperwork indicating their intent to find a job once they were settled. Some lauded it as a necessary move to address an ongoing problem while others complained about a bunch of layabouts getting a free apartment and lowering property values. Phoenix couldn't remember the philanthropist's name, but she remembered his sky-blue robe and his gray hair tied back in a bun, and how her father had called him a freak while begrudgingly admitting that he was doing some good. And then, a month after its construction, the building had been condemned. The philanthropist had been siphoning donations into his own private fund and using shoddy materials and the cheapest labor he could find. *Structurally unsound*, one report said. *A wonder of physics that it remains upright*, another said. *Certainly one way to fix the homeless problem*, one reporter darkly intoned. Her father, slamming down his morning coffee, proclaimed it a genocide on poverty.

All this Phoenix recalls as she stares at the brick high-rise, the plaque proclaiming the first Interim Shelter for the Homeless in the city now covered by a condemnation notice.

"Are we allowed to be here?" Phoenix asks, slowly realizing that she's been sitting in that building for the last four days.

Aisha laughs. "No, but there are a ton of squatters on the first floor. No one's brave enough to climb up past that. 'Cept me, of course."

You weren't the one risking your life all day in that place, Phoenix thinks.

"Come on, I have something to show you." Aisha walks down a side street to a lilac Mini and unlocks the door.

"You have a car?"

Aisha shrugs. "It's a loaner."

She drives half an hour to the town of Butterbin, a small mining town infiltrated by local artists. Phoenix visited once to try to sell some of her spirit orbs, but in the first store, surrounded by semi-precious stones in glass cases, the cashier had held the string between long turquoise nails and informed Phoenix that they sold art, not tchotchkes. Though there were plenty of other stores to try, Phoenix had the sense that the woman represented the spirit of the town, so Phoenix flipped her the bird on the way out.

Aisha drives through the darkened main street and up a narrow, winding road leading to the mountains. She parks in front of a sign that says "Warning: Toxic Waste Ahead," alongside several smaller signs telling visitors what not to do in stick figure form: don't swim, don't drink the water, don't dive in headfirst. Phoenix can't figure out the last one: a stick figure man and a stick figure woman walking hand-in-hand into the water. No suicide pacts?

Ahead is a small ticket booth with a boarded-up sign reading "Closed."

"They used to charge admission," Aisha says. "But since the world went to shit, it's no longer much of an attraction."

She leads them over a metal gate, nodding her approval when Phoenix easily vaults over the top, and down a winding path worn clear of footprints. As they round the bend, the whole world opens into a panoramic view of rainbow water swirling purple and red and blue. At first, Phoenix thinks lake, but then she realizes it is a pit surrounded by blasted mountain: cross-sections of sediment are streaked with orange. Four floodlights cast the mountain and its lake in brilliant pools of light.

"It's beautiful," Phoenix whispers.

"Terrible things usually are."

And then Phoenix realizes what she is seeing: an abandoned copper mine filled with acidic water. Her stomach churns with the poisonous beauty.

Aisha points to a structure in the distance, a long gray building topped by two cylinders.

"That's the water treatment plant. Keeps the level down so it doesn't poison the groundwater."

Phoenix nods. She isn't sure what to say.

"I know it's weird that I like coming here," Aisha says. "But it's like . . . we're totally fucked, you know? It's only a matter of time. But everyone's pretending that we've got this under control. Here, though, you can see how close we are to disaster, to the earth swallowing us whole. Makes you realize, you've gotta grab what you can while you can."

Phoenix edges closer to Aisha. She can feel the heat of her body radiating out into the night. Above them, the moon is a halved beauty. Phoenix isn't sure whether it is waxing or waning. Even incomplete, it radiates across the sky.

"Before I die, I imagine coming here and diving in headfirst, before any of those fuckers can get me."

Phoenix feels the ground opening in front of her. She imagines leaping from the edge, Aisha's hand in her own, screaming obscenities into the abyss.

Aisha reaches over and slips her fingers through Phoenix's. As soon as Phoenix is used to the pressure of her fingers, Aisha has pulled her in and they are locked together, lips and hands and skin.

At first, all Phoenix can feel is starshine bursting throughout her body. But then, slowly, she becomes aware of each separate sensation: Aisha's hand on the small of her back, the other in her hair; Aisha's lips, soft yet firm, just the right pressure; Aisha's skin warming under her touch. She is a fairy tale, she is a legend, and the beasts are gone, leaving only meadow. She imagines a compli- cated lock clicking open, a body finally at rest.

When Aisha pulls away, Phoenix knows she would follow her into the abyss.

Later, Aisha drives them back to the condemned building. Phoenix barely registers her earlier fear. There are much more pressing matters to consider, like what will happen when they get back to the room, what she even wants to happen.

And then they are climbing the stairs, and then they are inside, and then the twin-sized bed is empty and waiting. Phoenix's heart is a drum roll trilling without end.

Aisha stares at the bed, then turns and grabs Phoenix's hands. "Listen, the universe is expanding at an endless rate, but we don't have to move with it. We can stay still a while longer."

Phoenix nods, and inside her chest a cymbal crashes, reverberating into quiet. "Maybe let's just go to sleep?"

Aisha climbs into the bed and scooches her body toward the wall, leaving enough room for Phoenix to lay still and straight. She curls an arm around Phoenix's waist, suffusing her with warmth. Not all the warmth is conducive to sleeping, of course, but Phoenix knows that despite her body's urging, it isn't time. Not yet. Eventually, the late hour stills her gnawing and she falls asleep.

The next morning, Aisha is already in a maroon wrap dress, her rainbow wig firmly in place, by the time Phoenix wakes. She balances on the trash like a seductive surfer as she applies lipstick. As Phoenix shifts into wakefulness, she feels her furry teeth and greasy hair. How long has it been since she bathed? And there Aisha stands, put together and beautiful. Phoenix feels like a dirty child by comparison.

"What's wrong?" Aisha asks.

Phoenix tucks and re-tucks a greasy strand of hair behind her ears. She shrugs.

Aisha climbs into the bed, straddling Phoenix, and kisses her. Phoenix runs her hands along Aisha's legs, thick and muscled, up to her hips, her back. She pulls her down until she is covered with Aisha's touch.

"Damn girl," Aisha says, sitting up. "You're gonna make me late."

"For what?"

Aisha climbs off the bed and tosses several items into Phoenix's backpack: two giant water bottles, a wallet, keys, a few other things Phoenix doesn't see. "Hate to ask, but can you pack mule it up?" Aisha offers the backpack to Phoenix.

Phoenix nods. She feels a bit better holding something that is hers.

"We can get you a shower, too. After."

Phoenix is about to ask after what, but it is clear that Aisha is in a hurry. Today she is sharp, focused, her body radiating with purpose. She nearly pushes Phoenix down the hallway to the waiting car.

They pull up in front of a hotel at the back of a shopping complex containing a buffet-style family restaurant, two clothing stores, an ice cream parlor, and a CompleteMart. The hotel, a Sleep Well Express, has only a few cars in the parking lot. Phoenix follows Aisha inside, where she ignores the front desk and heads straight to the lobby. On one of the cream couches, a man in a suit skims the headlines from his WristBud. Aisha motions for Phoenix to sit in one of the smaller chairs while she approaches the man.

"Excuse me," Aisha says. "Do you have the time?"

The man looks up from his book and nods. There is a large clock on the wall above them, but neither of them looks up. The man takes what looks to be a keycard and hands it to Aisha. Then he walks to the elevator and disappears.

"Okay," Aisha says. Her voice is a little breathless. "I won't be long. Help yourself to some food. It's all paid for."

Before Phoenix can ask, Aisha disappears into the elevator.

Phoenix sits in the chair and waits. Several minutes pass. Out the window, the sky is a perfect, cloudless blue.

Phoenix walks over to the adjacent room where a continental breakfast is being served. A small family sits at one of the round tables, eating bowls of cereal. The children are poking the sodden, lumpy mess, trying to break their plastic spoons. The mother and father both stare at the wall, bleary and silent. Phoenix grabs a banana and then, without much thought, places the entire bunch in her backpack. She also grabs a yogurt and a muffin. These she eats back at her chair, glancing around her every couple of minutes as though she is about to be caught.

It is clear now that Aisha is a prostitute. There's no other explanation for the man in the gray suit. She's probably in his hotel room right now, her beautiful dress on the floor, her legs splayed open and . . .

Phoenix has lost her appetite. She eats a couple more bites of the muffin, but it feels gummy in her mouth, the saccharine sweetness false. She spits it out into the trashcan. She fills a tiny plastic cup with lemonade until she has washed away the taste.

She should leave. She has her backpack, her sun suit. She could leave Aisha's wallet and keys on the chair or she could take them with her. How far could she make it in Aisha's car? Maybe to a whole new state. She could start a new life, one that isn't dependent on the goodwill of a stranger . . . a stranger that screws random men for money. Here is yet another way that Phoenix is naïve. How much of last night was real and how much was Aisha manipulating her? Yes, Phoenix should leave. That is what she should do. There's certainly nothing keeping her here. She shouldn't even think about it. She should just go.

And yet, Phoenix remains seated, her eyes trained on the elevator.

This is so stupid, Phoenix thinks, her eyes hot and stinging. She wipes the tears threatening the corners of her eyes, snuffs into her arm.

She watches the clock on the pillar above where the man was sitting. In sixteen minutes, Aisha appears in the elevator. She looks the same, but she is not.

"All right," Aisha says. She seems to have caught her breath. "Ready for a shower?" She holds out the room key like an offering.

Phoenix shakes her head. She doesn't trust her voice.

Aisha raises an eyebrow. "You sure?"

Phoenix nods.

"Okay, then you can just watch me," Aisha winks.

Phoenix shakes her head. She wants to tell Aisha to do whatever the hell she wants, but she doesn't want to cry.

"Okay little chickadee, what's wrong?"

"What did you do up there?"

Aisha narrows her eyes. "I brokered a business deal."

Phoenix huffs. "That's a new word for it."

Aisha steps back. "Well, aren't we all dressed up and ready to hang?"

Phoenix is not in the mood for any of Aisha's euphemisms. "Did you sleep with that man?"

"No."

Phoenix glances up. She wasn't expecting that answer. "I don't mean sleep like—"

"I did not fuck him. All right?"

Phoenix nods, but she remains seated. "Then what did you do?"

Aisha motions for Phoenix to follow her. She leads Phoenix to an elevator. Instead of going up to one of the rooms, she takes them down to the basement. Down a narrow hallway smelling of mildew and burnt fabric, they come upon a room of industrial washers and dryers. A boy of maybe eleven or twelve, his eyes large and brown, is folding sheets while another boy loads a dryer. Aisha leads Phoenix further down the hall to a stainless-steel kitchen where three young girls with the thin, knobby limbs of pre-pubescents are dicing onions, carrots, and tomatoes. At a side table by herself, a girl with thick brown hair barely contained by a rubber band is carving radishes into flowers. She has the focus and posture of someone much older. She takes a bite of a Vitabar every couple of minutes and then returns to work.

"Twenty years back, the foster care system got overwhelmed. There were just too many kids. So, they started sending out some of the older ones to corporate apprenticeships. It's mostly the big chains—hotels, restaurants, factories—that can feed and house the kids. They're supposed to be learning a trade so they can get hired when they come of age, but mostly the chains just toss 'em when they're too old."

Phoenix looks back at the girl carving radishes. She hasn't looked up at them once. She doesn't look like a servant, but if Aisha is right, that's exactly what she is.

"And you're going to break them out of here?"

Aisha snorts. "Darling, this shit is legal. They even lowered the age a couple years ago to eleven or twelve . . . some crazy young age. No, I'm showing you this so you understand just how big the world is, and how awful."

"All right . . ."

Aisha grabs Phoenix's shoulders. "I'll tell you everything, I promise. Who I am. What I do. But for now, I need you to trust me, okay?"

Aisha's eyes are netted with green and gold. They are an invitation, a lure flashing in the silent depths, but does Phoenix want to be caught?

"Okay."

Aisha smiles. She holds out the room key. "Shower first."

They travel up the elevator to the third floor, room 310. Inside, the room is immaculate: freshly made king-size bed, tightly rolled towels in the bathroom. Not even the complimentary bar of soap has been touched. Phoenix imagines the tiny hands at work scrubbing the place clean. Will she ever be able to look at anything the same way again?

Phoenix closes the bathroom door and checks the shower timer: two hours. Who is this guy? Some kind of business tycoon? She strips off her grimy clothing and leaves it balled up on the floor. She lets the water run until it steams. It takes a moment for her body to adjust: she can't remember the last time she had a hot shower that wasn't a stolen couple of minutes at the Youth League Center.

Afterwards, she wraps herself in a large plush towel and streaks a window in the fogged-up mirror. She stares at her hacksaw pixie cut. Every so often, she still reaches up to brush back her long brown hair and finds it gone.

Phoenix walks out of the bathroom and into the chill of the hotel room. The air conditioner hums a pleasant 72 degrees. Aisha is lounging on the bed, flipping through the channels. She stops on a news report: a bomb has gone off in the Civic Center in downtown Humira. A group of Pro-Earthers in long white robes who believe that everyone should just stop procreating and let the earth heal from her wounds was trying to get signatures on a petition for mass sterilization. The bombing was almost immediately claimed by the Pro-Birthers. The reporter cuts to an image of a woman in a cream cardigan and matching capris clutching a protest sign: a cartoon newborn in a uterus prison saying "I Deserve a Chance."

"They're just so *selfish*," the woman cries.

"They can have each other," Aisha says. She flips some more and stops on a morning talk show. The opening credits roll with *Grace* written in cursive across the screen. Grace walks into the studio in a crop top and shimmering red pants. As part of a crossover segment, they show clips from the network's newest reality show, *Becoming Blue*. Images flash across the screen of men and women from across the country working normal jobs—bus driver, construction, fast food— and then putting on the uniform of the Enforcer.

Aisha rolls her eyes. "What a pathetic attempt at legitimacy."

Then a voiceover promises that tonight, the viewer will see the country's seedy underbelly. As the voiceover continues, a series of images flash: a pudgy guy in an Enforcer's uniform, a warehouse, a man in overalls. The man in blue and the man in overalls begin to fight while the voiceover promises a showdown like no other.

Phoenix stares at the screen. It is all looking so familiar.

Aisha sits up, her hands clutching the bedsheet. "Holy shit."

"Is that . . . "

"Yeah," Aisha says.

"Did that guy," Phoenix says, watching the marshmallow man somehow land punch after punch on behemoth in overalls, "save me?"

Aisha snorts. "No." She glances at Phoenix out of the corner of her eye. "I did."

Phoenix watches the end of the segment and the commercial that follows: a woman, wine glass in hand, gasping at the efficiency of her new hooverbot, only three payments of $45.99 or three years.

"Did that guy help?"

"That show is fake. It's all made up," Aisha says, exasperated. "I shot that asshole."

Phoenix's stomach lurches. "You did?"

Aisha tucks her legs under her. "Don't worry—I wiped it clean. And I assume you stole it, so no issue."

Phoenix thinks back to Davie's living room. Did he ever say whether or not the guns were registered to him? If they found him, he would tell them who stole his truck and the gun inside it, and what she did before she left.

Phoenix clutches the towel that is threatening to slip off, leaving her exposed. "I should get dressed."

"Oh yeah, I have a surprise for you." Aisha opens the tiny closet next to the bathroom and pulls out another dress. It is white, with a series of blossoming lines meant to look like tree branches. She lays it on the bed along with a bra and a pair of underwear.

Phoenix turns to the bathroom, but Aisha reaches forward and catches her arm.

"Hey, don't worry. Even if they tie that," she gestures to the TV, "to us, there won't be any us to find. We're not exactly living on the grid here."

Phoenix glances at the dress laid out on the bed, the black lines curling around the fabric. She imagines the branches curling, thorny and protective, over her and Aisha. "What should I do with my old outfit?"

"Burn it."

Phoenix pauses. "Really?"

Aisha chuckles. "No, just throw it out. You don't need it anymore."

Aisha turns away while Phoenix changes. Although the cotton is soft, it feels firm enough to hold her in her new shape. "Listen," Phoenix says, feeling a surge of confidence, "No more mysteries. If I'm going to stay with you, you need to start telling me what it is exactly that you do. That we do."

Aisha smiles. "Better that I show you."

It is less than twenty minutes to the very edge of town and one of the few Full Experience Portal Centers left. At first, a curated FEP promised any experience you could want, like climbing to the top of the highest mountain or relaxing on the beach. But once they introduced sexual experiences and greasy goateed men became their main clientele, everyone started calling them FAP Centers. It wasn't long before Home Experience Portals let stay-at-home moms live out their fantasies with bare-chested men and lazy teenagers fight hordes of undead in relative privacy. Now, the storefronts are mostly shut down.

Aisha and Phoenix enter the lobby. A man sits behind a glass counter and several mounted television sets beam a catalog of FEP experiences: the lost city of Narunli, fighting a dragon, your grandmother's living room, the moon.

"Hey Wally," Aisha says.

The man behind the counter nods without looking up from his magazine. He presses a button beneath the counter. Down the hallway, a soft click reverberates.

They walk past unmarked doors until Aisha chooses one seemingly at random. Inside is a small room with a single leather chair, an FEP headset, and several posters of mountainous landscapes with the tagline: A Multi-life Experience in an Afternoon. Aisha hooks her finger into a small depression on the floor that she opens onto a metal stairwell.

"Are you a secret agent?" Phoenix asks.

"Sometimes." Aisha winks and descends the staircase, triggering small domes lining the wall. They click off after a few moments, leaving Aisha and Phoenix stranded within a small oasis of light.

At the bottom, Phoenix follows Aisha down a narrow hallway— just tall enough not to crouch and wide enough for two—until the space opens into a terrific cavern. A dirt floor leads to a curved metal ceiling stretching far beyond them into the darkness. Punctuating the space is a rainbow of circus tents, red and blue and yellow and green, striped or polka-dotted or plain, their points reaching like gospel hands toward the ceiling.

Nuna had told her about the underground businesses selling everything from stolen WristBuds to sex. While Phoenix never doubted such enterprises existed, she didn't think they would be literally underground.

Phoenix tries to imagine what this space was originally. The curved ceiling and the damp chill remind her of a subway station. A low whistle of air occasionally sweeps down the dark, unending path, as though phantom trains are still running.

As though reading her mind, Aisha explains, "It was supposed to be part of the Bullet line, but they ran out of money, so they just abandoned it, like everything else."

Phoenix thinks back to the still-standing Interim Shelter for the Homeless. She is beginning to suspect that the architects of the city are a bunch of spoiled children who leave their half-finished block towers for someone else to clean up.

In front of the tents, a man sits at a rotting ticket booth from some long-abandoned carnival. He too flips through a magazine, the beefier cousin of the man upstairs. A sign on top reads *Hearts for Rent* in faded pink. A chalkboard lists three categories: *Bodies for Rent*, *Minds for Rent*, and *Hearts for Rent*.

"Hey Jeep. Boss in?"

Jeep nods and motions behind him.

Aisha walks towards the first tent, an orange and white striped behemoth, when a woman in a fitted black pantsuit and a cropped black bob appears. Her face is pale, with an almost bluish tinge, and every inch is outlined in black: her eyes, her eyebrows, her lips. Something about her face looks wrong, but it takes a moment for Phoenix to realize what it is: underneath all that black, she is hairless. It is as though, every morning, she draws herself into existence. Rather than making her look cartoonish, the outlines make her look purposeful, austere, intimidating.

"You know the rule about visitors," the woman says, her voice stilling the air around them.

"It's okay," Aisha says. "She's with me."

"Obviously. She didn't just wander down here. And yet, the

rule remains."

Aisha nods and pushes Phoenix back in front of the ticket booth. She takes a picture with her WristBud. Phoenix doesn't even have time to react, let alone smile. It isn't until Phoenix turns around that she sees it—fleshy, limp, nestled in a thicket of black—the man with the magazine has pulled down his pants and flashed the camera, inches behind Phoenix's head.

"Augh!" Phoenix jumps. "What the hell?"

Aisha winces. "Sorry, I know."

"That," Phoenix says, pointing a shaky finger towards the man, now fully clothed and reading his magazine again, "is not okay."

Aisha shrugs but she doesn't make eye contact. "That's leverage."

"Count yourself lucky," the woman in black drones. "Most visitors we put on their knees." She turns and walks past the first tent, Aisha at her heels. Phoenix trails slowly behind. "Update on the Tobias account."

"Got the name and address of the woman. She's single, 41. Isn't that kind of old?"

The woman in black smiles. "Old enough to feel the sting of regret." She fingers a tassel at the entrance to another tent. "The sting of missed opportunities."

A young woman in a full-body Lycra suit with a huge Kandy the Kat cartoon head peeks out from behind the tent. "Got a live one for me?" She takes off the cat head and locks eyes with Phoenix. "A girlie show? Yeah, I can do that. Basic or premium?"

"Sorry, Kendra. She's with me," Aisha says.

Kendra sighs dramatically and leans her body over the rope holding the tent closed. Her voice pitches to a whine. "They're always with you. Ugh, Ms. Bodice, I haven't had a customer in days."

"Chin up," Ms. Bodice says. "We have a big fish on the hook. 2.5 mil and half a dozen lifetimes."

"Okay," Kendra says, leaping to her feet. "Can I go home early?"

"And leave a gap in coverage?"

"Nah, April can cover for me—I've been teaching her the

moves. Anyway, nobody comes for the Kitty Katcher this early in the day." Kendra clasps her hands together. "Puh-leeze, pretty please?"

Ms. Bodice sighs. "Fine, but send April up here before you go. And don't forget to sign out."

"'Kay, thanks!" Kendra dashes off into the darkness.

"So," Phoenix says, her voice still shaky from earlier. "What do you do here?"

Aisha laughs. "What don't we do here?"

Ms. Bodice sweeps her hand across the vast space in front of her. "What's your pleasure?"

Phoenix glances around. In this subterranean space, Phoenix feels very far from the light. "Is it . . . sex stuff?" she asks.

Ms. Bodice chuckles. "Certainly."

"But it's not all sex stuff," Aisha interrupts. "Come here, I want to show you something." She motions Phoenix towards a light blue tent halfway down the cavern. Aisha pulls the flap back. "Look in there."

Inside is a small, warm space suffused with the glow of two gold-plated table lamps and a space heater humming in the corner. The air is thick with must and honeysuckle. There are a paisley couch and loveseat, a wooden rocking chair, and several end tables webbed with doilies. It reminds her of a grandmother's living room, the kind she's seen on old television shows.

"That's for our nostalgia clients. They bring us a photograph, and we recreate the lost space of their first childhood. We even have a few geezers on hand to act out the family bits, though some clients think it destroys the illusion."

Phoenix steps back from the inviting space. "Why?"

Aisha shrugs. "Dunno. I don't care who I was before, but some people think it holds the key to their future."

Phoenix turns from the warm, inviting room back to the chilly gloom. "The girls who work here . . . are they . . . " Phoenix flashes back to the man with the overalls. What if Phoenix didn't kill him? "The man who captured me," she says, her voice pitching into panic. "He works for you."

"The bag man? Eww, he wishes." Aisha rolls her eyes.

"Everyone who works here does so of their own free will, once they are of age," Ms. Bodice says. "We take care of our own. Many of the girls come to us in dire straits: hungry, homeless, all their lives sold. But here, they are taken care of, and each worker need only provide the services they feel comfortable with."

Ms. Bodice runs a hand through Phoenix's hair. "You, for instance. Let this hair grow out, and you could be one of the damsels for our heroism clients."

"No thanks," Phoenix says, stepping out of reach.

"She's gonna help me." Aisha slinks an arm around Phoenix's waist.

"Mmm, I see." Ms. Bodice taps a nail against her chin. "Since I have yet to hire her, her salary is coming out of yours, you realize."

"No problem."

"And the liability is yours, too. You've been a good worker, Aisha, but if you lose one of our big clients . . ."

"Don't worry. I've got this."

Ms. Bodice reaches into her coat and pulls out a small black case, which she hands to Aisha. "Remember, as close to the hand-off as you can."

Aisha nods and zips the case into Phoenix's backpack.

"You're meeting at Circle Park in South Burrington at 12:45 pm, Monday."

Aisha taps on the screen of her WristBud. "Got it."

Ms. Bodice smirks. "Make sure to get out all your rough-and-tumbles that morning. I need you focused and on time."

Aisha blushes and grabs Phoenix's hand. "Got it. See ya!" She pulls her towards the entrance. Halfway there, Phoenix shakes her hand loose and stops.

"We gotta motor, babe."

"Can you just . . . give me a second? This is a lot to process," Phoenix says, her voice coming out in waves.

Aisha frowns, her wig slightly askance.

Phoenix opens and closes her hands, her mind roving in circles. "I mean, you say you're not a prostitute, but you're working for them. And you've got all these mole-women sitting around in the dark . . . "

"We have men working here too."

" . . . waiting for some guy to fuck them . . . "

"Or girl," Aisha says, smiling. "We're equal opportunity here."

"That's not the point," Phoenix snaps.

"Then what is? Why are you so bugged?" Aisha snaps back.

Before she can say hey or stop or no, Phoenix is being pulled, tidal, back to that bleach-stained mattress, her shorts on the floor beside her, just out of reach. If she could just pause, stop the scene from moving forward . . .

"No no no no no." Phoenix walks away. She's not sure what direction she's heading, just away.

Instead of chasing her, Aisha lets her go. Once Phoenix has crouched in a dark corner, nothing but a wall in her line of sight, she takes a breath, and then another, focusing on a single bolt holding two sheets of metal together, her eye tracing the hexagonal edge: right, down, down, left, up, up, right. She imagines her head packed tight with gauze, soft and thick and obliterating. She imagines gauze filling her mouth, her throat, not choking her, not suffocating her, but filling her with soft, white emptiness. After a few minutes, she stands and returns. Aisha waits for her.

"Better?"

Phoenix nods.

"You want to talk about it?"

A couple tears slide down Phoenix's cheek. She hates crying. It makes her seem emotional, easily dismissed.

"I just . . . " Phoenix's voice cracks. She clears her throat and tries again. "I don't like the thought of those women down there, forced to do God knows what."

"Nobody's being forced to do anything."

Phoenix shakes her head. "Okay, maybe not gun-to-your-head forced, but they can't enjoy it."

Aisha's mouth is a thin straight line. "You know this? You asked them all personally?"

"Well, no."

"You want to? We can go back."

Phoenix shakes her head.

"The women—and men, by the way—they all made a choice. They need protection, not judgment."

"I'm not," Phoenix says, frustrated that she isn't being understood. "I just . . . " Her voice cracks and she shakes her head.

"Listen, I'm sorry about the picture. I'm sorry I didn't warn you first. I should have. I just thought, I don't know, you'd run."

Phoenix crosses her arms, stares at the ground. Aisha lifts Phoenix's face with her fingertips. "I didn't bring you here to do that. I'll never put you in a position where you're forced to do something you don't want to do, okay? If we're ever in a place that you don't like, just say, I don't know . . . ashes, and I'll get you out of there. Okay?"

The flash of green at the edge of Aisha's eyes fades into hazel and brown, a tree-lined path leading to the very center of the woods: dark with promise, lush with secret life. Phoenix blinks. The path is an outstretched hand.

"Okay."

Virgil stumbles into the Nest at dusk the next day. He tries not to think about the train ride back: pale, expressionless Phren, his face a wall of just-set cement except for the bruises blossoming on his cheek; the queasy feeling in Virgil's stomach from a metric ton of junk food; the camera crew glancing at them with knowing expressions.

He glances at the Reversal board before heading upstairs. There are two more names with check marks next to them. They haven't been assigned another resident yet, which might mean they're floaters: willing to accept whoever reverses first. That would probably be Mr. Patrovitch, a man with emphysema who lives with his sister and her mentally ill boyfriend. Are they part of the package too?

It takes a second for Virgil to see his name highlighted on the board. Up for review. Officially, it's to make sure that everyone is pulling their weight. But in practice, it's to evict any undesirables before their lease is up. Now, he'll have two weeks to either sign up to be a custodian or get kicked out.

Fucking perfect.

Inside his apartment, Virgil's WristBud trills his electric bill and an un-skippable sponsored message. As a woman breathily whispers fantasies involving the chocolate volcano at the Two Rivers Hotel, he wonders: will he sign up to parent a screaming child when he can barely take care of himself or will he abandon the only family he has? Christ, what a choice. There's absolutely no reason for them to be such bastards. He's a decent guy, the last couple days notwithstanding.

He's so absorbed in self-pity that he's not even surprised when he emerges from the bathroom and Trinity's perched on his bed.

"Make yourself at home," he growls.

"Someone has had a bad day at work." Trinity tucks her feet underneath her. "Share."

He tosses the camera to Trinity. "Knock yourself out."

She spends the next couple of minutes listening to the handful of conversations he managed to tape. At the end, she sighs. "That is fine. A good start."

"A good start? Did you hear the part where they talk about exterminating us?"

"Yes, and that will be a good sound bite, but they can simply apologize and fire the man who was speaking. We need something bigger, something they cannot just sweep under the rug."

"Speaking of big things, saw my name on the board downstairs."

"Yes," Trinity says, "I'm working on that. But you will need to do your part and capture something of magnitude."

Virgil sits on the other side of the bed. "How do you even know they do that kind of stuff? You might be on a wild goose chase."

"I am not," Trinity says. "We just have to try harder."

"We? I don't see much 'we' here. I see a whole lot of me sticking my neck out and you sitting on your ass."

"I can assure you that I am not *sitting on my ass*," she says, enunciating the last couple of words. "I am setting up quite a few moving pieces behind the scenes."

"And when will I see what's behind the scenes? This so-called movement?"

Trinity sits up straight. "You want to meet them?"

Virgil nods. He didn't realize he had the desire until the words are out of his mouth.

Trinity tucks the camera into her backpack and snaps it shut. "When you have something worth showing them. I will be back in a week. See what you can get."

Virgil is staring at the door where Trinity just walked out when he remembers that today is Sunday, barbecue day. Walking up those stairs feels impossible, like he's heading to his own execution, but he has to know.

The roof is packed, the sky a spreading stain. As soon as Virgil steps onto the asphalt, the tenor of the party changes. The once-boisterous mood plummets. Thirty heads turn, eyes sullen or angry.

Virgil threads through the crowd—silent, staring—to Tongs.

"Hey man," he says, his voice unnaturally loud. "Got a burger for me?"

Tongs slams the lid of his grill. "Where's your uniform?"

"It's my day off."

"Do Enforcers have days off? Or just temporary reprieves from all the killing?"

"Tongs . . . "

"Don't call me that. My friends call me that." He crosses his arms, his spatula slick with grease, just like Virgil's pose from the promo spots. "How can you do it?"

"Listen," Virgil says, glancing back at the gathering crowd. "Yesterday, I saved a bunch of girls from human trafficking. That's something."

"Have you killed anyone?" Mrs. Nyugen asks, her voice barely a whisper.

"Well . . . " Virgil recalls the old man in the hospital bed, his face leached of color and life. "Technically, I don't kill anyone. The Portologists take care of that." Even to Virgil, that sounds like a douchey thing to say.

"That's it, then," Tongs says. "Nothing more to discuss."

"That's not it," Virgil says, his anger swelling. "I'm sure you've all been enjoying that free rent. That's because of me. They were going to evict you or worse until I signed up."

"What a great company you work for," Tongs says, his voice dry. "Murder *and* extortion."

"I did it for you, for all of you!" Virgil's voice is higher than he would like. "You could at least be grateful."

Mrs. Silvers steps forward, baby Karl in her arms. His breathing is quietly labored. It sounds like an accusation. "If your actions are truly magnanimous," she says, "you'll sign up to be a custodian."

All of the anger whooshes out of Virgil. He turns to face thirty hardened expressions. "I thought you didn't want me. I thought I was a killer."

"You are," Mrs. Silvers says in a quietly assured voice. Her words slice right through Virgil. "But we can discuss your employment in more detail once you commit to your responsibilities here."

"I . . . need to think about it." Virgil's body is hunched, trying to cave in on itself.

"Asshole," a voice mutters from the crowd. Several more voices join in, overlapping.

"Murderer . . . "

"Bunch of roaches . . . "

"They're all the same . . . "

"Are they coming here . . . "

Tongs steps forward and lifts a hand. "Barbecue is for residents only."

"Yeah, fine," Virgil says, walking toward the door. Once out of sight, he lets the hot, angry tears pour out. He slams the door to his apartment—his now-temporary space—and paces back and forth between the bathroom and the bed, his head buzzing with aborted comebacks.

And then an idea, small and unsteady, starts to blossom. They need to see what he can do as a man in blue. They need to see him do something helpful, something selfless, something powerful. Mrs. Silvers asked Virgil to find her son. He can do that. He can get them to have a reunion, then air it live so everyone sees it. Then they'll drop this custodian business. Might even drop his review. He'll show them that he's necessary to the Nest . . . and someone not to fuck with.

The next morning, it only takes a few minutes of wandering the hallways of perfectly manicured women to find Benson. It takes another minute for Virgil to tell him his idea and get him to sign off on it. To find Ocean, Virgil assumed it would take a week, or at least a couple of days. Benson just grins. "Ask one of our lovely assistants. They'll find your boy in less than an hour."

Virgil shudders with the knowledge of how easy anyone is to find.

"Give me fifteen minutes," a woman in a tight reddish-blonde bun says. She begins clicking away, never once looking up.

Virgil wanders back into the break room filled with nervous energy. Most of the Enforcers are out on calls, so it's just him and all the free water he can drink. He opens and closes the fridge, turns on the tap, unable to sit still. He just wants to get moving.

Out of the corner of his eye, Virgil spies Phren. The muscles in his stomach tense, then relax. What the hell? He's fixing things today, so why not this?

Virgil jogs to catch up and touches Phren lightly on his back. Phren tenses before turning around, as though he knows.

"Hey." Virgil waits for Phren to say something, but he's just standing, his body squared off. He won't be caught off guard again. "Listen, about . . . well, you know. I was having a rough day. I'm sorry."

"Virgil," Phren says, his eyes soft and full of forgiveness, "go fuck yourself." He walks away before Virgil can react. Virgil watches him go, his mouth open, his body slack.

What a fucking asshole. Virgil apologized—sincerely, too. What the fuck else does he want: Virgil prostrate, on his knees, begging for forgiveness? Virgil scoffs. Yeah, he'd like that.

Finally, the reddish-blonde woman tick-ticks across the hallway and hands Virgil a manila folder. Inside is a picture of Ocean and some pertinent details: employer, address, relationship status.

"He's here in town?"

The woman nods, her face inscrutable. She looks odd standing here, like a hooverbot out of its dock. "At this hour, he won't be home. You'll want to visit his place of employment, Burrington Community College. He teaches Introduction to Literature from 9:00-10:30 and then Literature of the Colonized from 10:45-12:15. There will be a half-hour break for lunch. He'll be in the Peterson Building, Room 302. It's all in the folder."

"Yeah, okay, thanks." Virgil flips through the folder, skimming the information. Relationship status: single. Allergies: dust, mold, pollen. Medications: Omeprazole, Testosterone Enanthate, Zolpidem. Political views: no party affiliation, slight socialist leanings. Address: 422 Lake Street, Apartment 2B.

"Can I borrow the Barreler?"

The woman snorts, her first emotion show of emotion.

Guess not.

The main campus of Burrington Community College is sprawling and green, one of the few places with a manicured lawn. Virgil passes a brand-new Environmental Science Center, a large glass building complete with solar panels, and an aging Performing Arts Center before he finds the Peterson building tucked at the edge of campus. The brick exterior has been worn to a grimy grey. Inside, the scuffed black-and-white tile floor reflects small squares of fluorescent light. On a corkboard in the hallway, flyers promote campus events: an Honors symposium on multigenerational poverty and the environment, an after-hours mixer headlined by comedian "Lotta Laffs," and several flyers advertising the school's new Human Services degrees, including Assistant Transitional Life Coach and Multi-life Addictions Counselor. And then, in the top left corner, far from anyone's reach, is a white sheet of paper with a single phrase written in thick black marker: *Subsidized drugs = legal murder.* The corners have deep gashes in them, as though the paper has been torn down and tacked back up dozens of times. Virgil snorts. That's a bit much.

It's a couple minutes until noon, so Virgil paces outside of the room, occasionally peeking inside. Ocean stands at the front, a small man with dark hair whose arms are in perpetual motion:

circling and pointing, sweeping and pounding the desk. Everything about him is buzzing with energy, purpose, momentum. Virgil can't make out what he's saying, but he can hear the students guffaw loudly in response.

At 12:15, the students exit. Virgil waits for two stragglers who seems to be asking very involved questions. Once the room is clear, he strides inside before Ocean has a chance to escape.

Ocean is packing up a battered leather satchel but pauses when Virgil enters.

"Ocean Green?"

Ocean's legs buckle. He backs up against the board. "You must be mistaken. I have a full lifetime and a half remaining."

Virgil glances down at his uniform. Right. "I'm not here for that."

Ocean straightens and tries to look composed. "Then what?"

"I'm here on behalf of your mother."

Now Ocean's body tenses. He returns to packing up his bag. "Not interested."

"Now, wait a minute . . . "

"No," Ocean says, zipping his bag closed. "I have no minutes to spare, so if you'll excuse me."

"I can't do that," Virgil says, softening his voice. Beyond the two-day stubble, Ocean's face is round and scared. Virgil's eyes travel down Ocean's frame, past his thin collarbone, the kinked cuff of his polo shirt, past the delicate pouch of his stomach, to the pilled fabric of his trousers. Virgil blushes when he realizes what he's looking for. He clears his throat. "I'm part of this program where regular people become Enforcers. It's called *Becoming Blue*."

"Bully for you. I don't watch trash TV."

Virgil makes a fist and pushes it against his leg. "I live in the same building as your mother, and we'd like to do a little segment with you two, a reconciling." He searches Ocean's face for a response. "She misses you, and she's really sorry."

Ocean paces the length of the table, glancing from the window to the door. He stops and faces Virgil. "What do you know about me?"

Virgil glances down at the manila folder. Ocean follows his gaze, then snatches it out of his hand. He reads the printout, snorting every couple of seconds. "It's all right here, isn't it? I'm surprised you bothered to come down yourself—why not just send a drone to pick me up?"

"We don't do that."

Ocean narrows his eyes. "You sure?"

"Listen, I think we got off on the wrong foot." Virgil steps forward, and Ocean steps back in response. "I understand what you're feeling. I know what it's like to have a shitty mother."

"You understand, huh? You come down here to bond with me about HRTs? You want to commiserate about getting called a fag on your student evaluations and administration shrugging their shoulders? You want to talk about the insomnia and how the only thing that helps puts you in a fog all day? You understand all that?"

"Well, not specifically," Virgil admits, "but I have my own problems."

The area around Ocean's ears reddens. It's kind of cute.

"I don't think you're a fag, by the way," Virgil says. "I think you're quite nice looking."

Ocean throws his hands in the air. "Fucking perfect. I had to get the only closeted blue boy in South Burrington. Do us both a favor and go get your rocks off in the nearest men's bathroom and stop projecting all your mommy dearest baggage on me."

Virgil lifts both hands and imagines bringing them down like a wrecking ball onto this asshole's back. "I'm just trying to help."

"You're just trying to exploit me for ratings, you mean." Ocean takes a breath and closes his eyes. It looks like he's mouthing something silently. "All right. I have twenty minutes for lunch. This is all the time I'm willing to give to this conversation."

"But—"

"If you follow me back to my office, I will press charges. That will certainly give you some ratings."

Ocean flings the satchel over his shoulder. At the doorway, he turns. Maybe he's changed his mind, had second thoughts? "Did . . . has the cancer come back?"

Virgil shakes his head.

And then he's gone, and there are two students hovering by the door. "Are you done?" a girl in a ponytail asks. "Can we come in now?"

PHOENIX

The drive to South Burrington is long and uneventful. The desert turns to barren fields and dried-out riverbeds and then to the occasional bog that smells of rotten eggs. They skirt the areas that have flooded, where only the most water-logged, ornery residents remain. All along the highway, billboards for military recruitment (multi-life sign-on bonus!) and reminders not to Zoom and drive followed immediately by ads for government-subsidized "Rest Stations" eventually give way to chain restaurants and boutiques. They stop at a Chicky Chicky Bang Bang and toss the greasy bags on their way out. Once it grows dark, Phoenix nods off, her head lolling back and forth on the headrest. She sleeps fitfully.

She wakes to tall gray buildings surrounded by smog that blocks out the sun. Everything around Phoenix is dismal, lifeless. She knows that inside the buildings are people, that life pushes against these concrete boxes, but still, the view is depressing. Everyone thinks the desert is empty, but it is actually full of creatures thriving in extreme conditions. Here, though, all is sleek gray monotony.

Aisha loops around a small park in the middle of the mirrored buildings. She parks along a side street and turns to Phoenix. Her eyes are tired and bloodshot.

"We've got one shot at this. If she makes us, we're done. Keep close and stick to the script."

Phoenix rubs the sleep out of her eyes and nods. They walk toward the fountain in the middle of the park. Instead of water, plastic curves from the spout, iridescent and blue. It moves in waves toward the basin, where it meets a thin sheet of plastic acting as a pool of water.

"That's depressing," Phoenix says.

Around the fountain are long metal benches, empty except for a homeless man underneath a pile of blankets and several men and women in suits eating bagged sandwiches or checking their WristBuds. Aisha and Phoenix sit behind a woman in a matching floral blouse and skirt. Her shoulder-length brown hair and the way she tucks one leg underneath her as she chews on a half-unwrapped turkey sandwich peg her as quietly ordinary, maybe a little shy. Phoenix has no idea why she was chosen, what makes her special. They sit and watch the woman as she slowly eats her sandwich, occasionally sipping on a bottled iced tea. Then, when the woman stands, Aisha counts to five and stands as well.

The woman leads them past the fountain and halfway around Circle Street. Cars don't even wait for the light to turn green before blasting their horns.

They follow the woman into the subway, and Phoenix feels her knees buckle when she looks up at the board listing individual stops and fares: on-peak, off-peak, weekend, night. The writing is so tiny she has to squint to make it out. Aisha smiles and loops her arm through Phoenix's. She scans her Wristbud at the turnstile and both she and Phoenix walk through. They sit two rows back, then follow the woman when she gets off at Brickland Boulevard. Somehow, the woman does not notice them.

When they emerge from the station, apartment complexes have replaced office buildings. Otherwise, it is the same: towering buildings blocking out the sun, streets full of cars, the air thick and difficult to breathe. Phoenix wonders if this is the life her father imagines for her: trudging from one brick prison to the next, her only reprieve a hastily eaten lunch in front of fluttering plastic. Later, Aisha will tell Phoenix about the downtown area with local pubs and restaurants, a discount movie theater, even a small field of Turf4Real where screaming children throw their bodies against the springy ground. Phoenix doesn't see any of that, though; she simply follows the woman as she heads to one of the nondescript apartments.

The woman helpfully holds the door for them, and then the elevator. They follow her onto the eleventh floor, turning left as she turns right. Then they hover by a door behind which thrumming bass music reverberates. The woman enters apartment 4G.

"Doesn't she recognize that we don't live here?" Phoenix asks.

Aisha chuckles. "How many of your neighbors do you know?"

Phoenix thinks back to her community—her father and Davie Lynn and Boomer and Barbara—and a lump forms in her throat.

Aisha knocks, and after several long moments that their entire operation hinges on, the woman answers.

"Hello, Ms. Miller, we're with the Census Bureau, and you've been selected as a candidate for an extended interview. It comes with a hundred-dollar cash incentive, and you'll be entered in a drawing to win a trip to Bermuda. May we come in?"

Ms. Miller pauses for a moment before nodding. "You caught me on one of my early days. Normally I'm not home at this time."

"Lucky us," Aisha says.

Inside are a couple screenprints of birds and flowers, the kind sold at big box stores, and a small bookcase full of tattered paperbacks. They sit on a knobby blue sofa that smells vaguely of feet. Surprisingly, Phoenix doesn't find it unpleasant. Instead, the space feels warm and welcoming, if a little ordinary. The usual plastic blinds have been replaced by lacy blue curtains that match the sofa. Even closed, they let in soft white light.

"Would you ladies like something to drink? Coffee? Tea?"

"Tea would be lovely, thank you," Aisha says.

As soon as Ms. Miller turns her back, Aisha reaches into her bag and pulls out a small clear bottle and pours some liquid onto a hand towel. She quickly pads up behind Ms. Miller and covers her face with the cloth. Ms. Miller lets out a startled *mmmff* before going slack. Aisha grabs her limp body and lowers it gently to the floor.

Aisha shoves the cloth and vial back into her bag. She removes a syringe and sticks it into Ms. Miller's neck, depressing the liquid. "Help me get her onto the couch."

They position Ms. Miller's body upright, as though she is napping. Then Aisha walks into the kitchen and begins heating up a tea kettle.

"You really wanted some tea, huh?"

"The Sleepytime cocktail will buy us a little memory loss, but we need this scene to look as realistic as possible." Aisha opens cupboards until she finds the tea stash with mundane names like Energize and Relax. She places three Energize tea bags into three floral mugs.

A timid knock sounds at the front door. Aisha waits for a moment before another three knocks follow. She opens the door to a man in a suit holding a baby carrier. "Safe to deliver the package?"

Aisha nods and takes the baby carrier, containing a recently reversed Brandon Tobias, a tech guru who created the chip technology that allows seamless integration of multiple platforms on the WristBud.

The man with the baby carrier departs as quickly as he entered, leaving Phoenix and Aisha in a strange apartment with an infant and an unconscious body. Phoenix feels panic start to blossom in her throat. She thinks back to Aisha's explanation on the car ride up.

"A lot of billionaires like to hire yes men to guard their wealth once they reverse until they come of age," Aisha had explained over buckets of Chicky Chicky Bang Bang, "but some of the more creative types want to re-engineer the life that made them who they are."

"So, the woman we're following . . . "

"Is as close to his mother as Mr. Tobias could find. Looks, temperament, job, the works. He's spent a small fortune finding her, too."

"And how do we convince her to adopt him?"

"We dose her with artificial oxytocin. Helps with bonding. Then, we need to make sure that the first thing she sees is Brandon."

"So, she'll never know who he is?"

"Neither of them will know until little Brandon turns 25."

Phoenix lowers herself onto the couch to wait. A shrill whistle makes her jump up again. Her heart clenches: they've been discovered, it's all over.

"Teatime," Aisha chirps. She brings out the three steaming mugs and places them on the coffee table. She positions the baby carrier on the floor next to Ms. Miller. Then she pulls out a small wooden box and, opening it, places it under Ms. Miller's nose.

Ms. Miller shifts, shifts again, coughs, and then leans over and violently retches. She sits up, rubbing her eyes and looking around.

"Think you nodded off for a second there," Aisha says. "As I was saying, we represent the Forever Home Institute, and you have been selected as a custodian for little Brandon here."

"Custodian . . . " Ms. Miller mumbles. "Brandon?"

"As I mentioned before, upon your agreement, you will be provided with a monthly stipend to take care of necessary staples. You will also be provided with donated supplies: crib, carrier, etc."

Ms. Miller rubs her eyes, looks around in a panic. "I think there's been some sort of mistake . . . "

Aisha pushes one foot against the carrier, turning it slightly towards Ms. Miller. Ms. Miller turns and, locking eyes with the baby, closes her mouth. Baby Brandon curls his fingers over the blanket covering him. He opens his mouth in a small but tremendous yawn. Ms. Miller reaches out a tentative hand, as though discovering an exotic and potentially dangerous new creature.

And then, a memory clicks into place. Phoenix's mother sits cross-legged on a braided rug, her long brown hair in a loose braid. Phoenix strains to hear her voice, but the memory is silent and full of light. She can feel the itchy rug beneath her bare legs. She can feel the afternoon sun on the back of her neck. Her mother is holding out her hands. Her fingers are long and lean, her palms full of thick brown lines. There is nothing inside of them. She looks up to see her mother's face, to see what she is trying to communicate, but her mother is gone. The memory dissolves.

"You will of course be put on our list of Prime Members, should any additional donations be made."

"Donations . . . " Ms. Miller echoes. She has just touched the sunshine-fine hair of the baby's cheek.

Phoenix holds out her hands. She tries to remember the tributaries on her mother's palms, but nothing remains except for her own lined skin. "It's a sad story, really. His caregivers abandoned him next to the Circle Street fountain."

Ms. Miller looks up. "I eat lunch there."

Aisha stares at Phoenix. She's gone off-script. Phoenix continues: "Luckily, we were able to intercept him before the men in blue."

Ms. Miller places a hand on the carrier. "That's terrible."

Aisha nods. Her sly smile means she's caught the thread of Phoenix's story. "You're really his last hope, I'm afraid. So, if you would, please sign here and here and initial here." She places a packet of documents on the coffee table in front of Ms. Miller.

Ms. Miller glances from the documents to the baby and back to the documents, then seems to arrive at some sort of conclusion. She signs her name across the dotted lines. Then she pauses midway through the fourth page. "It's asking for his name. What did you say it was again?"

"Well, that's really your decision, isn't it?"

Ms. Miller looks up toward the ceiling. "Liam."

Aisha nods. "Lovely name."

After a few more minutes of polite chitchat, Aisha gathers the documents and promises they will be in touch. Outside the door is a box full of formula, diapers, burp cloths, and a few baby toys next to a bassinet. Aisha drags each item inside and leaves it all in the living room next to the couch. Ms. Miller is beginning to remove formerly Brandon, now Liam, from the carrier.

Phoenix breathes deeply after they close Ms. Miller's door. "Oh my gosh, I thought I was going to pass out."

Aisha smiles. "You did good."

"Sorry about the improvisation."

"No, no—I think that put her over the edge."

"Did we lie to her about the stipend?"

"No, though the Institute is just a shell for Brandon's . . . Liam's money."

A small glimmer roots in Phoenix's chest and begins to hum a feeling like hope, like future. "So, this is what you do?"

"Well, it isn't every day that a billionaire pays us to kidnap his own custodian, but yeah, I do the high-end work."

"Okay," Phoenix says, "I can get behind this."

Aisha chuckles. "Darling, I love ya, but if we get caught, we'll get twenty to life. Those drugs aren't exactly legal."

Phoenix grins. "You love me, huh?"

The elevator dings, and Aisha and Phoenix get on. As the doors close, Aisha grabs Phoenix by the waist and pulls her in. "What if I do?" And she kisses her, softly, insistently.

Phoenix is not at all surprised when Aisha leads her from the subway station to another one of her nooks: a small one-story apartment in town. This one is light and open and clean, with dish towels that have small blue flowers on them and wicker chairs painted white. It is exactly the kind of place where she imagines Nuna living. Phoenix is not surprised when Aisha unzips the back of her dress and pulls the straps down. She is not surprised when Aisha begins kissing her neck, her collarbone, her chest, and she is not surprised by the warmth spreading throughout her body. She is not surprised when Aisha asks her if she's certain nor when Aisha leads her to the bedroom. She is not even surprised by how easily it comes to her, how she knows exactly what to do. But she is surprised, so, so, so surprised by the waves building, building, oh god, and then crashing into mind-blank light.

VIRGIL

Virgil wakes to the sound of knocking. After the colossal failure that was his visit with Ocean, Virgil doesn't feel like dealing with anyone, but especially not Mrs. Silvers, currently standing on the other side of the door.

"Virgil," Mrs. Silvers clasps Virgil's hands in hers. Her eyes are wet. "My son, Ocean, called me today." She says each word carefully, her footing unsteady. "I don't know what you said to him but thank you."

"Oh," Virgil says, "Sure."

She squeezes Virgil's hand once more before returning to her apartment.

That motherfucker. That cocksucking piece of shit. All Ocean had to do was have a five-minute conversation on the air, and everything would have been fine. He and Mrs. Silvers would have reunited, and Virgil's name would no longer be highlighted. But no, he had to be a selfish prick.

Virgil sucks down two Zoomies back-to-back and flips through the channels. By the time he's on his third Zoomie, the most he's consumed in one sitting since his early twenties, he can feel darkness begin to blossom behind his eyes. He knows what he needs to do.

"Of course we have housing available," Benson says, politely ignoring Virgil's bloodshot eyes. "One bedroom or two?"

"One."

"We'll take it out of your paycheck, of course, but even so, we receive these rooms at a steep discount."

"Do a little finagling, move some lives around, no one's the wiser?"

Benson smiles. "I'll have the keys to you this afternoon. Would you like one fully furnished?"

"You bet."

"Anything you wish to keep from your old place?"

"Nope."

"One final question. The two years' rent your old neighbors are receiving—shall those contracts be nullified upon your departure?"

A dark pit yawns open and whispers a hoarse yes. "Everyone except Mrs. Silvers."

Benson nods. "Now, we have a man we've been tracking for weeks—he's overdue for his transition, which reflects poorly on our department. You'll be working as an E01—search and retrieval."

"Really?" Virgil asks, his stomach quivering. "Would that play well on TV?"

Benson chuckles. "Time to bite the bullet, my dear chap." He straightens his cravat. Today it is peach with small white polka dots.

Virgil meets Joe Serial Killer downstairs, whose name turns out to be Craig. He walks Virgil through the basics: they will scout out the location where the newest intelligence places the runner, and then, if he's there, they'll call for backup. No heroics, no camera crew until they know what they're dealing with. However, Virgil will leave his WristBud on to capture a little handheld action, just in case they can use it.

"Guys like this won't come quietly. You in shape?" Craig peers at Virgil's gut.

"I'll be fine." Virgil is certain that Craig McSquare Jaw, who probably runs marathons for fun, will leave him in the dust.

And then, with barely any pomp or circumstance, Craig places an electric baton in Virgil's hands. Craig explains that the baton has two settings: shock and incapacitate, though the second has the potential to be lethal if overused or if the person has a heart condition. Virgil should attempt to avoid the lethal option. "It's a ton of paperwork," Craig chuckles.

After a twenty-minute video of a woman droning on about proper baton use (DO aim for the midsection . . . DON'T leave it on while in your holster . . . DO remember to charge the battery pack once a week), and another half an hour of practice on a dummy, Craig barking corrections from the corner, Virgil is cleared. He assumed there would be weeks of intensive training, maybe some kind of final exam, but no—Virgil straps the weapon into his new and slightly uncomfortable leg holster, and that is that. Benson mentions something about bi-weekly training once the show finishes airing, but it is obvious Craig is impatient to get into the field, so Vigil doesn't clarify.

Craig drives out past city limits to Haught North, a forested park that hosts family barbecues during the day and brutal stabbings at night. They park in a well-lit area and change into civilian clothes. Virgil clicks his WristBud ZoomPro app and tries to remember to aim it at interesting things.

Craig and Virgil follow the path through a shaded area with cast-iron grills cemented to the ground. Then, the path turns sharply into the trees. They walk for several minutes while Craig tracks their progress. Virgil glances at a downed tree, its roots like withered fingers gripping the air, the trunk beginning to return to soil. A small patch of white-capped mushrooms blossoms near its base. Virgil stops. This is the way it should be. Not the tree growing taller and taller, suffocating the tiny tendrils of dogwoods-to-be.

At a nondescript cluster of pines, Craig suddenly motions left, away from the path. He winds a circuitous path that to the untrained eye looks like meandering. He taps a couple buttons on his WristBud every few moments and reorients himself. They pass what looks to Virgil like the same group of pines when Virgil steps onto the eviscerated carcass of a squirrel.

Virgil claps both hands over his mouth to avoid screaming like a girl. The lolling head and bushy tail remain, the rest of the body flayed open.

Craig and Virgil walk forward. They pass another squirrel carcass and then a rabbit. The rabbit is newer. Flies and other wiggly creatures have just begun to burrow their way inside. Virgil pauses for a moment, his vision tidal, a steady and insistent pull, but Craig is already walking toward something he sees in the distance. Virgil follows until they come to a small clearing, and tucked at the edge, a camouflage-print tent. With the sun coming through the leaves, speckling the forest floor with light, it is almost invisible. If Craig wasn't here, Virgil would have walked right past it.

Craig lifts his WristBud to his mouth, ready to call for backup, when a gaunt man with a wispy pubic hair beard wanders out of the tent. He unzips his fly and begins to take a piss. Then he makes eye contact with Virgil and Craig. For a moment, he watches them watch him, his thin stream hissing on the ground. Then he zips up and takes off.

"We've got a runner," Craig yells into his WristBud and sprints after him.

Virgil follows them, his airways closing almost immediately. Perhaps his constant diet of fast food and Zoomies isn't conducive to exercise. By the time he rounds the corner where he last saw a spray of dirt and leaves, he's breathing shallowly. Luckily, a man living on squirrels is no match for a well-trained E01, and across a small ravine, Craig has the man up against a tree.

Virgil walks toward them, trying to hold his WristBud steady. When he is close, Craig tosses him a zip-tie. "You gotta be the hero." Craig trains his own WristBud on Virgil. Virgil grabs the man's arm, ready for a fight, but the man is nothing more than loose skin in his hands.

As they walk back to the car, the man shuffling along obligingly, he turns to Virgil with eyes rheumy and yellow. "I don't want to die."

"Who does?" Craig shrugs. He grabs the man by the back of his collar. "You run again, I'm going to make this painful. Understand?"

The man nods and doesn't say another word for the rest of the walk back.

Later that week, when Virgil watches the episode from the comfort of his new leather couch, a voiceover will list the man's sins: fathering three children with three different women on their last lives, and then two more with a woman who owed thirty years, and then skipping town before he could pay his own lifetime support. If they couldn't find him, all four women would die once the kids turned 18 and the children would tick down to one lifetime each.

"She never told me she was pregnant," the man says in an interview before heading to the Transition Center. He's been shaved to look respectable, but his yellowing teeth and skeletal face give him away.

"That's bullshit! That's bullshit! I told him right soon as I knew, and he said honey I'll take care of you, I just gotta get some cash for us, you know, for the baby, and then I never saw him again!" One of the women, big and angry in a faded yellow dress, surrounded by three screaming children, waves her hands dramatically. A second woman remains silent. Her children sit quietly, clutching her long orange skirt, as the first woman's children run in circles around the studio.

Virgil clicks off the episode. He isn't sure what to do now. He hasn't spent much time in his new place, even though it is objectively pretty sweet—queen-size bed, sectional leather sofa, television with premium channels, and a bay window overlooking the city. Everything is sleek and modern, rectangular and black, meant for looking, not touching. There's a board filled with wine corks from bottles he never drank, a bookcase full of books he'll never read. The one thing that fills him with dread is a painting over the bed: an abstract image full of violent streaks of red and purple and green. If he squints, he can make out a face and a pair of hands. From one angle, the face looks angry; from another, in pain, and from yet another, the anger and pain arrive at different thresholds. Virgil considers taking it down, but he's not sure he's supposed to. Even though he pays for this space with his salary, it doesn't feel like his. If he left, the apartment would stay exactly as it was—same bookshelf, same sofa. Some asshole would move in and that would be that. He wonders how many ground-in stains he left in his old place. He imagines the new tenant on his hands and knees scrubbing out the piss stain from one too many nights getting bombed and forgetting where the toilet was. The image makes Virgil smile.

There is a knock at the door. Virgil wonders who would visit him, here, on a Friday evening. Craig stands with the hooded man from before. The man, whose name is Marco, is muscular, tall, with buzzed black hair that would probably sweep down his face in wavy locks if he let it.

"You up for a little overtime?" Craig asks.

"Uh, sure." Virgil looks behind them for the camera crew, but they are alone. "Where are we going?"

"To take out the trash," Marco growls. Virgil's stomach dips.

They drive to the part of town where businesses hide behind bulletproof glass and bars line apartment windows. Skinny boys trying to be men stand taut on street corners. They watch, turning slowly as the car drives by, rooted to the asphalt.

Virgil fiddles with his WristBud, but Marco shakes his head. Whatever they are about to do, wherever they are about to go, it isn't the kind of thing meant for public consumption. And then Virgil realizes that soon he'll be out there in his bright blue uniform with nothing but a glorified sparkler to protect him.

They park down a side street as dark as their car. Police cars have lights to announce their presence but theirs is black, a shadow slipping over dumpsters and ducking under street lamps to find that one fire flickering too long and snuff it out.

Once they emerge, the street is quiet, the boys gone. Virgil breathes a sigh of relief. It's kind of nice, this mollifying presence. Beats ducking at gunshots or listening to some strung-out couple's screaming match.

They stop in front of an orange door with a rusted security gate. "Game face," Craig says. Virgil nods.

Craig knocks and a woman, thin and pale with too much eye shadow, answers the door. She has a constellation of bruises on one arm. Her mousy brown hair hangs limp and defenseless. She looks at the three men at her doorstep and walks back inside, the door open behind her.

They follow her into a living room full of particle-board furniture, a ripped leather sofa, and bare, curtainless windows. The room, though cheap, is spotless. The smell of bleach is overwhelming. A man sitting hunched on the sofa clutches the neck of a beer bottle. "You fucking called them?" the man says through clenched teeth.

Craig scans the man with his WristBud and it blips green. He scans the woman and it flashes red. "Ma'am."

The woman walks over to a small purse hanging from a banister. It is a sleek red alligator purse, easily the nicest thing in the entire apartment. She pulls out a tube of lipstick and applies it with shaking hands.

"Ma'am," Craig says again.

"Y'know, it's funny," Marco says, stepping towards the man with the beer. "Wasn't her name that was flashing a few minutes ago."

The man lifts the beer like he's going to smash it on someone's head, then takes a swig. "What can I say? Tess was feeling generous. Isn't that right, Tess?"

Tess finishes applying her lipstick and pulls out a compact. She wipes away some of the smudged eyeliner beneath her eye. Then she clicks the compact shut and puts it back in the purse.

"Tess," the man says again.

"That's right," Tess says, her voice feather soft. She doesn't look up.

"Well, there you go." The man takes a long drink. He doesn't break eye contact with Marco.

Craig walks over to Tess and guides her by the elbow. He whispers in her ear and she shakes her head. It is a quick, sudden spasm. Craig looks over at Marco and shrugs his shoulders. "Ma'am, you'll need to come with us."

Tess turns and follows them back to the car. Craig does not zip-tie her hands, though it is protocol. The man watches from the window. He still hasn't put down the bottle.

Once Tess is ensconced in the back seat with Virgil, Marco turns around. "He can't hear you now. You can tell us the truth."

Tess is fiddling with her WristBud. Most of the pink has worn off, leaving a bright chrome finish. While most people opt for an upgrade every couple of years, this woman seems to have kept the same model for decades, perhaps an entire lifetime. Every few minutes, the WristBud vibrates, softly but insistently, the screen red. Finally, Tess removes the watch and sets it on the seat next to her. She turns to the window.

Once they are on the road, Craig glances in the rearview mirror. "Did he force you to give him those lives? Threaten you?"

Tess shakes her head.

"So, you gave him the rest of your life? Willingly?"

She nods.

"Ma'am, I'm going to need verbal confirmation."

"Yes." Tess's voice is barely audible.

Craig tries again. "If that man did something to you, if he has some kind of leverage, we can protect you. But you have to tell us."

Tess turns as far as the seatbelt allows her, until her whole body is facing the door.

Virgil wants to grab her by the neck and squeeze. "Do you know where we're going? Do you know what's going to happen to you? You're going to die! For no goddamn reason!"

"Virgil," Craig says.

"This is your last chance. In a couple minutes, it'll be too late!"

"Virgil."

"Why give up your life for that asshole? What's the point?"

"Virgil."

"Say something, you stupid bitch!"

"Virgil!"

Tess has turned as far as she can to the window, her arms curled around her stomach, her backbone visible through her thin shirt. Virgil slams his body back onto the leather seat with a grunt. "Fine, whatever. Have a nice death."

"You want us to drop you off?" Craig asks. His voice is sympathetic.

"Nah. I'm good."

Whenever Virgil pictures the Transition Center, which isn't often, he imagines a skyscraper, dark and impassive, looming over the city. The truth is much more mundane. A windowless three-story building arcs into view, a thick gray slab against a cloudless sky. No trees line the concrete path. No commemorative fountain breaks up the monotony. A long, low fence separates the building from the world beyond. At two different checkpoints, guards scan their WristBuds and motion them forward. It seems like overkill—who would try to break into this place?

At the entrance, a scowling woman taps a small plastic wand against their WristBuds. A small ping sounds and Virgil's Wrist-Bud flashes Clearance Level 1. They enter what looks like a waiting room with plastic chairs and tables bolted to the floor. The chairs are off-white, pockmarked but scrubbed clean, the plastic gouged at the base as though someone tried to rip them from the ground. Two men in white scrubs enter and grasp Tess by her arms. She has become limp, almost catatonic. Even though she doesn't resist, the men are not gentle.

"She'll have twelve hours to change her mind," Craig explains after she's led away.

"Do they?" Virgil asks.

"What?"

"Change their mind?"

Craig sighs. "Not really. Maybe they would with a couple months of therapy, but we don't have the resources or the time."

"So that's it, then. The lowlifes win and everyone else suffers."

Marco grunts. "Tell me about it."

Craig has been typing a series of notes onto his WristBud. After he finishes, he walks up beside Virgil. "I need to make one last stop. Room 105. You can wait outside if you like."

The last thing Virgil wants is to spend another second in this place, but he shakes his head. He's not going to be a coward.

Room 105 is long and cavernous, filled with bright white light from row upon row of fluorescent lighting overhead. Beneath the lights are gurneys—thirty to a row, twenty columns in all—each holding a body.

An itching begins at the back of Virgil's neck, then moves to his throat. The room swells with hundreds of bodies breathing their saccharine promise into his ear—soon, soon—but then he notices each body zip-tied to the gurney and hooked up to an IV bag. Not dead. Not yet.

"They're sedated before transition. Helps the Portologists do their job," Craig explains.

Between the rows of bodies walks a doctor followed by two nurses. The doctor sticks an IV bag with a syringe and then waits. The beeping slows, then stumbles, then finally transforms into one long drone. The doctor whispers to one nurse, who makes a note in her WristBud. The other flips the monitor off, stilling the sound. Then they move on.

"Want to see the Incinerator?" Marco asks.

"No thank you." Virgil's breathing is short and shallow. He feels like he's not getting enough air.

Marco gestures to the gurneys spread out before him. "One of our docs suggested composting the bodies—the healthiest ones—but the Alliance for Preserving our Humanity nixed that idea. Cheaper, better for the environment, but just like a bunch of humanitards to just sit around and whine."

They walk back through the waiting room to the small antechamber where the same scowling woman sits, waiting for more bodies to pass through the gate. Virgil is lightheaded. He is desperate to get some air, but both Craig and Marco turn and block the door.

"One more thing," Craig says. His jovial demeanor is gone. "Coming here is a privilege, and not one I take lightly. Without this place, or places like it, our planet would be used up. Leine rejected the Transition Centers, and we all know how that went."

"Nothing but a pile of rubble," Marco says.

"It's not pretty, but it's necessary. The public can never see what we do. The work is too important for politics, for agendas. We have to be perfect all the time, or we end up on the news. That's why you're so important—you and the other recruits are creating our new public face. At the end of the series, you'll be assigned a unit. They will become your brothers, your family—we take care of our own here."

Craig leans forward until Virgil sees, truly sees, his face: hours-old stubble just beginning to peek through, lines around the eyes and mouth that he didn't notice before. "Stay loyal, and you're in. Betray us, and you'll wish you were on the first floor with the others."

Virgil swallows but maintains eye contact. "Yeah, sure."

"Okay," Craig says, straightening. "Who's up for a beer?"

Bogey's Bar is a dive at the outskirts of town, a musty basement lit by a string of multicolored lights and citronella candles. Craig, Marco, and Virgil pull up a table near the dartboard and order a pitcher of beer. Inside are a couple other men and one woman: a flat-chested behemoth gripping the bar like she's about to bench-press it. It seems odd that no one reacts to their entrance. Even though they're off-duty and out of uniform, no one could look at Craig or Marco and think they're anything other than men in blue. And then, as Virgil glances from square jaw to buzzed head to clenched fist, he realizes they're all Enforcers. This is an Enforcer bar.

"So, how does it feel, now that we've popped your Transition cherry?" Marco asks.

Virgil thinks about brushing off the question, acting like it was no big deal, but now that he's away from that place, all his fight-or-flight spent, he's exhausted. "Truthfully? I'm a little queasy."

"Yeah, that's common." Craig motions to the waitress and orders three Heart-Stoppers: a half-pound ground beef patty with onion rings on an everything bagel. Virgil tries to wave his away, but Craig lowers his arm. "Trust me. You're going to want to eat something. Regain your equilibrium."

"And once you're done eating, we're gonna get you laid," Marco grins.

"What?" Virgil's face flushes.

"Nothing beats the Transition Blues faster. Reminds you that you're alive and everything's still in working order." Marco grabs some darts from behind the bar and begins lobbing them at the board with remarkable precision. He and Craig talk about their crazier cases: a woman who Ziploc-bagged her infants and sent them down the river, an underground fighting ring with 280 years on the line. Then Craig recounts the man living on squirrels in the woods for Marco. "Asshole thought he could outrun an Enforcer. But my boy Virgil got him in the end."

"Well, you got him. I barely kept up."

Marco lets his eyes drift down Virgil's frame. "Yeah, we'll have to get you on a training regimen soon. Can't be chasing down bad guys carrying forty extra pounds."

"We'll have to see which unit he's placed in after the show's done," Craig says.

"I don't know." Marco lobs a dart over Virgil's head. "Maybe he'll want to shave his head and join his new buddy, Phren."

Everything inside Virgil clenches. "That faggot. He wishes." The words, hot and venomous, arc out before he can take them back.

Craig chuckles and slaps Virgil's back. He grabs a handful of darts and lobs three in a perfect semi-circle. "By the way, the wife wants to have you over sometime for dinner. Still a couple of months to fire up the grill."

Virgil's stomach drops at the thought of the rooftop barbecue: Tongs at the grill, Tiny Tim mixing drinks. The feeling has the bite of guilt, the ache of regret.

"Jenise is a vegetarian, but I think I can sneak a few steaks on the grill for us." Craig winks. "We're out on Maplewood. Just outside the city."

"Heard that place is nice," Virgil says. "Lots of trees and shit."

"Jenn loves working in her garden. She's been growing zucchini, tomatoes, eggplant. She says out there with a breeze, underneath the shade of our dogwoods, she feels closer to nature, like the city doesn't even exist."

"Oh yeah, Selena said Jen showed her how to start an herb garden. She's gonna put it on our deck," Marco says.

"Is that your wife?"

"Daughter. She's five. Her mom died a couple years ago."

"I'm sorry."

Marco shrugs. "She's supposed to go to Westwood, but I'm gonna pull some strings and get her into Penbrook. We live on Longfish Avenue. It's no Maplewood, but they just cleared out a couple condemned buildings, put in a CompleteMart. I get a subsidy for living there. You know—Enforcer in the neighborhood, keeps people honest."

"Smart," Craig says. "Jenise says that Westwood just put in a second metal scanner. Selena doesn't need to be a part of that. Oh, that reminds me." He clicks a few buttons on his WristBud and beams an image of a woven floral handbag. "This here is a Go West bag, perfect for the office and out on the town, only $39.95."

Marco chuckles, "You switching careers on us? Or maybe you need to drop trou and show us what else you're switching."

"Not for you, dumbass. If you have any lady friends, let me know and Jenise can hook them up."

"Your wife sells handbags?" Virgil asks.

"She's a nurse, but she sells Go West bags as her second life hustle."

"Your wife's a nurse?" Virgil asks before he can stop himself. He struggles to find a plausible reason, aside from the obvious, why that might be such a surprise.

Marco scowls but Craig laughs. "I know, I know, it's hard to understand when you're on the outside. One of us saves people for a living and the other kills them. But she said herself the day I dragged a Zoombie who had peed on three different nurses out on his ass that me doing my job lets her do hers. If the hospital, not to mention the world, was packed floor to ceiling with assholes believing their precious life was worth more than the next guy's, she wouldn't have the resources to save anyone, let alone the kid who might one day grow up to cure cancer, but only if he's given a chance."

Virgil nods. "Makes sense."

Craig walks to the dartboard and grabs all five darts. He drops them into Virgil's palm. "You let me know a weekend for the barbecue. Don't wait too long, though. Summer's almost over."

A couple hours later, as they're heading out, police have sectioned off the sidewalk in front of a Stop-N-Go. A crowd is beginning to gather, peeking across the police tape.

"Probably another botched robbery," Marco says.

"Got a good crowd. Better do a scan," Craig whispers.

As they approach, the crowd shrinks back. A few people turn and begin walking quickly away. Marco's WristBud emits a steady series of beeps followed by green lights, and then, as he sweeps by a middle-aged woman carrying a tote bag full of groceries, the light turns red and the device emits a small ding, like a casserole that has just finished cooking.

"Thirty-two hours," the WristBud chirps.

The woman's face pales, and she turns and begins walking. In three quick strides, Marco has caught up to her. "Ma'am, we're going to need you to come with us."

"No," the woman says, stepping back. "I still have time."

"Barely a day," Craig says. He has stepped behind her, blocking her exit. Virgil moves to her left.

"Plenty of time," the woman gasps. She cranes her neck around as if looking for someone to save her.

"You can spend that time in our reflection room," Craig says. He places a hand on her shoulder. "You don't want to make a scene."

"My children . . . " the woman whispers.

"The front desk receptionist would be happy to arrange a final visit."

"What will they do without me?"

"Are your children at home?" Craig asks.

The woman nods.

"Are they with anyone?"

"My husband."

"Then they'll appreciate the opportunity to live out their full lifetimes."

"But what about the homecoming dance? I was supposed to be a chaperone."

"Ma'am," Craig says softly but firmly. "Your time is up."

The woman's legs buckle beneath her. Both Craig and Marco support her weight, leading her across the street and down the mostly empty sidewalk to their car. A young boy, maybe eleven or twelve, in a dirty t-shirt with the phrase "Fuck the Force" on it, jumps out from an alley.

"Fuck you, roaches!" he yells, tossing an empty bottle. Virgil jumps as it shatters at his feet. The boy turns and dashes away. Virgil steps forward as if to chase him, though there's no way he's going to catch up.

"Let him go," Craig says. "Not worth it."

"Christ," Virgil says, shaken. "We're just doing our job."

The woman has begun softly crying. Marco pats Virgil on the back. "Exactly."

PHOENIX

As the morning light drifts in through the curtains, limning Aisha's shoulder in blue, Phoenix feels a trilling in her chest. Yes, she is here. Yes, she is changed. She touches Aisha's skin, pulls her close: the warmth of Aisha's sleeping body surrounds her.

Aisha turns and kisses Phoenix's neck. "Morning."

The early morning light turns everything soft and filmy, a quietly sleeping cat. Phoenix is certain, if she concentrates, she can hear the room purr. "Let's stay in bed all morning."

Aisha smiles. "As you wish."

After a few minutes, Aisha falls back asleep and Phoenix pads to the kitchen. The light washes over the cupboards, the speckled blue countertop. Phoenix opens cabinet door after cabinet door, but they are all empty. A couple ant traps, but no food. Inside the fridge is the same story: several packets of soy sauce along with a stoppered bottle of white wine, but nothing else.

Undeterred, Phoenix glances out the window. Across the street is a Stop-N-Go. She can be the one to bring food back this time. Maybe surprise Aisha with some breakfast in bed.

There's just one problem: Phoenix doesn't have any money. And though she has plenty of experience lifting things she needs, convenience stores are too small, the cashiers usually too vigilant. She'll have to do this the legitimate way.

She finds Aisha's bag on the wicker chair and roots through it. Lip gloss, compact, nail polish remover, duct tape, two spools of wire, hairbrush, notebook, sunglasses case, used hypodermic needle (thankfully capped), but no wallet. Damn. The last item Phoenix finds is her WristBud. She's seen people use it to pay for things. In fact, most people just use their WristBud rather than bothering with cash or a credit card anymore. She's not sure if it links to a bank account or is used like a credit card to be paid off later. But she's certain Aisha won't mind—they have to eat, after all, and all she's doing is saving Aisha the trip.

She carries the WristBud down the stairs and across the street to the Stop-N-Go. She only has to wait about two minutes to cross the street. This early, it isn't busy yet. Later, the street will become a cacophony of horns and barely contained rage.

Inside the store, a middle-aged man reads a newspaper. When was the last time she saw a physical paper? It is a delightful anachronism, and Phoenix decides she likes this place, this man. She strolls from one row of items to the next: batteries, cat food, powdered donuts, sunflower seeds. She considers walking down the street to find a restaurant, maybe a Health King or something, but she doesn't want to get lost or have Aisha wake up to find her missing.

She grabs a package of Honey Beelites, oversized donuts wrapped in a honey-chocolate casing, and two bottles of cola. She also grabs a bag of chips and a package of sunflower seeds for later. She's always wanted to learn her father's trick of opening the casing with his teeth and then spitting it out without losing the seed. The thought of her father makes her stomach dip.

Snap out of it. This is nice. She is happy.

The cashier wordlessly scans her purchases, then nods his head at the total. Phoenix takes the WristBud from her pocket and, not certain what to do, offers it to him.

The cashier wrinkles his brow before nodding towards the scanner to the right of Phoenix. She holds up the WristBud, turning it until its face matches the quivering red line of the scanner.

Instead of a happy ping, she hears a noise like a buzzer. That doesn't sound good.

She holds the WristBud up toward the scanner again, but this time it doesn't make any noise. It just flashes red.

The cashier holds out his hand and Phoenix obediently places the WristBud in it. She's probably doing it wrong. He'll know what to do.

The cashier types a few buttons on a laptop in front of him, then scans the WristBud on a device on his side of the counter. "This your WristBud?" His voice sounds accusatory.

"No," Phoenix says, stepping back. "It's my friend's. She let me use it." Her heart is beating fast. "I'll go get her." The cashier has not given her back the WristBud, so Phoenix leaves it and her purchases and backs out of the store. She doesn't run—that would look guilty—but she does speed-walk back to the apartment complex across the street.

It isn't until she's inside the building that her heart slows down and she finally feels like she is no longer being watched.

Aisha grumbles when Phoenix shakes her, gently at first, and then more insistently.

"I lost your WristBud."

Aisha is suddenly upright. "What?"

"I went down to the corner store to get us some breakfast." Phoenix fingers the silky rainbow threads of Aisha's wig. "And the cashier took it. I guess it didn't work or something."

"No no no no no," Aisha mutters. She stands and begins pacing the room. "WristBuds are connected to their users' DNA. You can't just use someone else's. How do you not know this?"

"I don't really use them," Phoenix mutters.

"How have you not used one? Are you from one of those freaky desert communities or something?"

Phoenix continues to let the rainbow threads run, smooth and comforting, through her fingers.

"Holy shit, you are. That explains so much."

"So, what do we do?"

Aisha looks around the room, at the curtains letting in just a peek of mid-morning light, at the rumpled comforter and bed-sheet. She walks over to the third-story window and opens it.

"What are you doing?"

"Listen, we don't have time to get into the intricacies of WristBud technology, but that WristBud is so modded, they're gonna have some questions we shouldn't stick around to answer." Aisha climbs onto the small wooden balcony, nudging aside a potted plant crispy fried from the sun. "You coming?"

Phoenix glances out the window. It is a long way down. "Where?"

Aisha points up. "Roof, then over to the next building, then out of here."

"Uh," Phoenix says, imagining her body leaping and then falling, twisted, to the ground.

There is a knock on the door, and both women freeze. "Police. Open the door."

Aisha presses her fists together, then appears to come to a decision. "Don't tell them anything. They don't have anything on you—they'll have to release you. Next chance you get, go to the Health King on Main. I'll find you." Aisha kisses Phoenix's cheek, climbs out the window, and is gone.

The knocking resumes, and Phoenix can hear mumbling outside of the door. She glances from the window to the door and back to the window. She left. Aisha left her. Phoenix's panic reaches a crescendo and then her nerves short-circuit, and she gives up.

With nothing else to do, and no other escape, she opens the door.

The officers drop Phoenix off at the closest precinct, her hands handcuffed behind her. Another officer, a woman with a large mole on the side of her nose, takes down her information. Phoenix glances around at the only other person in handcuffs: a scowling man, gaunt and strung out, who keeps scuffing the carpet like he's trying to find a secret. The officer grows more and more irritated the longer it takes to find Phoenix in the system. Finally, she snorts and sits back in her chair. "Your family emigrated to a desert community. You're not a U.S. citizen. Where's your passport?"

"It was stolen," Phoenix says truthfully.

"Your father filed a missing person's report several weeks ago."

"I'm not missing. I left," Phoenix says.

The officer raises an eyebrow. "Don't you think you're a little old to be running away from home?"

Phoenix sits back in the chair.

"Why did you leave? Were you threatened? Hurt?"

Phoenix shakes her head, but she doesn't look up in case she starts crying. She can already feel the burning behind her eyes.

The officer leans in, her voice low. "We have asylum protocols, you know. In case your father . . . in case your home isn't safe."

"What?" Phoenix sits up. "No, he didn't . . . I just had to get out of there, you know?"

The officer snaps back to her former countenance. "Well, regardless of your reasons, you can't just enter the U.S. without a passport. You should know that. After we get this all sorted out, you're probably going to be deported."

Inside a small room with scuffed white walls, Phoenix tries very hard not to cry. She is handcuffed to a long wooden table. Shame pulses at her chest, her throat.

Her father is going to be furious.

She tries not to picture Aisha's eyes, those green lines speckled with gray. She tries not to fall, eyes closed, into that soft, mossy field.

Come back.

Eventually, the door opens and a man with a shaved head enters the room. His face looks soft, almost pleasant, but there is something hard beneath the surface. He sits down and hands Phoenix a cup of water. Phoenix drinks it and the man hands the empty cup to someone Phoenix can't see outside the door.

"My name is Phren," the man says. "And you are Phoenix Ibson."

Phoenix nods.

The man opens a manila folder with a small stack of papers inside. "Looks like you're a long way from home. Mind telling me how you wound up in South Burrington?"

Phoenix scowls. Not answering is incredibly difficult—she can feel this man's voice kneading the knots of anxiety in her throat, tempting them to unfurl their truth. His voice is a stream, carrying her gently but insistently to its destination. Maybe she could tell part of the truth, let the rest stay buried? But she knows that once she starts, she won't be able to stop. She'll tell him everything. Her only recourse is to stay silent.

"I see. So, this is the game we're going to play. I must tell you: this will be a lot easier if you cooperate." He waits a beat, not looking up from his folder. "Where have you been living?"

Phoenix glances toward the mirror that she knows from procedural cop shows is a one-way window. She imagines Aisha on the other side, her hands pressed against the glass, leaving five perfectly formed fingerprints. She imagines walking over to the window and placing her own fingertips on top, the heat transferring through the glass. She imagines the warmth buoying her against the tide that threatens to whisk her away.

Phren taps his finger against the table. "Stop me if I'm wrong. You ran away because you wanted to know what life was like on this side of the wall. Or maybe something happened, and you felt like you had to leave. You stayed with a friend for a couple of days, but then you met someone . . . a man who was older, wiser, seemed to have all the answers. Wavy dark hair, a little pudgy but in a good way. Solid. Like he could hold you and not drop you. You went out with him a few times, and even though he seemed to be doing some illegal stuff, you looked the other way, because he was good-looking and kind, and he took care of you. And then, one day, you wake up in an apartment that isn't yours with the cops beating down the door, and that man, that kind, sexy man, is nowhere to be found. He has betrayed you." Phren sits back and crosses his arms. "How did I do?"

Phoenix breathes a short, sharp exhale and looks down. If she looks up, he'll see the line of sweat forming at her neck and realize how close he was. Just switch the gender and there you go.

"Living on the reservation, you may not know that WristBuds are linked to their users' digital fingerprints."

Phoenix glances up. She assumed it was basically a fancy watch that could do a bunch of cool stuff. She hadn't really given the technology much thought.

"It's one of the ways we track people when their time is up. I won't tell you the other ways, but suffice to say, consumerism is our friend. This WristBud has been heavily modified. It was originally registered to a Paul Phillips from South Burrington. The only problem is that Paul Phillips is dead. It takes a pretty sophisticated amount of hacking to register the WristBud to a corpse and to link your own digital fingerprint to that corpse. Much more than a single person could possess."

Phoenix blinks. She needs some more water, but then she'd have to break her silence, and Phren would likely say no.

"We suspect an organization. One that performs illegal activities for those with enough money and time."

Phoenix discovers a small scratch on the metal table. She traces it to the edge, where it hooks into the side and then disappears. She tries to imagine how such a scratch could have gotten there, what amount of force would be required.

Phren sighs. "Additionally, one gun registered to a David Lynn Johnson was used in a homicide in Arridia two weeks ago. Mr. Johnson told us the gun and his truck were stolen around the same time you left."

Phoenix glances toward the window. She tries not to see it, she tries to push it down, but here it is: the mouth, open and gasping without breath, the sound of liquid leaving a too-small space. She can feel her own chest rising and falling, quickly, too quickly. She has forgotten how to swallow.

"Mr. Johnson isn't interested in pressing charges against the person who stole his property, just in getting it back. Do you know where his truck is?"

Phoenix shakes her head: a quick, jerking movement.

"Or who, perhaps, used the gun to shoot a known human trafficker?"

Phoenix shakes her head again.

"Perhaps the man, the owner of this modded Wristbud, pulled the trigger? Perhaps he was saving you from being kidnapped? Or perhaps he borrowed the gun without your permission?"

Phoenix shakes her head. It is a loose, slippery thing. If she isn't careful, it will pop right off. She lays her cheek on the metal table, the cold a sudden and sharp rebuke. She wishes she had her long hair back. She would pull it over her face, hide from this man and his questions. She remembers after her mother died, how her father would sit on the floor and comb her hair for hours while she sang the only song she knew. *If you're ever lost at sea / all alone and no dinghy / Just take a step and then one more / This is how we come ashore.* She only knew the first verse, so every time she finished, she would start again, and her father would pause, his wrist probably aching from pulling the comb hard but not too hard, and she would say, more, more, and he would continue, wordless, while she sang the first verse, deeply, soulfully, as if for the first time.

"Phoenix." Phren's voice is a tendril of smoke curling inside her. She lifts her head. "If you're mixed up with something, with this man or his organization, if he has you doing things, illegal things, we can protect you. But we need your help."

Phoenix presses her lips together, tears threatening. She shakes her head.

Phren sighs. He closes the manila folder. "All right, I'll be back later."

Time passes, but Phoenix has no idea how long. Hours, maybe. Less than a day. By the time the door opens again, Phoenix has a low-grade headache thrumming behind her eyes. She considers asking the officer behind the door for some medicine, definitely something to drink, but the man now standing in front of her with tired eyes and a receding hairline is not Phren but her father.

"Minmi?"

And now the tears that were threatening are flowing down her cheeks, down her neck, great waves of them, and she's hiccupping and coughing and he's there, his arms around her, holding her shaking body still.

"It's okay, it's okay," he says, over and over, even after she's stopped crying.

He pulls away to look at her, but Phoenix won't meet his eyes. "I'm sorry, Papa."

"Did he hurt you?"

At first Phoenix thinks he's talking about the fictitious man. She shakes her head.

"As soon as you went missing and Davie Lynn found Joey's body, we figured out what happened. I went after Jared myself." His whole face is shadow. "But he was already gone."

"Oh."

"Everyone's on the lookout for Jared. He can't hurt you now."

Phoenix doesn't say anything. Her tears have stopped.

"So, you can come home."

Phoenix nods. Her father pulls Phoenix into another hug, but this time, she doesn't return it.

"My little Minmi, what's wrong?"

There is so much packed inside Phoenix's chest that she can't begin to sort it out. She gestures toward the door.

"Don't worry." Fernal's eyes are nearly black. He begins pounding on the door, so loudly and so suddenly that Phoenix nearly falls back into her seat.

Eventually, Phren comes to the door. "Yes?"

"My daughter has told you all that she knows. If you aren't charging her, I'm going to take her home."

"We aren't charging her," Phren says, pulling a sheet of paper from the manila folder. "But you can't go home. She's a key witness in an investigation. The things that WristBud account is linked to . . . well, let's just say you'll want to stick around for a while. I've rented you both a hotel room in town."

Fernal takes the sheet of paper.

"We've also reactivated her. She's back on the grid."

Fernal's face drops. "You can't do that."

"She's been living in Arridia illegally for weeks, possibly longer, not to mention the possible criminal activity. If she's cleared of all charges, you can petition a judge for probation. But you'll need proof of residence after your deportation."

Fernal grips the edge of the table, and Phoenix wraps her arms around her stomach, waiting for the explosion. But he simply nods.

A police car drives them both to the hotel. It doesn't leave when they emerge from the car or when they walk through the automatic doors. Phoenix peeks out of the glass as her father checks in. Nope, still there.

Inside the room, Phoenix begins unpacking the small suitcase her father brought. Inside are a couple of his shirts and pants, underwear, and her clothes as well. She smiles, ready to thank him for his thoughtfulness, when she notices his arms held still at his sides. She waits for the storm clouds to burst.

"Papa," she says, hoping to forestall the inevitable.

Fernal holds up one finger. "Phoenix Ibson, I am so angry I can barely speak."

Phoenix nods and sits on the bed, though her father, his back still turned, can't see her.

"How could you do this? Do you know how worried I've been, what I thought might have happened to you?"

"I'm sorry, I—"

Fernal spins around. "I'm not finished. I've warned you so many times how dangerous it is to go running around with Enforcers lying in wait. And then I get a call and here you are, in jail."

Phoenix glances up at the painting above their bed: a calm blue ocean with a sailboat in the distance. The soft blue of the sky matches the soft blue of the ocean—only a thin brush stroke separates them. Phoenix thinks back to the apartment, the light coming through the curtains, Aisha's body radiating blue.

"And not only do you run away, but you don't call, you don't write, you don't try to contact me in any way. I have no idea where you are, if you are even alive."

Phoenix's eyes are starting to water again. She looks away from the painting to her father, pacing the length of the room. "I didn't want you to get exiled into the desert."

Fernal shakes his head. "That may have been true at first. But now? Now it is a choice."

"I'm sorry."

Fernal keeps pacing and then stops, turning to face Phoenix. "When we get home, after we make it through this, you are through. There will be no trips into town. There will be no truck privileges at all. You will work off your debt to Davie Lynn. You will go to your tutoring sessions and come home and that will be your life until I say so."

The word escapes Phoenix's mouth before she can call it back: "No."

"What did you say?"

"I'm not going back."

Fernal is tense, nearly vibrating. "Phoenix Ibson, if you think—"

"I met someone."

"The boy that has gotten you into so much trouble?"

"Not a boy. She's a girl. Actually, she's my girlfriend." The word floods Phoenix's body in warmth.

Fernal opens and closes his mouth.

"And I like her and she likes me. I know you want me to go to college, but maybe there's another way I can make a difference."

Fernal braces himself on the oak desk.

"It's not like at our community. I was just sitting around, using up resources, not really contributing. And now I'm giving back. Maybe not in a totally legal way, but since when have we been on the side of the law? Anyway, I can make my own decisions. I'm not a child anymore."

"Oh, you are definitely a child. And luckily for me, the state agrees. As soon as we are able, we are heading home. End of discussion."

The rest of the evening they spend amid the nullifying glow of the television. Fernal clicks through the channels, never landing on anything for more than a few seconds. Images flash, bright and meaningless: two women arguing, a self-sorting trashcan, the desert, a man falling down a flight of stairs, a necklace, the phrase "Do You Want Something Better." For dinner, Fernal orders a pizza, not trusting her alone in the room. When the light in the sky fades, he flips off the two bedside lamps and tells Phoenix goodnight in a voice of finality.

She watches the clock and waits: 10 pm, 11 pm, midnight. When it is 1 am and her father's breathing has the rattle of deep sleep, Phoenix slips a foot, then a leg, then her entire body out of bed. She pauses every couple of steps to make sure her father is still sleeping. Then, backpack in hand, she's heading out the door before she realizes that she can't just leave. Not like last time. She writes a quick note on the notepad on top of the oak desk, just three sentences:

I'm sorry

I love you

Goodbye

Any other details the police could use; any other justification would require more paper.

She slips out the door, down the stairs, and into the cool night air.

The Health King on Main is one of the few restaurants still open at this hour. She was afraid it would just be the drive-thru, but miraculously, the seating area is open as well. She tried to ask directions from a Nestless lying on a piece of cardboard, surrounded by lumpy trash bags, but he didn't wake at her shaking. The second man she asked stood on a corner in a shiny black jacket, his face an empty mask. He stared at her unwaveringly for so long, Phoenix wondered if she should repeat the question, until he finally lifted a hand to point in the right direction.

Now that she's here, she's feeling uncertain. The cashier, a girl about Phoenix's age, keeps glancing in her direction. She knows she is supposed to order something, but she doesn't have any money. How long is she supposed to stay? Hours? Days? In the morning, they'll notice she's gone and send a search party. And how will Aisha know she's here? Is she still waiting for her, or did she give up after she didn't come right away? Maybe she's back with Ms. Bodice and the other girls, waiting for her next assignment.

A woman in her sixties wearing a floral print cardigan walks slowly towards her. Just as she's about to pass, she tips her lidless soda directly onto Phoenix's lap.

"Oh my God!" Phoenix yells, leaping up and flicking the ice onto the floor.

"Oh dear, I'm so sorry, how clumsy of me. You better go to the bathroom to clean up."

"It's fine," Phoenix says, wiping off the seat with a handful of recycled paper napkins.

The woman grabs some of the napkins and helps. She leans close to Phoenix's ear. "I really think you should go to the bathroom."

Phoenix narrows her eyes, then grabs her backpack and storms into the bathroom. What a waste of a perfectly good soda. And why did that woman have to spill her drink in the exact spot Phoenix was sitting?

"Jesus Christ," Aisha says when Phoenix opens the door. "I thought you'd never get here."

Phoenix rushes forward, colliding them both into the bathroom door. Her lips seek out Aisha's; her hands are on her back, her waist.

Aisha runs her fingers through Phoenix's hair. "Missed you too."

"How did you know I was here? How did you even get in here?"
Aisha smiles. She motions toward the bathroom window: a

small rectangle barely large enough for a body to fit through.

"Why not just use the door?"

"I assume you didn't notice the unmarked car following you from the hotel?"

Phoenix looks behind her as though she would be able to see the car through the wall.

Aisha smiles. She whispers into Phoenix's ear, "What would you do without me?" Then she raps on the bathroom door. "Take off your clothes."

"Umm, not that I'm not happy to see you, but maybe let's wait until we're somewhere safer . . . and cleaner." Phoenix startles as a woman in a cinched hoodie and jeans walks out of the bathroom. When she removes the hoodie, Phoenix notices she is young: 19, maybe 20. Phoenix also notices her mangled pixie cut, just a little outgrown, and her terrible dye job. She could pass for Phoenix at a distance.

Phoenix and the woman change clothing. Aisha stands guard by the door. When they finish, the woman nods at Aisha and walks out, head down.

"That will buy us some time. By the time they figure out their mistake, we'll be gone." Aisha nudges open the window. It opens with a squeak so loud Phoenix is certain the men in the unmarked car have heard it.

Aisha boosts Phoenix and then shimmies herself over as well. She grabs Phoenix's hand and laces their fingers together. They walk, hands clasped, at a brisk pace: just a couple heading home after a night on the town. Despite her heart's cacophony, Phoenix loves the feel of Aisha's fingers interlaced with her own, the brief moments they appear, to any outside observer, like an ordinary couple.

After a few blocks, Aisha leads Phoenix down a side street, where they pick up the pace. It isn't until they're at Aisha's car that Aisha turns and surveys the pavement. "Looks clear." She opens the back door. "Best to lay low for a while."

Phoenix nods and stretches out on the floor, trying to ignore the dirt and trash and dead bugs near her face.

"Won't be for long. Just until we're at the next nook."

"We aren't leaving?" Phoenix asks, incredulous. "They're going to be looking for me, you know."

"I got you," Aisha says. She turns and runs a hand through Phoenix's hair. "Besides, we have one more job. This one's out in the sticks, though, so don't worry. They won't be looking for us there."

"They're not looking for you, anyway," Phoenix says. "They think you're a guy."

Aisha snorts. "Toxic heteronormativity saves the day."

Despite the unpleasantness of the floor, despite the contortions of Phoenix's body, despite the constant strobing of streetlights, Phoenix feels the tension of the past few hours begin to dissipate. Her father is still asleep. She still has a couple of hours before he finds the note, before . . . Phoenix tries not to think about what will happen next. Deportation, probably. Nothing worse, certainly. He didn't do anything, after all. Her mind circles and darts, a panicked, fluttering thing, before finally giving up. Nothing more to do tonight. As the engine weights her limbs with sleep, Phoenix glances up at the profile of Aisha's face, her arm slung lazily across the wheel. Everything's okay now. She's going to be all right.

When Phoenix wakes, the passing headlights and streetlamps have slowed. The sun hasn't yet broken through the clouds. Her neck and back throb from her awkward position on the floor. She heaves herself into the passenger seat.

"Morning," Aisha says. Except for the lines under her eyes, Phoenix wouldn't be able to tell she had been driving all night.

"Hope this is okay. I can't stay back there anymore."

Aisha nods. "We're far enough out."

Phoenix settles into the seat. The beltway of South Burrington has turned into a two-lane highway. The land is growing less and less cluttered: towering office buildings and skyscraper-tall Health King signs transform into strip malls and chain restaurants, and then again into roadside stands and two-pump gas stations. The land is long and yellow and flat. It as though the world has taken a deep breath and released it. Aisha turns down winding roads marked Route 636 or Route 641, bumping over washed-out potholes and tire-spinning gravel before returning to the highway.

"Gotta make sure we're not being followed," she says by way of explanation.

They stop at a gas station, its sign sun-bleached and rusted. While Aisha gets gas, Phoenix uses the port-a-potty out back. Inside the convenience store, they wander the aisles, thankful for a moment out of the car. Phoenix notices that Aisha no longer holds her hand. The cashier leans against the counter, his gut stretching his sleeveless white shirt. He scowls as Phoenix and Aisha walk through the store. It's hard to tell what about their appearance he finds most offensive. If Phoenix wasn't buzzing with anxiety, she might grab Aisha and pull her in for a little PDA, really get the cashier going. But if Aisha is keeping her head down, she must sense danger, so Phoenix follows suit.

They drive another half hour and then Aisha abruptly turns down a winding dirt road leading to a two-story farmhouse. The sun is directly overhead, so everything is simple and bright: yellow house, green shutters, blue sky. There are no shadows, no depth. Phoenix decides the simplicity is charming, welcoming, and not a paper-thin backdrop ready to collapse beneath them.

At the door, a woman in a bright orange sundress answers. She is even darker than Aisha. She grins, and Phoenix can't help but smile in return. "You made it. Come, we have much to discuss."

After Virgil's success with the E01s, Benson is all arm-patting platitudes. Though his ratings are still behind the single mother with the charming Southern accent, he's pretty high on the list of viewer favorites, way above former military guy who never speaks below a bellow and condescending pseudo-vegan who was caught last week eating a cheeseburger. In fact, Benson confides, he's planning to axe the bottom two sometime next week.

"Get them involved in a scandal, then let them go. Make us look like saints."

"What kind of scandal?"

Benson shrugs. "The kind of thing the public suspects us of doing anyway. Rounding people up and stealing their time. Something like that."

There are a couple days before Virgil's next segment will air, but Benson doesn't want them to get behind. He's been saving the most controversial job for last: an E03.

"You want me to be a Buzzard?"

"See, that's the problem right there." Benson begins pacing the small break room. "You're doing the exact same job as an E01, but now, suddenly, you're a monster."

"Well, they do murder babies."

"Those infants were adults mere moments ago. It's the exact same person, just . . . smaller." He tightens his cravat: pink and purple paisley. "We separated the Juvenile unit from the E01s our third year—we saw what a public relations nightmare it was. To be honest, it takes a special individual to work a job that reviled."

Virgil think back to the two knuckleheads that kidnapped him. "And by special, you mean a moron."

Benson smirks. "I will admit that particular unit is not comprised of Supreme scholars. But they are cleverer than they let on."

Virgil seriously doubts that last claim as he rides backseat with the two assholes who kidnapped him. Bunt, the tall fat one, drives the van while Zweber, the short fat one, fiddles with the radio, eventually stopping on a hip-hop station. He turns the bass up until the van vibrates with inventive cursing and racial epithets that both men shout gleefully into the closed-off space.

Virgil wonders if they play this station when they have children in the back. In the hollowed-out space where some might stick guitars or broken-down mowers, this van carries twelve children's car seats bolted to the floor. Above each is a large plastic container with a long neck leading to a small plastic nipple. Though empty now, each has the capacity to hold two liters of formula and, if necessary, a small amount of dissolved sedative. It reminds Virgil of when he was eight and his mother, in a late morning gin buzz she mistook for generosity, took him to the pet store to buy a gerbil. She brought him to a large cage where two of the gerbils had given birth. The wood chips shook with too many furry bodies all pressed together. His mother stroked one long red nail against the acned clerk's face and murmured pronouncements about the gerbils' vitality. The clerk flushed red, his body pulsing with hormones, unable to sort out his feelings towards this woman, sun-spotted and wrinkled but in a low-cut top. Virgil reached a finger tentatively into the cage. As though they too could feel the swirl of lust and repulsion, two gerbils leapt up toward Virgil's outstretched hand, tiny teeth gnashing. Luckily, he pulled his hand away in time. But later that night as he lay in bed, he could see their bodies thrashing against the plastic wall, that thin, translucent membrane, aching to be free.

Virgil folds that memory into a dusty corner of his mind. Once he reverses, all those memories will be gone, and he'll be free to fill that space with good thing, beautiful things, things that are worthy.

After twenty minutes on the highway, Bunt takes the Carrion Bridge exit and then pulls next to a squat brick building surrounded by a tidy artificial lawn. A maroon sign out front says *Perennial Care*. Inside, the smells of stale urine, boiled corn, and bleach swirl into a noxious mix. They stand at the front desk, glancing at the vase of plastic daffodils and brochures promising quality care, whether it is your first transition or your last. Finally, a nurse ambles over and hands them a clipboard. "Mr. Hooper took his leave of us a little faster than we anticipated."

Zweber scowls at the nurse. "You're supposed to call 24 hours in advance."

The nurse scowls back, and Virgil wonders who will win this miserable bastard contest. "We've had five call-outs this week and I've been understaffed for the past two years. You find me qualified nurses and you'll have your 24 hours' notice."

After Zweber fills out the necessary paperwork, another nurse carries a newborn swaddled in a blanket. Bunt grabs the baby and tucks him beneath his arm like a football. Virgil reaches a hand forward automatically, though the gesture is futile. But when he looks closer, Bunt isn't hurting the baby—it is secure in his grasp. He's obviously had plenty of practice. Bunt tosses the blanket to the nearest nurse. Neither nurse will make eye contact with Bunt or the newborn.

Bunt buckles the newborn in the seat closest to the door. He fills the plastic container with pre-made formula and lowers it until the nipple is within grasping distance. He then turns the temperature controls to 74 degrees.

"Why bother?" Virgil asks as Zweber checks his WristBud for the next address. "Why go through all the trouble of keeping the babies alive?"

Bunt shrugs, peeling out of the parking lot. "That's our job. Check the list, get the patients, bring 'em in. We do our job, the docs do theirs." There's probably a more sophisticated explanation involving government regulations and bipartisan agreements, but for these men, the checklist is king.

They hit up another nursing home on the west end of town and two assisted living facilities within five miles of each other. The process is the same: wait at the desk, fill out paperwork, receive newborn.

"Don't they have Portologists on staff?" Virgil asks after the fourth center.

"Nah, they only work at hospitals or certified Transition Centers," Zweber explains.

"But why? Wouldn't that be so much easier?"

Bunt shrugs, no explanation this time.

The next stop is a brick townhouse in the Silver Brook suburb. They walk up the stone pathway lined with rows of flowering bushes and knock on the door. A woman in green and white spandex greets them. She motions them in, jogging in place the whole time, as though they are holding her up from more important things. "It's my uncle. He just doesn't have any other family," she says, motioning towards the baby carrier on the floor beside the three pairs of neon sneakers. Even in the foyer, the hardwood floors and pristine white trim indicate that this is not a house with kids.

Bunt hands her a clipboard.

"Do I have to fill this out now? I was just about to go for a run."

Bunt crosses his arms, impassive.

The woman sighs. "Fine. But this better not take long."

When she finishes, she hands the clipboard to Virgil. She looks down at the baby carrier, where her uncle is making spit bubbles. She reaches a tentative hand forward and then abruptly straightens. "Well, if that's all. You gentlemen can let yourselves out."

And then she's out the door, running down the stone path as fast as she can.

The next two infants are abandoned on street corners a couple blocks away from each other, so the paperwork is quick. "More ghetto recycling," Bunt mutters to Zweber, who nods. It's nice to see the babies tucked safely in the car seats, sucking down the milk like their life depends on it, until Virgil remembers that it does. He faces forward and tries not to listen to their little gulps.

Their last stop before lunch is an hour out, the edge of the Burrington district. A husband and wife stand shaking in the doorway of a one-story rancher with toys strewn about the front lawn. Three girls in descending age peek out between their legs.

"We can't keep him. We just can't. I tried, you know? I got a second job, but they cut Burt's hours, and there's just not enough money or space or time . . . " the woman trails off, clutching a onesie in her fist. Her husband wraps his arms around her, but she resists.

"God damn it, I'm sorry!" she screams as they take the child away.

"Jesus," Virgil says once they're in the van. "That was rough. How do you do this every day?"

Bunt shrugs. "Money's good."

They stop at a Health King for lunch, and Virgil is relieved that it isn't his former employer. That would be a little more than he could bear. As they approach the counter, the place is a lot quieter than he remembers. It takes Virgil a moment to realize why: their presence is muffling cell phone conversations, children whining, people giving orders. Even the ticking of timers and the sizzle of oil seem dulled. After a morning of screaming women and fussy babies, the quiet is kind of nice.

They eat their crumbles in the car while the AC blasts on high. Virgil keeps waiting for one of the babies to start wailing, but they appear to be sleeping. Halfway through their meal, they receive a call from headquarters: a baby has been abandoned in Sun Stream Park.

The park is five square miles of forested trails, so Virgil is expecting an hour of walking in the 90-degree heat, but it turns out that they just have to follow the crowd. The infant is tucked inside an insulated lunch bag on top of a park bench. The baby wiggles inside its makeshift carrier, reaching up toward the occasional face that peeks over.

The crowd parts to let the men in blue through, everyone taking up as little space as possible. Men and women clutch their arms and press their legs together, each person uncertain and waiting for them to fix it.

Bunt scans the infant with his WristBud and then shakes his head. "This one's brand new."

The crowd begins muttering and everyone takes a collective step back.

"The mom's probably still here," Zweber whispers, his breath hot in Virgil's ear.

Virgil glances around at the terrified faces. Why would a mother who abandoned her child stick around? There aren't any women that look young enough or scared enough to be the culprit: two middle-aged women and a thirty-something in stretched-thin yoga pants and a teenager who is recording all of it on her WristBud. And then Virgil sees him: a young guy, late teens, his skin nearly translucent with sweat, wearing a CompleteMart shirt. The nearest CompleteMart is an hour away. He's shifting from one foot to the other, hugging himself, and craning his neck to see what's happening.

Virgil is debating whether or not to call the kid out when he meets Virgil's eyes, swallows, and then sprints in the opposite direction.

"Told ya," Zweber says.

"Should we chase him?"

Zwber shakes his head. "Not worth it." He grabs the handles of the bag and walks back to the van.

They pick up two more infants amid tears and apologies and hurried explanations, which Virgil is already sick of. Save the hysterics and just give them the kid already.

With every car seat filled, they head back to the Transition Center.

On the way, Virgil asks the question he already knows the

answer to. "What's going to happen to them? Will any of them be placed in the foster system?"

"Foster system's full. Can't find homes for the kids they have," Bunt explains. "Most'll be transitioned, but sometimes they find other places for 'em."

"Like where?"

Bunt shrugs. "Not my department."

As they pull up to the gates of the Transition Center, Virgil feels the now-familiar sinking in his gut. This time, he can more quickly push the feeling aside and focus on the tasks at hand: removing the patients from the van and placing them in the industrial eight-seat strollers. The fabric is a worn baby blue with a large bar on the handle that must be depressed for the stroller to be pushed.

Inside the Transition Center, the same scowling woman scans Virgil's WristBud and he receives a new clearance level: 2. They take the elevator to the second floor and another warehouse-long room with fluorescent lighting. Here, the gurneys are smaller, and each holds a sleeping baby hooked up to an IV and monitor. The walls and ceiling are the same baby blue, and Virgil suddenly remembers that blue is supposed to be calming. This blue, however, inspires nothing but dread. Gazing out at rows upon rows of infants drifting quietly out to sea, Virgil realizes why they're on the second floor: this is so much worse than the ready-to-be-euthanized adults. Several Portologists walk from gurney to gurney, just like the floor below, administering the proper dose into the saline bag. Except for the quiet beeping of the machines, all is silent.

Virgil lets out a small puff of air. It is the only sound in the room.

A nurse, followed by a Portologist, approaches them. The nurse is short with scowling, gnomish features while the Portologist's face droops as though his skin is melting off his body. The nurse holds out her WristBud to scan the infants Bunt and Zweber have brought in. For each that has any time remaining, the WristBud emits a small ding along with the time: two lifetimes, one lifetime, 17 years.

"What happens to all that time?" Virgil asks.

"Goes into the bank," Zweber says.

"And then what?"

Bunt shrugs. "Up to the government."

"People can petition the government for more time—desperate people, important people. It's often used for diplomatic negotiations," the nurse explains.

After the nurse wheels the infants away, and Bunt and Zweber head back toward the elevator, Virgil grabs the CoolStoryBro camera in his pocket and takes a single picture: a sweeping panorama of the room. He's not sure why he does it—it just feels necessary.

The only infant the nurse didn't wheel away is the abandoned baby. Bunt has him in the familiar football hold.

Virgil waits for them to talk him through what he's seen, maybe give him the familiar "this is a privilege" lecture. But they simply press the button to the third floor. Virgil wonders what atrocities await him there. Maybe this is the torture room for enemies of the state. A little waterboarding before your life is laid waste before you? But all Virgil sees when the doors open is a long beige hallway leading to a series of doors. Bunt, still holding the infant, chooses the third door on the left. Inside is a long oak conference table and sitting at the end of the table, his head outlined in sunlight from the only window in the whole goddamn building, is Benson.

"We won't be needing this," Benson says, tapping his Wrist-Bud. "I know exactly where that little tyke is going."

Bunt and Zweiber exchange a glance and then hand the baby over. Before Virgil can ask what the hell this room is for, they've left.

"I've gotten reports of both pictures and videos uploaded to social media of this little guy." Benson pulls a paisley handkerchief out of his pocket and wipes away a line of snot. "You are my ticket for getting the E03s on camera."

"You want to put Bunt and Zweiber on camera?"

Benson chuckles. "God, no. Even if I cleaned them up, I couldn't get them to manage more than a few monosyllabic grunts. How was your ride along with them today?"

Virgil purses his lips, as though he can trap the images into a soundproof vault, never to be seen again.

"I take it you won't be accepting a position as an E03 after your filming is complete, then?" Benson chuckles again. "Not to worry—Craig has already put in a request for you as an E01."

"Yeah?" Virgil straightens and breathes in his gut, as if Craig in the room.

"It appears you made an impression. So, for this one, we have a nice gay couple in lower South Burrington. They live in one of those lovely historic row houses. It'll look great on camera." He picks up the baby, who is busy watching his own wiggling fingers.

"Where would he have gone otherwise?"

"Probably one of the clean-up sites out West."

"Does he get any say in that?"

"Once he comes of age, he can choose to stay where he is or to come back here to the Transition Center."

Virgil flops into one of the padded oak chairs. "So, his choice is to either remain a servant or to die?"

Benson rolls his eyes. "Don't be so dramatic. It's not like they work 24 hours straight. He can still go out for a beer, buy discount groceries, fall in love, start a family. There's a whole community out there. Not a single person sent there has ever made the choice to return."

"Shocker."

"Is it high risk? Certainly. But many jobs are—construction crew, deep-sea divers . . . us, not to put too fine a point on it. We've found a way to preserve life and," Benson holds up a finger, "at minimal cost to the taxpayer."

"All right, whatever." Virgil is suddenly exhausted. He feels the last tentative tendrils of empathy whoosh out of him. He's ready to head home and spend the night in a B-bomb haze.

Before he can leave, however, Benson hands him the infant. The baby is heavier than he expected. It looks quizzically up at his face. No warm, fuzzy feelings, no maternal warmth at all floods through Virgil. He feels annoyed, and he feels a headache thrumming at his temple, but he feels nothing for this child. He just wants Benson to finish up whatever the hell he's doing so he can get out of here.

"Smile like you've just been rescued from certain death," Benson says in a syrupy baby voice. He aims his WristBud at Virgil.

Virgil grimaces, hoping they can edit in a smile later.

The filming at the historic row house goes smoothly. Benson finds a dorky-looking E02, someone like Phren who works with the police to investigate lifetime fraud, to dress up as an E03. Virgil and the fake E03 hand the baby off to the gay couple, two thick men in khakis and polo shirts. They are both clean-shaven, and it is obvious by the way they rub their chins and glance at each other's faces that this is a new development for both of them. They take the camera through a tour of their home, showing off their babyproofing efforts: outlet plugs, baby gates walling off the brick fireplace and stairs, and rubber corner guards for the stone coffee table. There is a gap over the mantle that they explain, off-camera, usually houses an abstract painting of two men in an embrace. Even in the abstract, they assumed it would be too much gay sex for a major network 8 pm time slot.

"Since we're adopting, the Bible-thumpers can assume we're just good friends," the taller man with a receding hairline jokes. Virgil smiles, but his mind is elsewhere. He's supposed to head over to Craig's after work, and Craig hinted that there would be a happy surprise waiting for him. A guy like that, with such a well-defined jawline, would have no trouble convincing a lady to meet his chubby friend.

After the cameras are off and the crew is packing up, the taller man delicately lifts the baby into his arms. The baby is in a light blue onesie, as close to the Enforcer color as Benson could find.

He doesn't have Bunt's ease in holding the baby—his whole body is stiff, even as he rocks back and forth.

His partner, a dark-haired man with a hook-shaped scar on his cheek, walks over and holds his finger out for the baby to grab. "Hey little guy. Hey. You're home now."

After filming wraps, there isn't much else to do, so Virgil is home before noon. He flips through the channels, trying to find something he'll watch for more than five seconds. A documentary on all the extinct sea creatures—definitely not. An episode of *'Til Death Do Us Part?*, where men and women who have committed to each other for two full lifetimes are suddenly forced to navigate a brand-new marriage and in-laws when they turn 18, all under the watchful eye of a documentary film crew? Okay. There's no cash prize, simply the brief, incandescent fame that flares from letting the public into the drama of the quotidian. Here, teenagers at the cusp of adulthood must wrestle with a marriage arranged by strangers—themselves a whole lifetime ago. Which one of them takes a shower in the morning and which in the evening? How will they react when they touch a counter sticky with jelly and crumbs? For how long can they listen to the other's entire collection of free jazz albums without jumping out a window? Which one of them has debt? How much? Do they want kids? A failure here signals a failure to step confidently into adulthood, into the people they are meant to be. A breach of union, an unraveling of the tapestry they wove in synchronous harmony, will sling each of them netless, Nestless, into the quivering gloaming of their final lifetime and a world that is prepared, practically salivating, to cast them into the pit in anticipation of the new. Virgil is several hours into a marathon and rooting through a drawer of take-out menus when he hears a knock at the door.

Tiny Tim stands in the doorway, looking exactly like he did the last time Virgil saw him over a month ago, except for a new patchwork of reddish-blonde stubble that evokes a creeper hanging outside of a playground during school hours. "Hey. Thought I'd drop by and see your new pad."

"Come on in, man," Virgil says with forced cheerfulness.

Tiny Tim wanders around the apartment, checking out the sofa, the television, glancing into the kitchen. "Nice."

"Yeah."

They stand there for another couple of minutes, looking around at everything but each other.

"Definitely a step up from the old place," Tim says.

"Yeah," Virgil chuckles. "It's amazing what you can afford when you don't make slave wages."

Tim nods. Another minute passes.

"Sit down, man. Want anything? Soda? Water?"

"Water?"

"Yeah, no worries. I don't have a counter." Virgil winces as he says it, feeling more and more like some rich asshole throwing his money around.

Tim snorts, though it sounds more like a cough. "Why the hell not? Fill 'er up!"

Virgil fills two tin water bottles—Enforcers are encouraged to stay hydrated, especially in the field—and brings them back to the living room.

"Thanks." Tim downs most of his immediately, so Virgil does too, even though he's not thirsty. Then he fills them back up.

"You can keep that, if you want," Virgil offers.

"Nah, man, it's cool." The rest is unspoken: what use is a water bottle without water?

After another awkward pause, Virgil is getting desperate. "Want to shoot up some SICKOs?" He motions towards the HEP headset.

"Nah."

"Want to get bombed?"

"I've gotta drive."

"Right." Now Virgil is pissed. It's not his job to prostrate himself when Tim's the one who came over, unannounced, acting all holier-than-thou because Virgil has water now. Virgil is about to turn on the TV to let someone else fill the silence when Tim turns and clasps his hands together.

"The reason I came over here," Tim says and pauses. He takes another drink of water. "I wanted you to know that there are no hard feelings."

"Oh?"

"Yeah, it was pretty shitty the way it all went down. Everyone was angry about the documentary that turned out to be a reality show but putting you up for review was a low blow. I mean, you still technically had two years to agree to custodian, not two weeks. And then when all the stuff with Mrs. Silvers aired . . . "

Virgil assumed, after the debacle with Ocean, that the Mrs. Silvers storyline had been cut. He feels the rumble of betrayal deep in his gut.

"Since you were gone, a bunch of the tenants turned on her."

"Wait, what?" Virgil straightens.

"Yeah, all that stuff with Ocean . . . and then someone leaked that her rent was paid for while the rest of ours wasn't, and they assumed she had made some deal with the Enforcers."

Virgil stands and begins pacing the room. "They've got it all wrong. She's not a part of any of this."

"Listen," Tim says, raising a hand. "Most of us knew she wouldn't do that, not without telling us, so we fought for her."

Virgil stops pacing. "So, she's okay?"

"Yeah, she's fine. I'm sorry, I thought you knew all this."

Virgil shakes his head and sits perched on the edge of the couch cushion. "You're the first person I've talked to since I left."

"Oh." Tim glances toward the floor. "I figured you and Mrs. Silvers . . . you two were always close."

Virgil shrugs, though the image of Mrs. Silvers in her floral cardigan floats cotton-candy soft into his field of vision. He shakes the image away.

There's another knock at the door, and Virgil panics, not wanting Craig and Tim to meet. For one brief, hideous moment, he imagines hiding Tim in the closet like some five-minute hooker. On the other side of the door, however, Trinity stands with her arms crossed.

"Well," Tim says, walking to the doorway, "that's my cue."

"No, listen."

"It's okay. I have to get going, anyhow." He narrows his eyes at Trinity and then at Virgil. Virgil opens his mouth to try to explain things, but it would take too long and at this point, Tim would just assume the worst anyway.

Once he's gone, Trinity walks inside. "Are you ready?"

"For what?"

"You wanted a meeting. It is a long drive, so we need to leave now."

Virgil glances at his WristBud. No message yet from Craig. He supposes this won't take long. "All right."

"You will need data to get in." Trinity holds her hand out, palm up, and Virgil places the CoolStoryBro camera on it.

Trinity looks at the single picture of the infant Transition room and listens to the brief audio file. "This is it?"

"Yeah, but you don't understand. That's where they're killing all the babies."

"We know this is happening."

But you don't know what it felt like, Virgil wants to say. It was over a decade ago when some kid snuck into a Transition Center and leaked photos of the babies about to be euthanized. The public pitched itself into a frenzy, screaming "Reform, Reform," and the Enforcers made a big show of putting all of the babies into the foster system. But then, suddenly, there were all these kids on the street, crying, starving, getting lost and picked up for human trafficking, not to mention the older ones, the ones who somehow survived, stealing shit, destroying property, forming these roving gangs, and suddenly both sides agreed that this couldn't continue, that things should go back to the way they were. The Enforcers said that they would try to catch everyone before they reversed, and the public said, okay, problem solved, and everyone bought incredibly large entertainment nooks and looked the other way.

"Okay, but the babies with extra time. They get killed too, and the time goes into a bank."

"Well," Trinity says, a note of uncertainty in her voice. "That does not sound illegal."

Virgil rolls his eyes. "I'm sorry if you want some crazy story where we beat a man to death and steal his time to use on hookers, but that's not what we do. The guys I work with are a little rough around the edges, but they're basically decent guys doing a shitty job as well as they can. And yeah, I don't really agree with sending Nestless babies on their first life out West, but what can you do?"

Trinity raises her head. "What?"

After repeating the last phrase again, Trinity breaks into a wide smile. Her teeth are the whitest Virgil has ever seen. "That we can use. Do you have proof?"

"Not really."

Trinity clicks a few buttons on the camera. "How long after you took this picture did you find out?"

"Uh, ten, fifteen minutes later?"

Trinity fast-forwards until she finds Benson speaking in the same tone and inflection as he did that day. Virgil hears his own reaction, too. He sounds mildly surprised, and then not surprised at all.

"But how did you . . . I mean, I didn't . . . "

"We programmed the audio to start recording when it registered certain code words. A back-up in case you were not able to click the button in time."

"But . . . that's my voice, too."

"We'll leave your name out of it."

Yeah, super. How many other people did Benson have that exact conversation with? He'll know immediately that it was Virgil. There's no way Virgil can let Trinity upload that audio.

Trinity places the camera in the small purse slung across her shoulder. "Ready?"

Virgil spends most of the two-hour drive considering ways he can get into the bag tossed casually across the backseat. Maybe he could offer to carry Trinity's purse in. No, that would be weird and suspicious. Maybe during a lull in the meeting, he could sneak it into the bathroom. No, someone would see him. As he ticks away each option, he digs his fingers into the fabric of the car seat. Why did he even agree to this in the first place? He's no activist; he's never gone to a protest, never cared about anything enough to risk tear gas or rubber bullets or worse, real ones. He's the guy that goes to his crappy job for eight hours and then gets bombed in his room by himself.

Why didn't he just throw the camera away?

The question's still kicking around in Virgil's brain when they pull up to a little blue farmhouse surrounded by a field of tall, yellow grass. There's a narrow stone path, slightly overgrown with weeds. He can imagine the husband outside, painting the white wood trim, the wife washing dishes in the kitchen behind the checkered blinds. And then, the husband knocking back a beer, maybe two after a long, hard day. The wife pursing her lips, trying not to nag. The husband's hours getting cut at work, and then him switching to something harder, just to take the edge off. The wife spending more and more time outside, in the comforting lines of the grocery store, her fingers trailing the uniform, colorful boxes of Vitabars and, on the fifteenth of each month, splurging a little on a bag of clementines, maybe even a whole grapefruit. The husband being late for work after one too many drinks and getting fired. The wife letting her hand fall against the rough linen of the checkout boy's sleeve, waiting to see if he pulls his arm away. The husband selling their valuables, and then their furniture, then their time. The wife locking the husband out one night and the husband using a rock to bash in the window. Glass sprinkling all over the pretty checkered blinds. The husband standing over the wife, rock in hand. He'll do it, unless she gives him the last of her time.

Virgil has seen the ugly, scuttling things behind closed doors. No longer does he believe in the inherent goodness of humanity, in each person's willingness to dig deep in the sands of their consciousness to scaffold a cathedral of the divine. No, he's seen too often what happens as the wind whips them against the rough stone slab of the everyday: the hours underground pressed tight against too many bodies struggling for air, an entire day cloistered in devotion to the unreal, and as each body hurls to the next place, the next task, always the quick tripping over the earth's sudden and irrevocable decay. All of it leads to the gradual erosion of dignity, of grace, of their very soul, leaving behind a body that looks whole but is nothing more than a collection of frayed synapses, all speaking the same essential tongue: mine, mine, mine.

Without even bothering to knock, Trinity opens the front door. Virgil's objective is clear. No matter what awaits him, he must aim his body towards his own Northern Light. They walk down a hallway, the wood floors creaking with each step, and enter a room that makes Virgil pull up short.

"I knew it, man, I knew it!" Tiny Tim stands and pumps his fist in the air. He's surrounded by nearly a dozen other people sitting on mismatched furniture: a corduroy sofa and loveseat, wooden chairs of many styles and sizes, an unraveling ottoman. A few people stand near the back while others sit on the hardwood floor. And over by the fireplace, where he hurriedly replaces a small potted succulent on the mantle, is Tongs. Virgil scans the room for other people from his Nest, but he doesn't recognize anyone else. Still, his heart begins to beat faster.

Trinity guides Virgil to the middle of the room. "Hello, everyone. This is our man on the inside." Everyone nods or smiles: politely, cautiously. "I hold in my hands the final piece of evidence we need to take down the men in blue."

The entire room bursts into cheering and applause. Tim reaches over and claps Virgil on the shoulder.

"Combined with the videos from our Arridia Unit and the audio from our LaKind Unit, this should be enough to start our disruption."

Arridia Unit? LaKind Unit? Virgil assumed this was a bunch of pissed-off kids posting screeds on the internet and occasionally hacking websites. He had no idea this was such a large and well-organized group.

"Toya, Paul, you two start working on the pamphlets. We will need about two hundred to paper the city. Hazel, Shonda, and Van, start working on the subway. We will need AV support along with our friend in corporate to give us access to the ad space. Aisha, Phoenix, you two know what to do with this." She tosses the camera over several heads into the outstretched hands of a girl in a rainbow wig. Another girl sits beside her with a badly dyed and slightly overgrown pixie haircut. Pixie haircut girl whispers into rainbow wig girl's ear, and the way she touches her inner thigh tells Virgil not to waste time on charm.

"Everyone, I want to thank you for all of your hard work. It has been a difficult journey. We have lost some friends along the way."

The crowd begins murmuring their assent. Someone whispers the name Brin.

Trinity opens her arms. Her voice is sonorous, tidal, a great swelling crescendo ready to envelope the room. "But I'm here to tell you that their sacrifice has not been in vain. We now have evidence that they are sending children, first-life infants, into the tent cities out West."

More murmuring from the crowd. Virgil looks back at rainbow wig girl. She places the camera in a small bag looped around her shoulder.

"Our man on the inside has risked his security, his reputation, his very life to secure this information for us. You may recognize him from the reality show, *Becoming Blue*."

"Selling our souls to work with the roaches," a woman, small and waifish, possibly a teenager, mutters. "How much of our integrity are we willing to compromise?"

"Like you know anything about integrity," another woman stage-whispers. "I saw you eating a Vitabar. Did you forget that they use foster contracts in the factories?"

"Enough," Trinity snaps. "I will not have this conversation again. Tonight, we will begin the second phase of our disruption.

Once the package is secure, we will rendezvous at destination Alpha and begin the loadout. We will have to act fast to get our message into as many eyes and ears as possible. Please set your watches to 8:42 pm."

It is then that Virgil notices that not a single person in the room is wearing a WristBud. Instead, they are all wearing old-school watches, the kind he's seen on documentaries. When he glances down at his wrist, he notices that his WristBud is also gone.

"Hey, where's my—"

"I have it. It is safe. Do not cause a scene," Trinity whispers in Virgil's ear. Then she turns to face the room. "To protect today, we must sacrifice tomorrow. To the Pro-Fin!"

"To the Pro-Fin!" everyone bellows.

Then, as quickly as the crowd unites, they break up. People get up, stretch, begin breaking off into smaller groups. A few drag chairs out of the room. Trinity walks to a couple near the door and begins gesturing emphatically. She looks so tall, so self-assured. Virgil had had the sneaking suspicion that it was either racist or sexist or both that she had what he assumed to be a minor role in this organization. During her speech, though, it was obvious that she was a star, a blue giant about to go supernova, pulling everyone into her orbit.

Virgil walks to a side table and pours himself a cup of cold coffee while keeping an eye on the two women with his camera. They're sitting away from everyone else near the window, tucked behind the corduroy couch. They're still whispering, still in constant contact with each other.

Tim and Tongs walk up beside Virgil. Tim is grinning, his whole body vibrating with his excitement. "Man, I'm so glad to see you. You really had me—I thought you had become one those fuckers."

"Ha, yeah," Virgil smiles.

Tongs stands with his arms crossed. He's in a striped button-up shirt, his thinning hair slicked back. He looks out of place without his tongs and grill.

"I mean, when Trinity stopped by your place, I assumed you two were . . . "

"Nah, she's not my type." Virgil winks, though he feels a hollow in his gut.

Tim steps back and forth, nearly tripping over Tongs in his excitement. "I knew it, I knew you wouldn't fucking do that, man. Aargh!" He slaps Virgil on the back again, then calms down. "I wonder why Trinity didn't say anything."

Virgil shrugs.

"I guess that's between you two." He winces and glances over at Trinity, who is still gesturing emphatically to the couple by the door. "Whatever, man. I'm here, you're here, it's all good!"

Virgil glances back at the women with his camera. He's going to have to make his move soon, but he still has no idea what it should be. He's trying not to get panicked as his opportunities for subtlety slowly tick away. "Is anyone else from the Nest here?"

"Nah, it's just us. Trinity's a genius at knowing who to approach and who to leave alone." Tim looks over at Trinity again, his face soft with lust. "But hey, this changes things, you know? Tongs and Trinity both have an in with the board. There's no reason why you can't move back in."

Tongs sighs and then lowers his arms. "Yeah, I can do that."

The couple Trinity was talking to have finally walked away. Virgil nods and then jogs over to Trinity before she can get mired in another conversation. "About that audio."

Trinity claps her hands together. "It is brilliant, is it not? We have an official admitting to significant transgressions on tape."

"Yeah, I was thinking, this is just the tip of the iceberg. I bet I can capture much worse."

Trinity looks doubtful. "I can give you another camera if you like."

"Well, see, that's the thing. Once you air this audio, my cover will be blown. I won't be able to go back. So why don't you give me that camera and I'll see what else I can get for you? Really make sure your, uh, disruption is successful?"

Trinity shakes her head. "No, we are moving into the second phase tonight. I appreciate all the work you have done."

Virgil nods and walks back to the corduroy couch. Even before he reaches it, he knows the space behind it is empty.

Virgil takes a breath. Now isn't the time to panic. They can't have made it very far. He walks as quickly and calmly as he can to the window, where he catches a glimpse of rainbow wig next to a beat-up electric purple mini. He doesn't acknowledge Tim or Tongs or even Trinity as he marches out the door, down the weed-infested walkway, and into the backseat of the car.

"Yo, blue boy. You lost?" Rainbow wig bellows through the open window.

"Nope. Trinity told me to come with you."

The woman in the wig turns and storms back into the house. Shit, Virgil thought he could bluff his way through this.

The small girl with the overgrown pixie cut looks toward the house and then back at Virgil. She bites a piece of skin from her nail.

Virgil tries to remember the names Trinity just said. "Are you Aisha?"

"Phoenix," the girl says.

"Phoenix, right. Your girlfriend always this angry?" Phoenix smiles and nods. Virgil scans the backseat and the floor of the front seat, but he doesn't see the bag with the camera.

Finally, Aisha returns from the house with Trinity. She flings open the driver's side door and, narrowing her eyes at Virgil, gets in. Trinity climbs into the backseat as well.

"You would like to be dropped off?" Trinity asks.

"Nah, I figure you all could use another set of hands. This second phase sounds pretty intense."

"Yeah, pass," Aisha says. "I'm not babysitting some psychopath for hire."

"Hey, I'm the reason you're even having a phase two."

"No," Aisha barks, locking eyes with Virgil in the rearview mirror, "Trinity and her years of grassroots effort, her constant and unwavering sacrifice are the reason there is a phase two."

"That is enough. If you would like to help, we accept," Trinity says.

"And if you fuck with us," Aisha says, a slow smile creeping across her face. "I'll reverse you right out the fucking window."

PHOENIX

The man in the backseat, whose name turns out to be Virgil, drums his hands on the seat. He seems nervous. He keeps making popping sounds with his mouth.

"So, how do you know Trinity?" Aisha suddenly asks.

Virgil shrugs. "We lived in the same Nest."

"Past tense?"

"Well . . . I live somewhere else now."

"Probably some swank condo built on the backs of dead babies," Aisha stage-whispers to Phoenix. "So, you kill anyone?"

"No," Virgil answers. "Not really."

"Of course, you just steal them away in the dead of night so some other asshole can do your dirty work for you."

"What about you?" Virgil snaps. "You kill anyone?"

Aisha purses her lips together. Phoenix notices that Aisha's wig is askance. She reaches over to straighten it, but Aisha swats her hand away. "None of your goddamn business."

Phoenix finds a loose thread at the hem of her dress and twists it between her fingers. She isn't naïve—she knows Aisha has done ugly things, maybe even terrible things. But the question she's unwilling to ask is for whom and will Aisha do them again?

Aisha turns on the radio and flips through the stations, mostly religious and country music amid swaths of static. They cross a small bridge, pale yellow reeds rising from the sludge, the smell of rotten eggs drifting into the car. The sun droops below the horizon.

Aisha turns down a back road. She follows it as it twists and turns, until they come upon a long, unbroken stretch surrounded by trees. Through the evening breeze, the trees shake their shadowy burden of branches. It is beautiful, and yet Phoenix can't stop the tremendous beating of her heart. It feels as though they are about to drive off a cliff. They pass a small white church with an even smaller graveyard and then, in the center of a field, a raised platform behind three wooden crosses lit below by spotlights. Though the sign says "Worship Center," it looks like a gallows.

Finally, they turn onto a gravel road that winds around and around, eventually ending at a one-story house set far back from the road. Nobody comes out to meet them. A chorus of crickets calls, hidden among the overgrown grass, while pinpoints of light punctuate their cries. Phoenix nearly gasps—she's never seen fireflies before. Her eyes track each burst of light across the darkness: two here, one there, then a cascade across the field. The whole world is alight for one brief, joyous moment, before the car doors slam and she's pulled back.

The four of them walk up the overgrown walkway and knock on the front door. A man in a wrinkled linen shirt, his face gaunt, opens it a crack, peeking through the chain.

"Oliver," Trinity says.

Inside, every available surface is paneled wood: the floors, the wall, the ceiling. It is the kind of house that looks like it should be beside a dock, not tucked in the middle of a grassy field. Large bay windows overlook the field, or they would, except they are covered by thick light-blocking curtains. Most of the overhead lights are turned off. A handful of lamps cast circles of yellow on the paneling, making everything look jaundiced, slightly haunted. The man motions them to a couch and roots around in the small kitchen nook. He returns with a loaf of bread, two bags of deli meat, a block of cheese, and an entire chocolate cake.

"Thought you would be hungry."

Trinity shifts in her seat while everyone eats. Finally, she stands. "Oliver, we are moving on to Phase Two."

"I know, I got your message."

"We should shoot the video now."

Oliver takes a small cylinder, O2 on-the-go, and takes a long hit of it. He replaces it into the pocket of his linen pants. His body is all hard angles: cheekbones and chin and pasty white elbows. His shirt flops against his skin, a flag at half-mast. "All right. Give me ten minutes."

As he wanders off to some other room, Phoenix can feel the food settling in her stomach, weighting her jittery limbs with reassurance. For the moment, they are no longer in flight. And even though this space is temporary, as are their bodies inside of it, she feels like she can focus her thoughts on more than her immediate surroundings.

"If you were ever in trouble," she asks Aisha once everyone has moved to separate areas of the living room to wait, to ruminate, "would Ms. Bodice rescue you?"

Aisha pauses, her eyes scanning Phoenix's face. "Why?"

Phoenix shrugs. "Just curious. I wasn't sure if she was just your employer or your family."

Aisha smiles and seems to relax. "Well, she wouldn't come herself. That would be like the CEO walking into a factory to fix a broken cog. But she would send someone, yeah. We all look out for each other. Like Crystal's mom, for instance, was a B-bomb addict, and Crystal was born a micro-preemie, like 29 weeks old, a pound and a half, barely breathing, that sort of thing. But that's why we have a self-funded medical plan—we're able to budget for the problems we know about as well as the ones we don't. When she reverses, we know she'll go all the way back to 28 weeks, so we're ready for the hospital costs."

"And what if Crystal started doing B-bombs like her mom?"

"Well that's part of it, yeah. She'll have to detox while still in the NICU and then monthly rehabilitation therapy will be built into her plan."

"Wow," Phoenix says, staring at a place on the wall where the wood panels don't precisely line up. It caught her attention a moment ago and she can't stop staring at it, mentally trying to fix it. "That's pretty amazing."

Aisha brushes a smudge of dirt off of Phoenix's forehead. "Why all the questions?"

Phoenix smiles. "I was just thinking about what's next. You know, after all this?"

Aisha threads her arm through Phoenix's and pulls her close. "Don't worry about that. I got you."

VIRGIL

The cake has left Virgil's teeth furred, his whole mouth sour with too much sugar. Everyone is sitting around, making polite chit-chat, so Virgil walks to the bathroom. He needs to take a piss, but he also wants to splash some water on his face, take a long drink and get the taste of syrup out of his mouth. Unfortunately, the bathroom is just an empty basin with an empty plastic jug beside it. There's no counter, no toilet at all. Guess he's going to have to squat over some hole out back.

Virgil stomps back into the living room and begins pacing back and forth. He knows he should calm down, because the more agitated he gets, the more Aisha locks eyes with him as if to say, *I see you, fucker.* Finally, he walks out the front door and swings around the back until he finds the port-a-potty.

Outside, a soft breeze ruffles the grass. Inside, the air is thick with molten shit and flies circling their bounty. A roll of toilet paper sits on the floor, misshapen, moisture-warped. Virgil sits on the wooden seat and clenches as a geyser erupts. God, he needs to get the hell out of here and back to the soft comforts of his apartment, the pipes flowing with fresh, clean water.

Virgil runs his tongue over his teeth, his body pitched forward in desperation, and then, etched on the dark wood before him, Virgil sees his face. Not as it is now, but as it was that night. Virgil watches his mouth pop open in joy and then shock. Virgil watches his body twist backward to escape his blows. Virgil feels his body heave forward, wanting to press his weight against him, stop him from moving, stop him from crying, wanting to slam him against the wall, Virgil's hands on his chest, his legs, wanting, fuck, to be inside him. And then Virgil watches his body, bruised and bleeding, crumple to the floor.

Virgil flings open the door until it makes a satisfying crack. Enough hiding out here like a goddamn pussy. Time to man up and do what he came here to do.

Back in the living room, Trinity holds out her hand. Aisha places the camera inside. Virgil sucks in his gut, tenses his legs. This is his last chance.

Trinity points the camera at Oliver, who takes a deep breath before beginning.

"My name is Oliver Brent. I work for Veritas Biological, or at least I did. We were a company that provided full genome mapping to individuals hoping to change their future. We weren't the most profitable or the least profitable . . . we were somewhere in the middle. We mostly serviced the greater Burrington area."

The adrenaline formerly surging through Virgil's arms and legs has started to wane. This sounds like it's going to take a while.

"Even though there is at least one company per tri-state area, we weren't really in competition with each other. Most of us have a common parent corporation: Bien Global. So, we shared information that would help us better increase our profit margins. Anyway, a funny thing starts to happen when over 70% of the population is using genome mapping: you start to notice trends. Maybe if we were in competition, nobody would have noticed. Maybe if our boss had found it first, we wouldn't be here. But the fact is, we started to notice some interesting epigenetic changes. These changes were technically errors but ones that didn't cause any known disorders.

"One of my colleagues decided to map the changes. It wasn't long before my supervisor, and then my supervisor's supervisor, and then finally the CEO of Bien Global caught wind of our discovery. We were expecting accolades, but instead we received a tersely worded memo that the data was to be discarded. Turns out, when the government mandated three reversals per lifetime, they also made it illegal to actually research the reversals. Luckily, or unluckily, depending on your viewpoint, I had already made a copy of the data to share with my old college roommate. I managed to get the information out before they started the random searches."

Trinity clicks a button on the side of the camera, possibly to zoom in. "And what is the meaning of these changes you discovered?"

"Well, we think it has something to do with the Reversals. Now, I need to be clear: we can't be sure these are the genes responsible for the Reversals. We would need much, much more data, and for that, we would need to lift the ban on research. And even if we are able to conclude that this pattern of changes is responsible for the Reversals, it would still be many years before we were able to control all of the transcription factors. That said," Oliver says, breathing more heavily, "this really is the first step in understanding the Reversals in a way we never have before, and it is the only viable option we have of reinstating human cellular death as it was meant to be. So I implore you to vote Yes on Proposition 38, to allow research into the Reversals again."

At this point Virgil is standing, though he's not sure when he stopped sitting. His hands are at his side, loose, fingers tingling. This can't be it. This can't be the ace in the hole that Trinity was talking about. But it makes sense—it's not enough to show the Enforcers are corrupt. You have to turn the tide against the reversals themselves. Mount enough public pressure to prevent the solution from getting swept under the rug. But then, Virgil would only have this one shitty life, a quarter gone, and he would never get rid of these memories: his mother, the men on the couch, the feel of sugar against his teeth, Phren's face, it all would be with him, permanently, until . . .

Later, he would say it happened so fast, he didn't have time to think: he was all action, an electric impulse from fingertips to toes.

But that wasn't entirely true. He had enough time to think, okay, yes. He had enough time to give up the rooftop and the grill, Mrs. Silvers and baby Karl. He had enough time to whisper "you win" to the Enforcers, who would have his life, his soul, until the next round. And maybe next time, he would be good, he would be kind, he would stand for something noble, something greater than himself. There was a chance, anyway.

He clicks the baton to its highest setting and leaps forward.

PHOENIX

The first thing Phoenix sees isn't her mother's body, which she never witnessed, but the beach. The sun is a hint of red cresting the horizon. The sand under Phoenix's toes is still cold. She is holding a tiny vial of glass, green, with edges worn smooth like the sea. Why is she there? Are they on vacation? They never lived by the ocean. She glances at her mother sitting on a white bath towel. Her arms are wrapped around her legs, and a knit brown afghan is draped over her shoulders. She stares out at the sea. Phoenix wishes she had something to cover her shoulders. She is in her favorite swimsuit, the polka-dotted one. It is turquoise, a word she has just learned how to say. Her chubby little fingers keep tracing the circles as though she can unlock that small jolt of pleasure when she first saw the swimsuit and place its warmth across her skin-prickled shoulders. She shivers, but it isn't unpleasant—it is the shiver of a secret she has managed to keep. The beach is empty except for the two of them. Phoenix sticks a foot in the water and gasps. It is much colder than she expected. As the water recedes from the shoreline, tiny bubbles form across the sand. A small white-and-brown sandpiper skitters down the shore, prodding each hole, closer and closer, until—quick, run!—the water returns. Phoenix wants to chase him, but he is already too far down the beach.

She remembers a song her mother sang on how to be brave—just take one step and then one more—and so she does. The water is thigh-high, then waist-high, and she looks back at her mother who sits and stares. Phoenix is about to walk further when a wave crashes on top of her head and knocks her down. She tries to get up, but the pressure is too firm. She panics, flailing her arms and legs, but it is no use—her tiny body can't resist the pull of the tide. Finally, the wave recedes, and it turns out that she was only a foot from the shoreline. She sits, coughs, and wipes the sand from her face. Her mother is still in the same spot.

She climbs into her mother's lap, and her mother begins to finger-comb her hair, which is tangled and full of sand. She's about to ask what's for breakfast until she sees the ocean in her mother's eyes.

Her father walks up behind them and places a hand on Phoenix's shoulder. "Don't you think it's a little early for a swim?" He looks at Phoenix's mother and his face goes dark. "Jesus, Nell, it's barely 7 am."

Phoenix's mother turns and smiles. The waves in her eyes are crashing with a dull certainty. "The sky is so beautiful this time of day."

Her father grabs Phoenix's hand and pulls her roughly inside. He runs a warm bath and scours the sand with a washcloth. Then he opens the door to release the steam. It is not the same bathroom he will later seal off for two weeks, telling Phoenix it is off-limits, nor is it the bathroom of the trailer he will build without a door, only a thin sheet. This bathroom is white, spotless; it will hold all they have cast off—dead skin, globs of toothpaste, wet towels, an empty vial the size of a broken promise—for an hour, two at most, before it is all scrubbed clean once again.

Virgil replaces the baton. At his feet, Trinity's hand cups Oliver's shoulder, her fingertips completing the circuit. Both stare sightless at the ceiling, their bodies slumped with sudden weight except for Oliver's knee, which is raised at an unnatural peak. Virgil holds out his hand until he receives both the camera and the keys to the car. Then, wordless, he leaves.

Aisha turns and wraps her arms around Phoenix, whose body is stiff and trembling. "Are you okay?"

"Uh, no," Phoenix says. She tries to chuckle but it comes out as a cough. "Are you?"

Aisha looks down at the bodies and then back up at Phoenix. "It's not what I was hoping for, no."

Phoenix looks at Aisha. She wishes she could have remained in the woods, within the lush green canopy of Aisha's eyes, where it was quiet and warm and safe. But eventually the forest ends, and it is time to turn your face to the setting sun. They were never there to help Trinity with Phase Two. The knowledge arrives, perfect and whole, along with the contents of Aisha's bag: a small black case with a needle full of poison.

"I'll have to call for a new car. Ms. Bondice isn't going to be thrilled, but she'll understand. Well, at least we have this." Aisha touches her CoolStoryBro camera, which was looped through the belt on her pants. She then grabs a handful of papers from her bag and sprinkles them across the bodies. Phoenix notices the phrase "Embryos, Not Eggs!" She doesn't need to read any further to realize what kind of scene Aisha is setting up.

Even now, though, Phoenix isn't thinking about Aisha or Virgil or even the bodies that were once Oliver and Trinity, two people just trying to make the world a little less shitty. She's thinking about her father waking up in that hotel room by himself, reaching across the now-cold sheets, clutching the fabric between his fingers and wondering what he did wrong. She's thinking about the men in the police car handcuffing him and leading him into a cold, dark cell for questioning. She's thinking about their skeptical faces when her father says he had nothing to do with it, has no idea where she went. She's thinking about his body hunched over the table, bruises forming on his face, his arms, his chest, the red recording light of the cameras turned off. She's thinking too of her father whisking her from the beach that day, gathering only what he could carry.

Phoenix walks outside. Her feet crunch the gravel, though the sound is very far away. She stands before the grassy field, the call of the crickets rising in both pitch and volume. Then, all at once, the sound stops. Phoenix looks up to see a bat gliding and banking, pitching and reeling, all in complete silence. Each turn is whip-fast, a blur of darkness amid the faltering light. For once, she is not afraid. She remembers from Mrs. Green's lessons that bats have more than two dozen joints in their wings, just like a human hand.

Phoenix will tell herself that she had a feeling about the poison in Aisha's backpack, but of course, during Oliver's interview, when she grabbed Aisha's Wristbud and tiptoed into the kitchen, she felt only the cold, smooth floor beneath her feet, the breath she inhaled fluttering inside her chest. There wasn't anywhere to scan the WristBud like at the gas station, so Phoenix slipped it on. Hunched in a corner, her body on the precipice of panic, she clicked past screens until she arrived at what looked like an online store. Only a couple more presses until she heard the same angry buzz, saw the same flash of red. Before she left, she whispered "ashes" to the screen, imagining her breath imprinting her emotions, her memories, her very soul onto the device, the only apology or explanation she would ever give. Then, heart racing, she slipped back inside Aisha's arms.

Now, as the crickets swell without crescendo, the sky empty and black, she waits for the single squeak in the still, humid air to let her know they are here.

ABOUT THE AUTHOR

MELISSA REDDISH's stories have appeared in *Gargoyle*, *Raleigh Review*, and *Grist*, among others. She is the author of a collection of stories, *My Father is an Angry Storm Cloud* (Tailwinds Press), and a novella, *Girl & Flame* (Conium Books). She lives on the Eastern Shore of Maryland.

www.ingramcontent.com/pod-product-compliance
Lightning Source LLC
Chambersburg PA
CBHW021138190726
48288CB00008B/2723